---- ★ ----

"Has everyone touched this?"

"Molly found it. And then I handled it as well. Once we found out what was inside, no one else wanted near it."

On the chance there might be a usable print or two, I didn't pick it up. I lifted the lid by two opposing diagonal corners, using the tips of my thumb and third finger, avoiding the box's flat surfaces. There inside, on a soft bed of cotton, lay a darkened, shriveled finger.

Lunch rolled over in my stomach but settled in place. I bent to get a closer look at the stiff digit. I guessed it to be the index finger of an adult. It lay on its cotton bedding, slightly crooked, bluish-gray with a longish, dirt-encrusted nail. The severed edge had been cut cleanly with something very sharp. There was no blood to be seen.

---- ★ ----

Connie Shelton

COMPETITION CAN BE MURDER

WORLDWIDE®

TORONTO • NEW YORK • LONDON
AMSTERDAM • PARIS • SYDNEY • HAMBURG
STOCKHOLM • ATHENS • TOKYO • MILAN
MADRID • WARSAW • BUDAPEST • AUCKLAND

For Dan, my soul mate always.

COMPETITION CAN BE MURDER

A Worldwide Mystery/June 2005

First published by Intrigue Press.

ISBN 0-373-26531-X

Printed in U.S.A.

Acknowledgments

Thanks first, and always, to Dan for putting up with life with a writer, for sharing his helicopter skills, and for catching all my technical errors. To Dad and Wendy, who made possible the Scotland trip that gave inspiration for this story. To Susan Slater for her editorial expertise and dear friendship. And to Simon Wood and his buddies on the North Sea oil rigs—your information was invaluable, and if there are mistakes they are my own. Finally, to the warm and lovely people of Inverness and Aviemore, Scotland, for your hospitality and friendliness, and for introducing me to haggis.

ONE

THE ROLLING gray waves of the North Atlantic stretched beneath me to the horizon in all directions. For a kid from New Mexico who'd always had a mountain, a rock, or a tree as a focal point, all that gray shimmering undulation felt a bit unnerving. I glanced again at the waypoint I'd programmed into the GPS and gripped the cyclic a little more firmly. I was right on course.

Eyes on the horizon, I refused to think about the water's depth and my stomach settled back into position. In the distance, between the heavy gray sky and the steel-gray water, I thought I could see the tiny dot I was aiming for. It appeared to be too far to the north. I was going to miss it by a half mile at least. But I resisted the temptation to change course. The main thing I'd learned from Drake during my flight lessons was to trust my instruments, not my eyes. I re-checked the GPS reading once again.

The two men in the back seat, both burly, rosy-complected Scots, watched the back of my head. They both nodded curtly when I asked over the intercom if they were doing all right back there. The one whose red-checked shirt showed above his survival suit raised the corners of his mouth in what might have been taken for a smile when I glanced over my shoulder at them. The other held his lips in a straight line that made me wonder if he was naturally stern or was struggling to keep his breakfast down.

"Almost there, guys," I announced in the most chipper voice I could manage.

The outline of the oil rig was becoming clearer now, its assortment of blocks and protrusions made it look like some kind of tenement apartment building that had collided with a communications tower, all stuck onto a couple dozen stick-like legs coming up out of the water. I approached from the south, eased the right pedal so we made a gentle turn, and circled the rig to come into the wind. The big yellow H on the deck was clear, and I flared slightly and set the JetRanger's skids squarely on it.

A dark-haired crewman, ducking to avoid the spinning rotor blades, approached and opened the back doors for each of my two passengers. They shook themselves a little, like dogs out of the bath, when their feet touched the solid platform. Gathering a bulky pack each, they headed toward the crew headquarters without a backward glance at me.

I tightened down my cyclic stick and removed my headset so I could give the ship a look before taking off again. Improperly latched doors have caused more than one helicopter crash and I wasn't taking any chances out there over the water. The crewman glared at me from under heavy black eyebrows as I circled, rechecking the doors he'd just handled. I gave him a smile and a nod, and made a show of checking the cargo door and fuel cap just to let him know it wasn't personal. He backed away from the ship and stood at the edge of the helipad, hands on hips, waiting for me to leave again.

Colin Finnie, the crew chief I'd met for the first time yesterday, stepped out of his office and gave me a wave. Several other men waited in the background, talking quietly among themselves.

"Anyone going back this trip?" I asked as Finnie met me halfway.

"Not this time, Charlie. Tell Drake we'll have five transfers on Thursday."

"Got it." I shook his hand and turned back to my aircraft.

As I re-checked my controls and brought up my engine speed, I noticed the other crewman talking behind his hand to

Finnie. His eyes darted toward the helicopter as he spoke, those black brows dipping ominously.

What was that all about I wondered as I pulled pitch and lifted off the platform. An hour later, bringing the aircraft in over the Inverness airport, it was still on my mind. I'd have to remember to ask Drake about it when he got back.

THE WARMTH INSIDE the tiny office at Air-Sea Helicopters hit me with force the second I stepped out of the brisk, cool outdoors. I reached for the zipper on my red survival suit, ready to peel it off.

"Drake left you a message, Charlie," Meggie piped up. "He'll be in by three and wondered if you'd still be around?"

Meggie Flanery came with the job, and I was thankful that she knew the ropes and was willing to work with me. We'd taken this summer job in Scotland as a favor to an old friend of Drake's. Brian Swinney had known Drake back in their years of flying tours together in Hawaii. He'd returned to his native Scotland a few years ago and started his own helicopter service. But an illness in the family forced him to London just after he'd received a lucrative contract servicing the oil rigs in the North Sea. Since Drake's fire contract had ended in July, we'd just been able to get away from New Mexico, get to Scotland, and take all the tests and check rides to get our U.K. licenses by the first week of August. Brian was paying good money, but truthfully, Drake and I were really here for the adventure.

Meggie looked at me expectantly, her wide blue eyes and cupid's-bow mouth pursed in question.

"Sure, I can wait." I glanced at my watch. It was only another hour. Maybe Drake and I could grab some dinner together at a pub in town before we headed back to our rented cottage.

Meggie picked up the radio's microphone and transmitted Drake's call sign, the tail letters for the company's other aircraft. His voice came over the speaker and I could hear the Eurocopter's turbine whine in the background. I loved the way his voice sounded over the air, calm and professional at all times.

"Looks like you're all set, then," Meggie said after she signed off with Drake.

I slid the padded survival suit off my shoulders and freed my hands. "Whew! That thing sure feels good out there over the water, but I'll tell you, it's hotter than blazes indoors."

Meggie watched me with something bordering on awe. For all her twenty-one years, she had that flawless skin that comes only from a lifetime of exposure to cool, moist air and the pure blond, blue-eyed purity handed down from her Nordic ancestors. Still, she hadn't worked with many women pilots and never one who'd been known to double as a private investigator once in a while. I got the feeling at times that she'd like to adopt me as a big sister.

"Can I make you a cup of tea, then, Charlie?"

"Um, sure. That sounds nice." I tugged the legs of my jeans straight and rolled the sleeves of my plaid shirt past my forearms. "Let me wash up and run a brush through my hair."

I remembered something. "Meggie? One other thing—"

"Sure," she replied.

"The flight manual for the JetRanger. It's not in the aircraft. Have you seen it around here? I'm not supposed to fly without it on board."

"Haven't seen it here. Sorry. But I've got the information on the computer. I can print out another one."

"Thanks."

She turned to her monitor, made a few clicks with the mouse, and the printer began to feed out sheets of paper.

Ten minutes later I was sitting in the spare office chair, feet up on the wastebasket, with a warm mug of tea in one hand and a buttery shortbread cookie in the other.

"Karen called," Meggie said. "She says Brian's mother is a wee bit better today."

"It must be hard on them, watching her go through the chemo and all."

"Yes, I think so. I can't imagine me own mum bein' sick like that. How about you? Your own parents in good health?"

I told her how I'd lost my parents very suddenly when I was fifteen and Drake only had his mother now.

Meggie gave me another of those awestruck looks when she learned I'd basically been on my own since my teen years.

"But I have a neighbor who's like a grandmother to me," I assured her. "And two brothers. It's about all the family I can handle."

The radio crackled, Drake announcing, "I'm beach-in. Fifteen minutes ETA."

Now that he'd cleared the coast, I swigged the last of my tea and went outside to tie down the JetRanger's rotor blades and get everything secured for the night.

I'd just finished my duties when I caught the distinctive sound of the Astar's blades beating the air behind me. A British Air flight had just departed five minutes earlier, so I assumed Drake would be cleared by the tower for immediate landing. Sure enough, he brought the sleek red and white aircraft in smoothly and set her down on his designated pad. He grinned at me from the right seat as he gently pumped the rotor brake and the turbine engines wound down. As always, my heart did a little skip when I saw his gorgeous smile. Nearly two years of marriage haven't dampened things a bit for us.

An hour later, we'd secured both aircraft for the night, let Meggie go home, and driven into town in search of a pub and dinner.

At the Lantern Wick I was debating whether to brave it and try the Scottish delicacy, haggis, or to go with the less scary roast beef.

"You know how they make that haggis, don't you?" Drake teased.

"Please, I really don't need the details." I only knew that they used just about everything from the inside of a sheep, but didn't really want the whole play-by-play on how it was made. Every Highlander I'd asked about it simply said that it was very good and very rich. "Okay, I'm hungry tonight. I'm gonna' brave it. If I don't like it, I'll get a sandwich to take home.''

Drake opted for shepherd's pie, which smelled good enough to make my knees weak when it arrived. For a few minutes we didn't have much to say, as we dug into our meals. The haggis did turn out to be very good and very rich, with a warm whiskey gravy and a side dish called clapshot that tasted a lot like mashed potatoes. After I'd rolled my eyes and moaned pleasurably with the first bite, Drake even bravely tried a little.

''What's with that attitude I'm sensing out at the oil platform?'' I finally asked him after we'd curbed our initial starvation pangs.

''Did someone give you a hard time?''

''Not really, it's just a sense of hostility I get when I go out there.'' I told him about the crewman who'd openly glared at me when I landed. ''Today wasn't the first time.''

''Brankin, I think that guy's name is,'' Drake said. ''He's one of the union leaders.''

''Uh-oh. Are we getting into the middle of something nasty here?'' I asked.

''I don't know.'' His face was solemn and I knew he was trying to be straight with me without alarming me.

''Well, let me in on what you do know. I don't want to get hassled out there.''

''I met a few of the union guys yesterday,'' he said. ''I remember Robson, Ewing, Barrie, Tolliver...some of them. But I haven't managed to put the names and faces together yet.''

We'd agreed that I'd handle some of the flying in the JetRanger, an aircraft I was used to flying at home, while Drake would take the bulk of the time flying the French machine. It was more complicated, with some of the controls operating the opposite ways of those I was accustomed to. The contract called for nearly constant use of that machine, while the secondary one, mine, would probably only be called out once or twice a week.

''There's some kind of union squabble going on between the

boat operators and the helicopter operators. The oil companies like the convenience of using aircraft, but the boat operators don't want to lose the business. They've got some of the oil crews steamed up against us. A few of the men have refused to fly, wanting to only be transported back and forth to shore aboard the boats. Some of the ones you saw today, by the sound of it."

"But Brian has a contract. Would they actually try to harm us?"

"I don't think so. I think the real beef is with the oil company. But Brian's in the middle."

"And since he's in the middle, that means you and I are in it too, aren't we?"

He nodded and drained his glass of ale.

TWO

I ROLLED OVER and slowly worked my eyelids open. The window looked out on acres of emerald green lawn, bordered by low heather and tall pine forest. Gray sky gave the room a feeling of pre-dawn gloom, but a glance at the clock told me we were well past that. It was after eight o'clock.

Drake had left sometime before daylight, needing to get to the airport and be ready to fly early. I'd checked Meggie's calendar yesterday afternoon and noticed that, even though the oil company didn't have any flights for him today, she'd booked a couple of sightseeing tours for the morning and a recon of a farm later in the afternoon. Rain speckles on the window made me wonder if the weather would end up nixing the day's work.

I threw my legs over the edge of the bed, instinctively watching for the dog I was accustomed to seeing asleep on the floor beside me. Unfortunately, we couldn't bring our big red lab, Rusty, with us. The U.K.'s laws on quarantining pets that come into the country made it impractical, which was probably the real point of the law anyway, more so than the supposed one of keeping the country rabies-free. Well, it was only for a couple of months that I'd have to do without canine companionship.

After a quick trip to the bathroom and brushing my teeth, I slipped on jeans and a light sweater. A sound outside caught my attention and I went to the window and peered down. From our second-floor bedroom I couldn't see the source so I padded down the stairs in my socks and pulled aside the drape covering the sliding glass door in the living room. The noise had elevated and I picked out two male voices in a heated exchange, although I couldn't make out the words. No one was visible here, on the south side of the cottage, so I went into the kitchen.

From the small window over the sink I could see a young man stalking toward our driveway, two border collies trotting along at his heels. His back was to me and I could only see that he had reddish-blond hair and wore khaki work pants, heavy boots, and a plaid shirt. He carried a long shepherd's crook. The two black-and-white dogs stayed right with him and I was suddenly overcome with the need to pat a friendly doggy head. I sidestepped quickly to the front door and went out, belatedly realizing that I didn't have shoes on and that it was raining a steady, light drizzle.

The man looked my way as I closed the door behind me, somewhat louder than necessary.

"Hi," I ventured.

The golden brows, which had been pulled tightly together over an upturned nose, relaxed somewhat and his expression became a tad less surly.

"I'm Charlie Parker," I said, putting more perkiness than necessary into my voice. "We're renting the cottage here for a couple of months."

He was gentleman enough not to ignore the hand I extended to him. "Ian Brodie," he replied as he stepped forward.

"Are you a neighbor?"

"Near enough." His head tilted toward the long drive that led to our cottage.

"Beautiful dogs," I commented. "I really miss ours." I leaned forward and the two collies came immediately to sniff my hands. I ruffled their ears and patted both heads at once.

Ian softened considerably now that I'd gotten down on one knee and was letting the dogs lick my face. "Aye, I can see that ye do."

"We're just here for the rest of the summer," I said. "Not long enough to try to bring him with us." I told him about Rusty and his friendly manner.

"These are working dogs," he said. "We run sheep."

"Nearby?"

"Here on the property. We rent from the Dunbars, too." Something hardened in his face but I had no clue what caused it.

Our landlords were, I guess in the most literal sense, *land lords*. The family Dunbar went back just about to the dawn of time, and the thousands of acres where we now resided contained a few rental cottages, plenty of farmland, and one real, authentic castle. I could see its turrets from our upper windows, but had caught only the merest glimpse of the whole structure the day we arrived to pick up our keys from the estate manager's office.

I told Ian briefly what we were doing here and suggested that he drop by anytime, and bring the dogs.

"Well, my wife and I are around a lot. You can always find a friendly dog or two with us. Our place is the second turn after the bend in the road."

"I thought I heard voices a minute ago," I mentioned.

Ian stared pointedly at my feet, which were clad in thoroughly soggy socks now, and shrugged. "Was nothin'." He turned and gave a sharp whistle to the dogs, who immediately snapped to attention.

I stood slowly and watched the three of them follow the drive toward the road. Something had sure touched a nerve.

THREE

THE PHONE WAS ringing when I opened the front door. My socks made squishy noises as my feet hit the tile in the entry-way. I reached to peel them off, trying to hop toward the kitchen phone, and nearly landed on my face in the effort. It took about three giant stumbling steps to recover and reach the telephone. I managed a breathless, "Hello?" as I slid the last two feet and knocked one knee into the refrigerator. "Shit!"

"Excuse me?" a cultured female voice answered.

"Oh, I am so sorry," I breathed. "I was outside."

"In this weather? No wonder." She paused a long few seconds. "Is that Charlie Parker, then?"

"Yes, yes it is," I stuttered, wondering who on earth had our number here. Meggie was the only female I'd spoken to, and this voice was a few decades older.

"Yes, Charlie. It's Sarah Dunbar, up at Dunworthy."

"Oh." Brilliant, Charlie. What a charming answer to the lady of the castle. "I'm sorry, Mrs. Dunbar. I didn't mean to be rude."

"Oh, nonsense, girl. The weather's a fright today. I should give you a minute to towel off. Would you like me to phone back later? And, please, it's Sarah."

"No...Sarah, this is fine. No need to make another call. I'm doing just fine." I was, in fact, toweling off as we spoke, rubbing a kitchen hand towel vainly over my hair in an effort to keep the water from dripping into my eyes. Why hadn't I noticed how wet I was getting while I petted the dogs?

"Actually, I just phoned to see if you and your husband might be free this afternoon for tea? Say around four?"

Tea with the gentry? I wondered if she extended this invitation to every renter on the castle grounds? "Four would be lovely," I said, picking up on the few manners I'd once possessed. "I'm not sure what time to expect Drake in, though..."

"Well, then, you come—with or without him. I'm looking forward to meeting you."

I replaced the receiver softly and caught a glimpse of myself in the reflection of the microwave oven's small door. Shoulder length hair hanging in damp strands, bangs pasted to my forehead, no makeup. And my dripping socks had now made sizeable puddles on the tile floor. Yes—I'm going to tea at the castle. I couldn't help it, I broke up laughing.

I peeled off the socks and squeezed them out over the kitchen sink. Thirty minutes later I'd changed clothes and dried my hair, toasted an English muffin, and switched on the electric fire in the fireplace. It glowed orange through its fake logs and emitted a surprising amount of warmth. Stretched out in a hugely padded armchair with feet on a matching ottoman, I nibbled my muffin and contemplated my plans for the day. Buying an umbrella or two should definitely be part of the plan, I decided. I'd known, leaving New Mexico, that we would need them but since we didn't own any, the purchase had been put off.

The keys to our rented Vector hung on a hook by the door. Drake had been driving Brian's company vehicle and I'd been watching the way he handled the right-hand drive and getting a feel for the art of driving on the "wrong" side of the road. I thought I could handle it, at least for the short ride into the nearby village where I'd spotted a tiny general store, one gas pump, and the offices of the Royal Mail. Tackling the bigger town of Inverness, where they had traffic lights and everything, would have to wait.

The rain abated during the time I'd eaten my breakfast and tidied the kitchen, so I donned boots and pulled on a light jacket from the hall closet. The air felt cool and pleasantly damp as I walked the short distance down the cottage's flag-stone path to the grassy area beside a stone wall where we'd been directed to park the cars. From habit I walked to the left side of the car and almost sat in the passenger seat before I caught myself and circled back to slip in behind the wheel. Luckily, no one had seen me; I felt like such a tourist.

I took a few minutes to familiarize myself with the con-trols—gearshift on the left, pedals the same way I was used to, locating the wiper switch and turn signals. Finally, I felt ready to tackle the driveway.

The three miles into the village went uneventfully and I be-gan to get the feel for thinking in drive-on-the-left mode. I pulled into a small dirt parking area beside the one all-purpose building. Inside, the small store was a combination gift shop and general store. Touristy items like mugs, scarves, and ce-ramic models of Nessie filled the gift shop portion, while the rest of the store clearly catered to locals. Bins of staple food items like potatoes, onions, and other vegetables stood along the wall near the cash register. Three short aisles carried a surprisingly complete selection of groceries, while high shelves along the walls were filled with household items ranging from extension cords to toasters to lampshades. A portly woodstove in the center of the room told me that this was a year-round operation, frequented by local residents, and not merely a sea-sonal tourist shop.

I browsed the shelves, getting a feel for the stock, and tried hard to resist the smell of the freshly baked bread being set out on the counter by a plump lady in tweed slacks and a heather-gray sweater.

The door creaked open while I was involved with deciding between chicken noodle or tomato soup for lunch, followed by the sound of male boots clumping against the wooden floor and the door swinging shut with a solid thump.

"...believe the price we're given?" one of the male voices muttered.

"Makes ye ill, doesn't it?" the other said.

"I'm goin' broke, I'll tell ye. We don't get wool prices back up, there's no point in doin' this."

The two sets of boots made their way to the counter, where the clerk apparently pulled bakery goods as they pointed. I heard the rustle of paper and the clink of coins. When I stepped to the end of the aisle and looked that direction, I noticed both men held some kind of puffy pastry in a slip of bakery tissue. The tall, dark haired one dropped a few more coins onto the counter and the woman passed across two paper cups of coffee. The man took a large bite of his pastry and picked up the coffee in his other hand. The shorter man was Ian Brodie, the farmer with the collies I'd met this morning. I took one step back so he wouldn't see me.

"Aye, this bein' dictated to by the government—" The dark haired man mumbled an expletive as he stuffed more pastry into his mouth. They had nearly reached the door again.

"Well, I for one ain't standin' for it," Ian agreed. "Somethin' bad's gonna'—"

His words were cut off as the door thumped shut behind him. I stepped to the window in time to the see the two men approach a dark green Range Rover with a crooked front bumper. Ian brushed powdered sugar from his fingers onto his pant leg before he reached for the door handle. His face was contorted in anger as he said something to the other man, who had climbed into the driver's seat. The vehicle backed sharply out of its parking spot and turned left onto the road. I glanced toward the woman at the counter, but she seemed busy stacking boxes of shortbread and didn't indicate that she'd paid the men any attention.

I'd gathered a small basket of grocery items—some cans of soup, fresh fruit, and salad makings—and took them to the counter.

"Umbrellas?" I asked.

"Oh, in the gift shop," the woman told me. "Just pick one up. You can pay for it in here with your other things."

I spotted a display spinner and pulled two umbrellas from it.

"Guess we didn't come very well prepared," I commented to her.

"Staying long?"

"A couple of months. I'm sure I'll become a regular in here over the next few weeks."

"Aye, well you'll need these, then." She finished totaling my groceries and told me what I owed.

As I was struggling to remember the denominations of the strange-looking coins, she spoke again. "You the couple who's renting out at Dunworthy? Those pilots?"

Beauty of a small town. You never have to introduce yourself. I grinned at her. "Yes, we're the ones."

"Amanda Douglas," she said. "Think you got some mail here."

"Mail?" I couldn't imagine what we'd be receiving so soon.

Amanda stepped through a doorway that led to the third section of the small building, the post office.

"Yeah, here you go," she announced, bringing a small parcel with her. "Looks like it's from New Mexico, USA."

I looked at the return address. The box was from Elsa Higgins, my surrogate grandmother and neighbor who was watching Rusty for us during our stay in Scotland. What on earth could she be sending? Probably some little item I'd forgotten, something she thought I couldn't live without.

Amanda was watching me with frank curiosity.

"Let's see what she sent," I suggested.

A pair of scissors appeared like magic from below the counter and Amanda watched as I opened them and used one blade to slit the tape on the package. Beneath a cushion of crumpled newspaper sat six small cans of Hatch green chilies. I couldn't suppress the laugh that bubbled out of me.

"Whatever...?" Amanda was examining one of the cans, her face screwed up in puzzlement.

"It's hard to explain," I chuckled. "Guess she knew Drake and I wouldn't last long without a chili fix."

She set the can back into the box with the others.

"It's a Southwestern thing, I guess. Kind of like, if you went to live in the U.S. for a while and couldn't find haggis."

"Ah…" She nodded in complete agreement. "Like that."

FOUR

THE SKY HAD lightened considerably now that I owned two umbrellas, and by the time I got back to the cottage there were patches of blue showing. I puttered around, organizing our few belongings and re-arranging a couple of pieces of furniture in the living room until it was more to my liking. I spent the afternoon exploring the tiny garden that surrounded our little home and getting some exercise walking through the forest.

After a quick shower, I donned a pair of slacks and cashmere sweater, hoping the outfit would be casual enough for afternoon tea and dressy enough for my first visit to a real castle. I envisioned the lady of the manor wearing a Chanel suit and pearls, tasteful black pumps, and little button earrings.

I arrived promptly at four, guiding my rented Vector down a storybook lane flanked by rows of trees whose trunks were close to four feet in diameter and whose branches had become so entwined with time that the overhead canopy was nearly solid. I emerged into an open area and spotted two other vehicles—a brand new Land Rover and a fifty-year-old Bentley—sitting to the side of a circular drive. I pulled to the side, staying a respectful distance from the Land Rover.

The castle itself towered five stories above me, a tasteful gray stone edifice with turrets pasted to its sides in seemingly random fashion. Wings extended from either side of the central structure, and archways led to unseen courtyards and other mysterious places. Turning my attention the other direction, I noticed that I had, in fact, crossed an old moat, which was now a grassy swale with precision-manicured lawns extending at least fifteen or twenty acres before thick forest took over. An English-style box hedge formed a maze to my left and led the eye upward to a rock garden with plantings of brilliant flowers. A rose garden, easily fifty feet in length, grew along the side of the castle itself, with bushes that reached the lower edges of the first floor windows. I was just noticing how small all the windows were, narrow slits in some cases, when a commotion behind me caught my attention.

"Ruffie! Ruffie, get over here!" a woman's voice shouted.

Bounding toward me came a small furball, some kind of terrier with white hair that dragged the ground and a high-pitched bark that sounded like a midget with the croup. Behind Ruffie, a blond woman trotted with a dangling leash in her hand. She wore a baggy pair of tweed slacks with a large mud stain on one knee and a brown sweater whose cowl collar lay askew over one shoulder. One sleeve was pushed up nearly to her elbow while the other flopped down around her wrist. She tugged at it while vainly trying to catch up with the dog.

"She won't bite," the woman called. "She's just a bit exuberant."

I knelt down, keeping my knees off the wet lawn and extended a hand to Ruffie. As soon as I reached out, she came to a halt, planting her tiny feet and staring suspiciously at my hand. The nose wriggled, but at least the barking had stopped.

"I'm so sorry," the woman said, breathless from her dash across the lawn. "I'd just reached down to attach her leash when your car pulled up. Once she saw you there was no stopping her."

"It's okay. I love dogs." I didn't mention that yipping little ones weren't usually my favorites. We'd see how Ruffie decided to treat me before making that judgment. For the moment the dog was keeping her distance, so I stood up.

"You must be Charlie," the woman said. "I'm Sarah Dunbar."

She tugged her flapping sleeve up and righted the cowl collar with one gracious flip before extending her hand to me.

"I'm dreadfully sorry to greet you this way, Charlie. I'd

meant to be done with the gardening and walking the dog, and planned to have put on something a bit more decent before you got here.''

''Would another time be…'' I began.

The picture of the pink Chanel suit blipped out of my mind instantly. This woman was completely down-to-earth with her mud-smeared knee and the blond hair tossed out of place. I guessed her age to be somewhere in her sixties, although her slightly thickened torso and a few spots on her hands were the only things that gave it away. Her complexion was smooth, with the texture of a baby peach and none of the sun damage so common in our part of the world.

''Oh, not a bit. Let's just go on in.'' She ushered me toward a massive wooden door. I noticed the family crest carved in stone above the lintel, a shield shape with some kind of animal entwined with something else. My quick glance didn't reveal much.

We stepped into a narrow vestibule that opened immediately into a larger hall. Sarah draped the dog leash over a wooden peg on the wall where coats and hats had been deposited. She knelt and caught Ruffie by the collar.

''Molly!'' she called out. ''Molly, can you bring a towel for Ruffie?''

A plump girl in a housedress and apron appeared with a small towel and she set to wiping the dog's tiny paws and blotting the dampness from the fur that had trailed in the grass.

''Pesky bit,'' Sarah commented, fluffing her own hair in front of a hall mirror. ''I don't know why we don't just shave her down so we aren't constantly minding that thick fur.''

I stood aside, unsure what to say to that.

''You can set your bag here, if you don't want to carry it.'' Sarah indicated an empty peg, and I deposited my shoulder bag there. ''Now let's see about that tea.''

She bustled through the hall, past a set of double doors, and into a huge, modern kitchen, cautioning me to ''mind the step'' as the uneven floor dipped downward.

''There we go now,'' she said, after filling a kettle with

water and setting it over the gas flame on the stove. She took a deep breath and surveyed the spacious kitchen. "Heavens, Charlie, take a seat—just there—while I find something to go along with this."

I perched myself on a stool at the long counter that edged one side of a center island made of butcher block.

"This kitchen is probably the biggest one I've ever seen," I told her.

"Humph—can be a damn nuisance, when you're hiking from one end to the other just cooking for two," she snorted. "But it's nice when we entertain and I guess it came in handy in the old days."

"So, are there only two of you here now?"

"Usually just Robert and me for dinner anymore. The children—well, they're in their forties—hardly children. They've gone to the bigger cities. One in London, one in Edinburgh. Grandchildren scattered all over. The nearest one's Richie, going to school just outside Inverness. He's still on summer holiday and he pops in. He and two chums are here now. You'll probably see them all, hanging about, while you're here."

"But doesn't it take a huge staff to keep a place this size?"

Sarah bustled around the big kitchen, pulling a cake under a glass dome from a pantry, a box of chocolate cookies from a cupboard. She cut several narrow slices of the cake and arranged them, along with some of the cookies, on a crystal plate.

"Oh, goodness, yes. We're lucky that the farm still supports us all. So many of our friends have resorted to opening their homes to tourists just to cover their taxes. It's a burden, that's sure."

The water boiled just then and I watched Sarah expertly pour from kettle to teapot, steep the leaves, warm the cups, and set everything on a silver tray.

"Let's do have a civilized tea in the drawing room," she said, lifting the large tray. "Get that smaller tray with the cake, would you?"

I picked up the second tray and followed as she butted a swinging door open at the far side of the room. It opened into a narrow hall, which led directly to a lovely room furnished in celery green and persimmon. Soft, upholstered chairs flanked a fireplace that had been freshly stoked so that a warm glow lit the room. We set the trays on a huge ottoman that stood between the chairs and Sarah poured tea while I eyed the cake.

"There now, that's better," she said after sinking into one of the deep chairs and taking her first sip of tea.

"This land has been in your family forever, I'd imagine." I pressed my fork into the raspberry filling between the delicate layers of white cake.

"Since the eleventh century," Sarah answered. "Scotland has such a rich history, you could study it for years and still not get it all. I'm foggy on many of the details myself and I've had this fed to me from the cradle." She chuckled at the memory of early school years. "I guess my interests always lie with the gardens and the animals. Didn't care much which clan killed which, or which king held power at what time."

She set her cup back on the tray. "Have you any Scottish kin, Charlie?"

"I'm not sure," I confessed. "I guess I haven't taken the time to study much of our family history either."

She patted my knee. "Well, I can't hold that against you," she said. "But if you're interested, I have a book. What's your family name?"

"Well, Parker on my father's side. My mother's maiden name was Davidson."

"Ah, Davidson!" Her face lit up. "Now that one's an old Scottish name. Want to take a look?"

I set my cup down and she led the way through two more connecting rooms to a library. Shelves filled two sides of the room, floor to ceiling, and most of the books were bound in leather and appeared very old. Sarah opened one of the glass doors on the front of a section and pulled out two books, one a small, modern paperback titled *Scots Kith & Kin,* and a thick, leather-bound edition of another.

"This little one's available at all the tourist shops. Just gives an overview, but it's a handy little thing," she said, handing it to me. "Now, this thing—this one'll tell you all about your clan. If it doesn't throw your back out first."

I offered to take the big book from her, but she'd already hugged it securely to her chest.

"Let's take these back in the drawing room," she suggested. "We don't run the central heat in the summer months, and no one's set the fire in here. Feels chilly to me."

The shadowy room did, indeed, contain a chill so we carried our books back to the warmth of the other room where Molly was in the process of stirring the fire.

"Shall I clear the tea things, Mrs. Dunbar?" she asked.

"Oh, leave them a few more minutes, Molly. We may pour another."

The girl actually dropped a slight curtsy as she left the room. Sarah poured us each another cup of tea and spread open the large clan book. After a minute or two of paging through it, she came to the spot she wanted.

"Here we go, Clan Davidson," she said, turning the book to face me.

I felt a sense of pride and an odd sense of connectedness, learning that my mother's family name went back to the twelfth century and earlier. Me, whose only sense of family came from my one brother who is my business partner back home, and another brother I rarely see. I felt a wide grin coming on, and I looked up to see Sarah watching me.

"Sorry," I said, "this is just the first time I've known any of this existed."

She reached over and squeezed my hand. "Borrow the book if you'd like," she said. "You'll have fun reading up, I imagine."

"You must think I'm being silly," I told her as I closed the large book and pulled it toward me. "You've known your own family history forever."

"Well, there've been Dunbars in this house since the 1500s. And my family, the Murrays, allied themselves with the Dunbars and other clans as far back as the 1100s. So, yes, I guess you could say we go a way back."

"I'll get the book back to you in a day or two," I promised. I could see that this new fascination with family history might begin to occupy me on my days off from flying.

A deep thud that sounded like it came from several rooms away interrupted my thoughts.

"Sounds like Robert is home," Sarah said. "Come, I'd like you to meet him."

I set the clan book on a round library table and followed her back through the halls to the entry. A rotund man of about seventy, with white hair that dipped in a wave over his forehead and intense blue eyes, focused on taking off his hooded parka. He patted each of the side pockets, and then flung the jacket onto one of the wall pegs. He seemed to be muttering something under his breath.

"Robert!" Sarah called out, stopping him in mid swing.

"Damn it all," he bellowed. "Two more lambs are missing!"

FIVE

"ROBERT, WE HAVE a guest," she said quietly.

He glanced up and noticed me for the first time. "Oh, sorry." His florid face went another shade brighter.

"This is Charlie Parker, the lady who's renting the Red Fern Cottage. Remember, she and her husband are flying for that helicopter service."

Robert dusted off a hand and offered it to me. "Sorry, miss, I didn't mean to go off like that with company around."

"It's okay. Really." I noticed his grip was firm and he had a winning smile, once he turned it on.

"Wash up, dear, and come have your tea. We're in the drawing room." Sarah bustled her husband toward a small powder room off the central hall, while she and I headed back toward the cozy fire. "I'd best just give this a little re-warm," she said after feeling the side of the teapot. "Be right back."

I browsed the room now that I was alone. The soft green wallpaper was silk and it perfectly matched the fabric on the chairs that showed just a genteel bit of wear. Bright persimmon pillows picked up the same shade in an Oriental carpet. Family photos covered one tabletop—modern pictures of the Dunbars and their offspring, some posed and some casual. A windowsill displayed a grouping of porcelain figurines, one of which I recognized as Chinese and very old. The others were traditional English figures and I assumed they were also antiques.

"There, this should hit the spot," Sarah said, bustling back in with the tea.

As quickly as she'd reheated the pot, I had to assume that

even ancient castles had microwave ovens in the modern age. She glanced up at the door.

"So, what was that you were saying about missing lambs?" she asked as Robert entered the room.

"Rrrr," he growled. "Two more. From the same flock as before. Don't get me started—I'm angry as hell about this."

"Here, have your tea," Sarah soothed, offering him a cup that she'd poured and laced with milk and sugar.

He took it and eased back into one of the overstuffed chairs.

"What do you think has happened to the missing lambs?" I asked, not catching Sarah's warning glance in time.

"Same damn thing." The growl was back in his voice. "Stolen."

"Now, Robert, you don't know that for a fact," Sarah said quietly.

"I bloody well do!" He glanced at me. "Excuse my language."

I waved it off.

"That young bloke...whatever his name is. You know bloody well that he'd love to increase his own flock. And he's made no secret that he thinks I'm part of the problem with price controls on wool. I wasn't one of the MSPs who voted that in, you know."

Ian Brodie, I thought, remembering the snatch of conversation I'd overheard at the store this morning. I almost opened my mouth, but didn't.

"Always griping about the cost of feed, cost of medicine for the sheep. Damned ingrate doesn't even appreciate that I'm giving him the lowest lease rates around for pasture."

"We're not *the* lowest," Sarah murmured, not very loudly. "And your position in Parliament certainly doesn't make you anti-farmer. He's just spouting off, I'm sure."

"And that attitude of his, like we owe him something because we've got it all and he has nothing. Huh. Man has no idea what a struggle it is to keep a place like this afloat. Trade places with me, he wouldn't last a month." He paused to take a sip of his tea.

"Enough of this," Sarah declared. "Let's get to know Charlie. Robert, she's the first female helicopter pilot I've ever met."

"Is that so?" he replied. "Are you really? Guess I thought your husband was the pilot."

"Well, he is. He taught me to fly and we share the duties." I explained briefly that we'd come to help Brian Swinney while his mother was ill. "Drake has had some fascinating experiences during his career. I think you'd enjoy meeting him."

"And is this what you do at home, too? New Mexico, did someone tell me?"

"Actually, back home I'm a partner in a private investigation firm. With my brother, Ron. I help Drake out in his own helicopter business there, but just on a limited basis."

"Investigator, eh?" Robert picked up on that tidbit right away. "Well, maybe you can find these lambs for me."

I chuckled at the thought. "Believe me, I wouldn't know one lamb from another and watching me try to catch one would probably be a spectacle worth selling tickets to."

"Ah, a little extra cash flow." He laughed, a deep, rich sound.

I finished my tea and told them I better be on my way. Sarah reminded me to take the clan book with me, and Robert offered to walk me to the door.

"We'll plan dinner sometime soon. You've been delightful company and I'd like to meet Drake." He patted me on the shoulder and held the heavy wooden door open for me.

DUSK DARKENED the sky as I arrived back at the cottage. Red Fern. It was the only time I'd lived in a house with a name. For the first time I noticed that there were thick patches of ferns growing around the little garden wall. A mist had begun to rise over the open moorland to the north. Southward, the pine forest appeared dense and black, with tendrils of mist playing at the tops of the trees. I hurried into the cottage and fired up the electric logs again. Drake should be here within the hour.

After two cups of tea and two slices of cake, I wasn't particularly hungry. But Drake would be, with all that sea air and adrenaline drawing at his reserves, so I decided soup would be a good choice for dinner. I opened a couple of the cans I'd bought this morning and added a few extra vegetables and a dash of wine to spark them up. Simmering gently on the stove, the scent filled the cozy rooms. I made a quick salad and put it into the fridge to stay chilled, then opened a bottle of wine and set it out to breathe on the counter.

I was just trying to decide between switching on the TV set or pulling out the book I'd begun reading nearly a week ago on the airplane. For some reason, I just wasn't getting into the story, but maybe that was because of the week's distractions. Before I'd made a choice, I saw the headlights of Drake's company van pull into the lane. At least this was a welcome distraction.

"Whew! It's getting chilly out there," he said as he breezed through the front door.

"Misty, huh? Dampness going to your bones?" Our high-desert climate at home in Albuquerque brings cooler temperatures with nightfall, too, but there's rarely any dampness associated with it. We were learning to adjust, and pulled out our sweaters often.

"How was your day?" Drake asked, planting a kiss on my mouth before pulling off his jacket that smelled of sea breezes and jet fuel.

"Very interesting. I'll fill you in during dinner."

"Something sure smells good. I'm starving."

"Wine first? Or with dinner?" I headed toward the kitchen as I made the offer.

"Mind if I have a quick shower first? I think I smell."

"Well, I didn't want to say anything…"

He'd come up behind me and he grabbed a dishtowel and gave me a quick pop on the butt with it.

"Hey!"

"Pour the wine," he suggested. "I'll step into the shower

and, unless you join me in there, I'll be ready to relax in about ten minutes.''

I thought he was going to give me another quick peck, but the kiss lingered and became one of those that sends tingles clear to the toes. Before I knew it, I was, indeed, in the shower with him and it was more like an hour later that we poured the wine.

''*Now* I'm relaxed,'' he murmured, as I ladled soup into bowls and quickly set the table. He carried the glasses to the table and we opted to switch off the overhead light and burn a candle instead.

I filled Drake in on my day, including the bit of overheard conversation between Ian Brodie and the other man, and Robert Dunbar's suspicions about his lambs being stolen.

''I'm sure it was Ian he was talking about when he said the young farmer probably took the lambs. Unless, do you suppose they have a number of different men leasing grazing pasture?''

''Hard to say, hon,'' Drake answered. ''This place is huge. Didn't they tell us the whole property was around 20,000 acres? Dunworthy runs a prize herd of Angus cattle, quite a number of sheep, and they've also got land planted in barley, which they sell to the distilleries. And that's in addition to the parcels they lease out so others can farm them.''

''Really? Well, in that case maybe there is any number of suspects.'' I caught myself. ''Listen to me. I'm talking like this is a case I have to solve.''

''Well, watch out, or you will be solving it. You're gonna' be up to your neck in it, just like you usually are.''

I ignored his gentle jibe. It wasn't meant to be critical, just a reminder that I do tend to get myself into things I don't want to do, and I've found myself in life-threatening situations on more than one occasion because of it.

We finished off dinner with some fresh fruit and I noticed Drake's eyelids drooping. ''Why don't you relax in front of the TV for a while, or just go on to bed?'' I suggested. ''Isn't tomorrow another early day?''

''Yeah, and I forgot to mention it's an early one for you

too,'' he said. "We're supposed to start service to a new platform and I want you to go along with me and learn where it is. You can get a little time in the Astar that way, too.''

It was only nine o'clock but the long day was suddenly catching up with both of us. I went around the small cottage, closing drapes, even though there was nothing out there but open moor on one side and forest on the other. Before bolting the front door I decided to step out and see whether the mist had cleared. If anything it was thicker. Tiny droplets of moisture beaded on my face and hair. Beside the cottage, the cars were barely visible beyond the garden wall. Somewhere in the distance a dog howled with a mournful sound. I shivered and rubbed my upper arms, giving myself a reassuring hug before turning to go inside.

SIX

IT WAS STILL DARK in the room when the alarm clock shrilled. Drake rolled over and silenced it and I rolled toward his back, wanting nothing more than to snuggle up to his warmth and stay there for another three hours. Five o'clock was no civilized hour to be up. I groaned as Drake sat up and stretched.

He headed for the bathroom and I walked to the sliding glass door that led out to our tiny balcony. I pulled the drape aside and squinted into the darkness. Last night's mist looked thicker than ever.

"I don't think we can fly in this stuff," I called to him.

"Still socked in?"

"Big time. It's not fit out for man nor beast, as they say, so my suggestion would be to crawl right back under those covers while they're still warm." I aimed myself toward the bed with just that intention.

"Not so quick," Drake cautioned, grabbing my arm just as I was about to dive. "The forecast is for sunshine today, so the mist will burn off pretty early."

I groaned again.

"It won't be so bad once we're out," he tried to assure me. "Get dressed and I'll get the coffee started."

I took a deep breath and headed for the bathroom. Splashing water on my face helped a little, as did brushing my teeth and finding my clothes. I felt a pull of longing as I smoothed the sheets and made the bed, but by the time I reached the foot of the stairs I'd adjusted. There's that point of no return when it's simply easier to start the day than to go back to bed and find that cozy dream-state again. Drake was clearly already there.

Coffee scent filled the kitchen and he'd already poured bowls of cereal for both of us.

"Here, this'll help," he said, handing me a mug of steaming coffee.

I took careful sips of it, staring out the windows for some hint of daylight beyond. There was none.

"Okay, breakfast's ready," he announced, carrying the two cereal bowls to the table. "Cheer up, things could be worse."

"Five o'clock's pretty bad."

"It could be pouring rain and we'd still have to go."

"Oh." I accepted the other half of the banana he'd sliced over his flakes and added it to mine. "Well, in that case…" I forced a fakey grin, just to show that I'd be a good sport about it.

Twenty minutes later we'd finished our breakfast, put the dishes into the dishwasher, and poured more coffee into thermal mugs for the road. We bundled into layers of shirts and jackets and headed for the company van. By the time we reached the airport, the dark mist had turned pale gray, although I couldn't tell that it had thinned at all.

The two helicopters stood on the tarmac, cushioned in the mist like delicate ornaments packed in soft cotton after Christmas. We headed toward the Eurocopter, a seven-seater, painted in Air-Sea Helicopter's trademark red and white.

"Are we waiting for passengers today?" I asked.

"Not this morning. We've got some gear to take out. It's loaded in the cargo compartment already. We may be bringing people back—I'm not sure."

We circled the aircraft, Drake briefing me on the pre-flight checklist. There were a few items unique to this craft, things I didn't have to do on the JetRanger, but overall it was much the same. He showed me what to check, I did the actual procedure, then he checked it off on the list. When everything was done, we took our seats, Drake at the controls, me beside him in the front seat.

The mist had thinned considerably and I noticed a patch of pure, pale blue overhead. It would probably be completely clear within thirty minutes. Just to be sure, Drake called out to the rig to verify their weather conditions.

"Same as here," he reported. "It should be clear by the time we get there." He started the engine and the turbine whined its way to life. The triple rotors slowly spun up.

"I'll probably have you fly it on the way back," he said. "Give you a little practice."

I nodded and adjusted my headset.

We got radio clearance from the tower and gently lifted off, clearing the small metal building that housed Air-Sea's offices and setting a course away from the airport's normal traffic.

"Did you file a flight plan with the airport, or did Meggie know our schedule?" I asked, once we'd cleared the area.

"She knows the general route," he said. "We're going to platform twelve first, then on to number six. I left her a note last night before I came home. And we've got the guys on the rig watching for us."

I was curious to see what the reaction would be from the guys on rig six, after the hostility I'd felt yesterday, but I didn't say anything to Drake. He hadn't seemed too concerned when I'd mentioned it before.

We climbed through the thinning white vapor until we saw blue sky above us and good visibility all around. He'd been right, the mist was rapidly burning off and we would have clear skies well before we needed to land. The water today looked nearly glassy as we flew over it, taking on a blue-gray cast as the sun came through. In about fifty minutes I spotted the new rig in the distance, its pointy cranes and struts sticking out at awkward angles.

Within an hour we'd finished our work there, cranked into action again and were on our way to Platform 6.

Drake spoke on the radio, letting them know we'd be landing, while I watched him, learning as much as I could about the new aircraft and how I'd need to handle it. I didn't see the man dash across the helipad until it was nearly too late. There was just a blur of blue jeans and green shirt. An impression of light hair.

"Drake! Look out!" My heart felt like it had gotten an injection of white lightning.

He pulled up and swung the aircraft in a sharp right arc. "Damned idiot!" he cursed. "What was that fool doing?"

"I don't know," I panted. "I just saw him at the last second."

He brought the aircraft in a complete circle around the rig and hovered beside the landing pad for a full minute, waiting to see if there were any other problems or anyone trying to get our attention. Everything appeared perfectly normal and quiet. He finally eased her to the left and set the skids gently down.

"I'm gonna' have a word with their crew chief," he told me over the intercom as we waited for the turbine engine to wind down. "You can go ahead and open the cargo compartment so they can unload their gear, if you'd like."

"Okay, no problem." I glanced sideways at my husband. "You doing all right?"

He blinked once then looked at me. "Yeah, fine. You?"

"I'm good. Just scared the hell out of me is all."

He reached over and took my hand, giving it a squeeze of reassurance. He pulled the rotor brake and shut down the engine. Tightening the cyclic and pulling off his headset, he opened his door and stepped down. I followed suit, noticing that Colin Finnie was walking across the platform. He extended his hand to Drake.

No one else had come out yet, so I followed Drake, curious as to how the conversation would go.

"Sorry about that, man," Finnie began. "I don't know…"

"What the hell was that all about?" Drake demanded. I didn't think I'd ever seen him so angry. "Who was that asshole?"

"Now wait a—"

"Okay, sorry. Who was that *guy?* And what did he think he was doing out there?"

Finnie shrugged. "I'll find out."

"He's just lucky I wasn't coming in any faster. He'd be a dead man right now."

"Look, I'll find out who it was and he'll get a reprimand. Okay?"

"Actually, we could have three people dead now and a million dollar aircraft destroyed. I think it's worth a little more than a reprimand. This wasn't some cute little teenage prank," Drake continued.

Finnie's mouth closed in a tight line and his face had gone a new shade of pink. I could see that Drake was losing his sympathy. I touched Drake's sleeve unobtrusively.

"Thanks, Mr. Finnie," I interrupted. "We just want him to understand the seriousness of the situation."

Three men came walking out just then, headed toward the helicopter. None of them wore blue jeans and a green shirt. I walked over to open the cargo doors for them to unload their supplies. Twenty yards away, I watched Finnie turn on his heel and head into his office. Drake turned back toward the aircraft, watching the men carry boxes away from it. As they walked away, he said, "If I got the introductions right, those three guys are Tolliver, Robson, and Barrie."

I looked after them, wishing I'd paid more attention. Then I noticed, standing in the shadows beside the structure, the man who'd given me such a dirty look yesterday. Brankin.

SEVEN

HIS DARK HAIR and blue shirt ruled him out as the man who'd run across our path, but I'd just about be willing to bet money that he was somewhere behind the stunt. He glared at Drake's retreating back before he realized that I'd spotted him. A mocking smile appeared on his face and he touched his brow, as if in salute to me, then turned and went through a doorway.

My blood pressure went up about ten points. What was this guy's game? His attitude toward the helicopter was pretty clear, and now it looked like he'd come to include Drake and me in his hatred. Well, know thine enemy, I thought.

"Can you watch things here a minute?" I said to Drake when he reached me. "I've got to do something."

Before he could object, I stalked toward Finnie's office and pulled the door open. It was one of those like on a ship, where you have to step up a few inches to clear the sill. I stepped inside and closed the door behind me just as he looked up from his paperwork.

"Mr. Finnie, I want to apologize for Drake's outburst out there," I said, stepping closer to his desk. "He's normally a very even-tempered man. It's just that whoever did this really gave us a scare."

"I know," Finnie replied. "I didn't see it happen, myself." He seemed to remember his manners. "Here, sit," he said indicating a chair in front of the desk. "And call me Colin."

"Thanks, Colin. Look, we don't want to cause trouble here. We're just trying to do a job."

"I know. And I don't think this is anything personal. No

one knows you and your husband. They're not out to hurt you.''

"Then why the dirty looks and why this stupid attempt to crash our helicopter?''

He fiddled with a pen and straightened the edges of the papers on the desk, stalling for time. "The oil men here are union,'' he began patiently. "The boat operators out there are union.''

I'd seen a number of boats come and go from the rig and wondered about their purpose.

"The company wants to go toward using helicopters for various services, including emergency evacuations, as well as transporting crews back and forth.''

"And the union boat operators want the business instead,'' I interjected.

"Exactly. They've been lobbying the government to create some regulations that would restrict the helicopter operators so severely that they wouldn't find it practical to do this kind of work.''

"As if we don't already have enough regulations to deal with,'' I mumbled.

"Probably so,'' Colin agreed. "That bit of it isn't my department, as they say. I don't know what's involved from any side of it. Except that I've got to keep an oil rig running as efficiently as possible.''

"Do you think any of these guys would actually go so far as to sabotage an aircraft or cause an accident?'' I asked, knowing full well that one had just tried it.

Colin rubbed his scalp with both hands. "I think most of 'em are men, just like men everywhere, and they want to do their work and get their paychecks and go out for a beer on Friday night and that's about it. I just don't know how serious their leaders are about getting rid of the competition.''

"Some of them are pretty openly hostile, though.''

"Some are,'' he admitted. "And I'll try to keep an eye on them.''

I sensed he was being straight with me. I thanked him for the information and headed back outside.

Drake gave me a questioning look as I approached the aircraft, but he didn't say anything. Two men were carrying away the last of the tools we'd brought in the cargo.

"Shall we go in and see if they'll offer us some lunch?" he asked.

"Um...I don't know. Maybe it's best if we don't leave the ship unattended."

"Why? What did you find out?" he asked.

"I'll tell you all about it later. Do we have any passengers or cargo to take back with us?"

"I thought that's what you went inside to ask Finnie," he said.

"No...that was something else. Let's just see how soon we can get off this rig. I'll stay with the aircraft if you want to find out," I suggested.

He gave me a look of curiosity but didn't push it. I found a bottle of window cleaner and a soft cloth while he went to ask for the manifest. I proceeded to wipe the salt spray off the Plexiglas windows of the aircraft while keeping a sharp eye out toward anyone who might approach.

Drake returned in a couple of minutes, shaking his head. "Nothing going back this trip," he said. "That was certainly an expensive run for the company."

"That one express shipment from Houston must have really been urgent, huh?"

I put away the cleaning supplies and we took our seats, this time with me at the controls. We put on our headsets and Drake went over the startup procedure with me.

Once we'd lifted off and safely put the oil rig behind us, I told him what Colin Finnie had explained to me about some of the rig's crewmen siding with the boat operators. He clamped his mouth shut and didn't say anything, but I could tell it was eating at him because he has this way of grinding his teeth so one little jaw muscle jumps. I gave him fifteen minutes before I spoke.

"So, what are you thinking?" I finally asked.

He turned to stare out the side window for a minute, then his eyes came back to me. "I'm thinking that I'd like to go back there, find that black-haired SOB who's probably the one behind all this, and thrash him."

I started to open my mouth with some platitude about how that really wouldn't do any good, but thought better of it.

"And I'm thinking that for our safety," he continued, "it would probably be smarter to call Brian and tell him we're off the job. He didn't exactly warn me that we had enemies out there."

I waited again, re-checking my GPS heading and making a minor course adjustment.

"At the very least I should talk to him tonight and let him know what's going on. Whatever it comes down to, I'm gonna' do what it takes to protect your life and mine. But he stands to lose a couple million dollars worth of equipment if things get really nasty." His voice had become calmer during this last statement and I figured the worst of the storm was over.

"I wonder if Brian would want to consider putting the two helicopters in a hangar at night, too. They're pretty vulnerable out there on the ramp after everyone goes home," I suggested.

"True. I better see if I can get through to him before we leave for the day."

In the distance, I could see the coastline looming ahead. Twenty minutes later, we'd crossed it and were making our approach to the airport. Drake had me practice a couple of touch and goes once we'd determined that no other air traffic would be affected. I had a little trouble getting used to the fact that the pedals operated in the opposite directions than those I was used to, but otherwise I was beginning to feel much more at ease with the French machine.

By the time we'd shut down and tied down the rotor blades, I was starving. I suggested heading into town for lunch, as I peeled out of the clumsy survival suit.

"I think I'll see if Meggie has a daytime phone number for

Brian. I want to get in touch with him before the end of the day, if I can.''

I could see this stretching into another hour, minimum— more if Brian gave him alternate instructions for storing the aircraft overnight. I left Drake to the final cleanup and I opted to walk over to the main terminal building and see what I could come up with in the way of sustenance. The General Aviation building was only a hop away from the main terminal if one could cross part of a runway to do it, but since that's severely frowned upon, I had to follow a chain-link fence for about a quarter of a mile before I found my way into the other structure. Once inside, I located a vendor who sold sandwiches and chose two that looked fairly fresh. Bottled iced tea and tiny bags of potato crisps rounded out the meal. I fished through the pockets of my jeans until I came up with some Scottish pound notes and was soon on my way. The hike back went more quickly, now that I could smell the bread and ham scent from my purchases.

Balancing everything precariously in the crook of my arm, I turned the knob of the little office at Air-Sea Helicopters and nearly dropped the whole burden as I looked inside.

Meggie was sprawled on the floor in Drake's arms with blood running down her cheek.

EIGHT

"OH MY GOD," I groaned, the words coming out no louder than a whisper. Meggie's face was dead white, her body completely limp.

The room had been trashed. File folders and papers carpeted the floor and every other horizontal surface. Brown liquid—accompanied by the sharp scent of coffee—coated the papers on the desk and trailed across the room where it saturated the cushions of an upholstered sofa.

"Get me some wet paper towels," Drake ordered as soon as he saw me. He continued to pat Meggie's cheek calling out to get her to wake up.

I planted my burden of food in the midst of the coffee soaked papers on the desk and ran to the cubbyhole bathroom in the corner. Ripping a length of paper towels from the roll, I doused them in cold water and squeezed out the excess. I dashed back to Drake with the sodden mass dripping in my hands.

"What happened here?" I asked stupidly.

"She was unconscious when I came in," Drake said. "I've gotten a few groans out of her, but she hasn't—"

I pulled the bunch of wet towels in half and handed one gob to Drake, who pressed it to Meggie's forehead. I dabbed at the blood on her cheek, then decided I might do more good by cleaning her up later. I ran the cold towel over her wrists and forearms, then dabbed her eyelids and temples, anyplace I could think of.

Gradually, her eyes began to twitch behind closed lids and she mumbled.

Drake coaxed her. "Meggie...Meggie. Wake up and talk to me. It's Drake and Charlie. We're here and everything's okay." His soothing voice that had comforted me many times began to reach her.

"What..." A little color rose in her face and she began to look less dead.

"Meggie," I said, "you're at the office. Charlie and Drake are here. Everything's going to be okay."

I looked at Drake as her eyelids fluttered. "Should we call 911 or whatever they have here?" I whispered.

"No, no, I'll be okay." Meggie moaned, stirring awkwardly. Her eyes opened and she jerked when she realized Drake was cradling her in his arms. "What happened?" she asked, pulling free of him and sitting up.

"We were going to ask you the same thing," Drake told her, smiling at her progress. "Get a little frustrated with the paperwork?" he joked.

Meggie propped her elbows on her jeaned knees and held her head. Her eyes focused for the first time on the layer of papers carpeting the floor.

"What!" She reached out and noticed blood on her hand. Turning it carefully, she examined the palm and the back. "What has happened to me?" she queried with frantic eyes.

"We found you here," Drake said. "We've just come in from Platform 6. We left early this morning, before you came in. Someone must have attacked you."

"That man—" she said. Her eyes darted between Drake and me, then around the room.

"No one's here now," I assured her. "Who was it?"

"A man... I'm trying to remember..."

"It's okay," Drake said. "It'll come to you. Let's just find you a more comfortable place to sit."

He helped her to her feet and kept an arm around her waist as she tested her legs.

"Sit over here," he said, pointing her toward the couch.

"Not there," I interrupted. "It's been soaked with coffee. How about the chair?"

I held Meggie's office chair steady and Drake led her to it.

"Coffee?" Meggie said, as she settled into the chair. "There was...I was just making the coffee..."

"Do you remember what time you got here?" Drake asked.

"Oh, eight o'clock. My usual."

Drake and I exchanged a look. Had she been unconscious nearly four hours?

"But I got your message about the extra early flight, so I didn't make any coffee right away. I—I think I returned some phone calls first." She pressed her fingertips to her temple.

"We better get you some medical attention," I suggested. "If you don't want an ambulance, let me at least drive you to a doctor."

She nodded. "That man came in...I didn't know him." Her face went white again and I put my hand on the back of her head and shoved it down between her knees.

"Do you know where there's a hospital?" I asked Drake. He nodded. "You better drive her to the ER. I'll stay here and straighten up. Maybe I can find some evidence that will tell us who did this."

"Lock yourself in," he said.

Meggie's color had returned somewhat when she raised her head, but I wasn't confident that she wouldn't faint again any minute. Drake and I got on either side of her and helped her to the car. He got behind the wheel while I fastened her seat belt and reclined the seat to make her a bit more comfortable.

"Wait just a second," I said. I rushed back into the office and located her purse, apparently untouched by the assailant, and carried it out to her. "She's bound to need her ID and some kind of insurance card or something at the hospital," I told Drake.

"Meggie, you just relax. I'll call your mother and she can meet you there."

At the mention of her mother, her eyes welled with bright moisture.

"What's her number?" I asked.

"Two four two nine," she said.

That meant it was local. The prefixes in the area were all the same. And it meant Meggie probably wasn't in too bad of shape, if she could call numbers to mind that quickly. I squeezed her hand through the open window.

"Take care. I'll come along later."

I watched Drake slowly back the car out of its spot and gently guide it past the speed bumps in the road. I turned back to face the mess in the office.

It hadn't miraculously gone away, and I wasn't sure how much help I'd be in getting it straightened out. I had no idea about Meggie's filing system, but it was a good bet that the intruder had scattered most of it to the wind. I slumped into her chair to reconnoiter the situation. All four drawers of the tall file cabinet stood open, most nearly empty. My guess was that the man had pulled handfuls of folders out and flung them across the room. The floor of the entire office was at least an inch deep in paper. He'd then evidently grabbed a pot full of coffee and flung it as well.

Was Meggie watching all this, or had he hit her first and she lay unconscious on the floor as he ransacked the place? If we were lucky, maybe she'd remember more details and help fill in some of the blanks.

Thinking of Meggie again reminded me to call her family. I punched in the digits and listened as it rang four times, five, six. I was just about to hang up when a breathless woman answered.

"Mrs. Flanery?" I inquired.

"Yes?"

I introduced myself and she apologized for the fact that she'd been hanging clothes on the line and had taken so long to answer. As gently as I tried to break the news, there is just no easy way for a mother to accept that her child is on the way to the hospital. After she'd nearly hyperventilated, I asked whether she'd be all right to drive and she assured me that her older son was there and he could do it. I hung up with my fingers crossed that everyone would make the trip without further incident.

There seemed to be nothing more to do than to tackle the disaster at my feet.

Well, if I couldn't put the files back into shape, I could at least clean up the mess. In the bathroom, I commandeered the entire roll of paper towels and began ripping sheets off to blot up the places where coffee was still wet. Much of it had dried, leaving wrinkly brown smudges on everything. The sofa was the worst, where it seemed that pure vengeance motivated the drenching of the pale blue fabric. I pressed towels into the spots and soaked up a lot of it, but much had penetrated the foam beneath and only time would dry that. With luck, an upholstery cleaning service with some good detergent might salvage the thing.

Trying to organize the paperwork looked like a nightmare to me. I had no idea where anything went. About all I could do was to gather papers into piles and leave it for Meggie in a day or two. Hopefully, she wouldn't decide that the job was too dangerous and quit, because I doubted Brian Swinney had any clue how his files should be organized.

I made stacks on the desk, stacks on the file cabinet, stacks in the drawers, and stacks on the floor. Against the wall on the south side, I came across dangerous shards of glass, where the coffee carafe had apparently landed with some force after its contents were gone. I gingerly gathered them and swept up the tiny pieces with a broom I'd seen in the bathroom. I applied more wet paper towels to the brown stains on the walls, re-hung pictures and certificates that had been ripped from their hooks and smashed on the floor, swept up more glass, and straightened the furniture. Drake walked through the door as I was stashing the broom and dustpan.

"Well, this is a big improvement," he said.

"How's Meggie doing?"

"Sitting up on an ER gurney waiting for a doctor to get around. Her mother and brother arrived and there was a lot of wailing, but basically I think she'll be okay. I suggested that she not discuss the incident in great detail with anyone other than the police, or us. Don't know if she'll contain herself, but

I didn't think it would be good if everyone in town knew about this just yet."

"Want a sandwich?" I asked, retrieving our lunch from the spot I'd hastily dumped it nearly two hours earlier.

Drake picked up his portion and looked around. "How's that couch for sitting?"

"A lot of coffee soaked into the cushions. I don't think I'd park my butt there yet."

He chose a side chair and pulled it up to the desk. The ham sandwiches were about a day and a half away from fresh but at this point I didn't care. I'd thought I was starving two hours ago. By the time I took my first bite, ravenous was a better word for it.

"I'd better call Brian," Drake said ten minutes later as he brushed the last of the crumbs off his shirt.

"Yeah, we thought we had bad news for him when we left the rig. This is gonna' be a double whammy."

I located the Rolodex for him and he rifled through it until he came up with a number where he thought Brian could be reached. I puttered, tidying a few last things while he made the call.

"Brian says he'll try to get away from London tonight. Meanwhile we should just make everything as secure as possible and not worry about it. He suggested that neither of us make any flights out to the rig alone, though. He knows that union guy, Brankin, and says he could be trouble."

I'd come across keys to the file cabinet in Meggie's desk, so I stacked as many of the papers as I could into the file drawers and locked them. At least they'd have to perform some serious breakage to get in there, or cart the whole cabinet off with them. I suspected they'd already taken anything they really wanted.

We checked the office's two windows and made sure the deadbolt locks were secure on the only door. Drake disconnected the batteries on the two helicopters, secured all the compartment doors, and locked the passenger doors. It was about as secure as we could make them without putting them into a locked building, and Brian hadn't seemed to feel that was necessary.

In the U.S. it's a federal crime to tamper with an aircraft, and I assumed the U.K. would have the same kind of rules. The only problem was that I didn't think these thugs were exactly worried about the legal aspects of their actions. It's also a crime to assault someone but that hadn't stopped one of them from knocking Meggie unconscious and leaving her.

It was nearly three o'clock when we climbed into the company car and headed back toward our cottage.

The grounds of Dunworthy appeared on our left more than a mile before the turnoff to the castle, and the turn to our cottage was around a bend another quarter mile down the road. I debated about stopping in to introduce Drake, remembering Sarah's casual invitation to drop in any time, but decided a nap before dinner sounded more appealing.

I awoke in darkness, pulled from leaden sleep by the ringing of the telephone downstairs. My foggy brain registered only that Drake must have answered it because it quit ringing about the time I rolled over. My body said stay; my brain nagged that I really shouldn't or I would be asleep until about midnight, when I'd become fully awake. Logic finally won the argument and I dragged myself from bed and splashed cold water on my face in the bathroom.

"That was Brian on the phone," Drake said, nearly scaring the socks off me as I blindly groped for a towel. "He said his mother's taken a turn for the worse in the last hour and he doesn't think he should leave just now. He asked me to go back out to the airport and get the aircraft stowed in one of the hangars out there. He's already called ahead and arranged it."

"Now?"

"Yeah, I better go. If something happens to them outside and he hasn't taken 'reasonable precautions,' his insurance company's likely to give him a lot of grief.

"Apparently these union threats have been going on for some time, but this is the first time they've actually done anything. He's worried."

"And you have to deal with it." I really didn't want to sound bitter, but an edge crept in.

"For now." He pulled me into a close embrace and rubbed my back. "Want to come along? We could get some dinner in town afterward."

I gave him a quick kiss and went to look for my shoes.

The trip to the airport, moving both craft into a hangar—supervised by Fergus, who "yes mum'd" me a lot—and dinner at a decent seafood place took hours, and it was nearly ten o'clock as we approached Dunworthy. Rounding a bend in the road I caught sight of flames leaping high into the air. My heart sped into high gear.

"The castle! Drake, turn in at their lane."

NINE

THE TIRES SQUEALED as Drake made a hard left turn into the lane. I lost sight of the flames as the heavy canopy of trees closed in, but an orange glow to our right peered through at intervals. We followed the winding lane until we came into the open area at the front of the castle. The flames were still to our right.

"It's not the castle, thank goodness," I said as Drake brought the car to a halt beside the family Bentley.

"It's in the direction of our cottage," he replied tersely.

We both took off running at the same instant. A fruit orchard covered a couple of acres, beyond which Sarah had told me there were a number of small cottages and a few old buildings from ancient times. We stumbled between the apple and cherry trees, the glow becoming brighter and the heat from the fire already warming the air around us. We emerged into a small clearing past the orchard and saw the flaming structure.

The thatch roof of a small building was completely ablaze, with flames shooting twenty or thirty feet into the air. Its stone walls stood invincible, while several people raced around not accomplishing much of anything. I spotted Sarah Dunbar off to one side, wrestling with a fire extinguisher.

"Sarah!" I shouted.

She didn't hear me. I nudged Drake and we headed toward her.

"Can Drake help with that?" I asked.

"Oh, Charlie! I'm so glad to see you. Yes, please," she said, handing the extinguisher over to Drake.

His look told me he knew the small extinguisher would be useless, but he took it and ran to join the others, pulling the pin from the canister as he went.

"What happened?" I shouted above the roaring fire and the shouts of the people.

"I don't know. We just discovered it," she said. "Robert's trying to get the pumper out here."

At that moment a garden tractor appeared, with Robert driving, pulling an antique contraption of some kind. It jounced over ruts and onto the unmown turf surrounding the little hut. Men ran over to help him and they were soon unwinding a hose and cranking up a generator. Water pumped from the hose, in fitful spurts at first, then as a steady stream which was at least wet, if not forceful.

"What kind of building is that?" I asked Sarah.

"Oh, it's a crofter's hut," she said. "Dreadfully old. Hasn't been occupied for two or three hundred years, I'm sure. Old thatch ceiling must have been like a candle wick, you know."

I guess I gave a puzzled look.

"They burned peat fires in those huts, fire ring on the floor, meat hanging from the ceiling to cure. Interiors of those places are coated in grease an inch thick."

"Well, I can see how that would burn easily," I said. "Maybe I should see if I can lend a hand."

The men worked their way around the sides of the crofter's cottage, dampening the flames on one side, just to have them flare up on another. I joined Drake, who'd set the fire extinguisher aside the minute the pumper showed up. We helped unwind some extra lengths of hose and then to bear its weight as it filled with water. At last, it looked like we were making some headway. The roaring flames had settled into smaller ones, with thick billowing smoke everywhere.

"At least we kept the surrounding grass damp enough," Robert commented as I stepped aside to let the men finish it up.

"Thank goodness it didn't spread to the orchard," I said.

Robert turned to issue an order to the men.

I scanned the surrounding forest, contemplating the amount of potential destruction had the fire run unchecked. A slight movement caught my eye beneath one of the trees in the orchard. A man huddled behind one of the thick trunks, watching the scene. In the dying light of the fire, his red-gold hair glowed. It was Ian Brodie.

"Charlie, here take this," Robert said, handing me the wrench he'd used to crank open the water valve. "It goes in that toolbox on the other side."

I reached out for the wrench and when I looked up again, Ian was gone.

Now what was that about, I wondered, circling the pumper to put the wrench away. If Ian were this close, why hadn't he come over to help?

I remembered Robert Dunbar's comments yesterday, his suspicions about Ian being the thief who'd stolen his two lambs. Was Ian really at war with the Dunbars? Could he have set the fire? I walked back around the pumper to the spot where Robert stood watching the last of the dousing efforts.

"Any idea what started the fire?" I asked.

"No," he mused. "Canna' figure it out. No lightning tonight. That's usually what does it. Lucky we have old Betsy here," he said, patting the pumper's flank. "Closest fire department's almost all the way to Inverness. Take 'em twenty minutes to get here. Used to have a volunteer fire crew here in the village, but they're all gettin' old like me. Canna' do it anymore, that gettin' waked up in the night." He patted the pumper again. "Betsy here's old. Think me grandda' brought her in more than eighty years ago when we pulled her with horses. But she still works."

He supervised the rewinding of the hose, then climbed aboard the tractor to drive Betsy back to storage. Sarah came around the corner of the still-standing stone walls to survey the wreckage. Now that the fire was out, the night had turned dark and chilly. Everyone was finding their way around by the beams of a couple of flashlights someone had brought.

"Oh, Charlie, there you are," Sarah said. "I'd like you to meet my grandson, Richie."

A gangly kid of about fifteen stepped forward. His large hands flopped at his sides, as if they weren't quite sure they belonged at the ends of those long, skinny arms. His blond hair hung over his forehead, having received a few too many sprays of water to stay in style. He wore baggy black pants and a black pullover that hung halfway to his knees. In his case, I wasn't sure whether he was trying to be stylish or if virtually any clothing would hang on his skinny frame. He nodded jerkily toward me and murmured a hello that almost made it past his lips.

"And Richie's friends, Lewis and Alisdair," Sarah added, summoning two other boys over. Lewis was a bit more filled-out than Richie, and I noticed that he and Alisdair went for the same baggy clothing. They each gave me a polite nod but I sensed teenage sullenness just under the surface.

"Let's go inside," Sarah suggested. "I'll make us some cocoa."

We trooped through the orchard in a line, one of the torch-bearers at the head and one at the end of the scraggly procession. When we reached the castle three men, presumably groundskeepers, left. Richie and his friends informed Sarah that they were off to town.

"Now where—" The slamming car door cut off her inquiry.

Drake and I were now the only ones standing with Sarah. I introduced them and included Robert as he came walking back from one of the outbuildings with a flashlight in hand.

"I'm afraid we should beg off staying for cocoa," I told Sarah. "It's been a very long day. I'll have to tell you about it sometime."

"Let's do plan on dinner one evening soon," she insisted.

Turning to Drake, she added, ''I understand you have some fascinating stories to tell.''

I could have almost sworn she winked at him but he didn't seem to notice.

''I'm going to figure out where Ian Brodie is leasing land and which cottage they live in,'' I told Drake in the car on the way back to our place. ''I think I need to pay him a little visit.''

TEN

BRODIE'S COTTAGE stood among a collection of old barns and wooden-fenced corrals. The land was somewhat hilly with gray-white rocks that jutted up through the rich, green grass. In the distance, a flock of fifty or sixty sheep grazed in a low spot at the base of a rocky promontory. I'd followed the sketchy directions Ian had mentioned when I met him and found the place without any trouble.

Three grown collies and a half-dozen puppies bounded out to meet me as soon as I stopped the car. One of the adult dogs, a female with nipples hanging inches below her belly, sniffed cautiously at my fingers before slowly wagging her tail and giving her tacit approval for me to touch her babies. With acceptance by the adults, I stooped down and became instantly covered in puppies. Their small bodies wiggled uncontrollably as they crawled over my shoes and worked their way up to my knees and lapped at my chin. I got a case of the giggles; there was no way not to erupt in laughter.

"Sorry, ma'am, there's not another show until twelve-thirty."

"Show?" My confusion must have registered on my face with a look of stupidity.

"The dog shows? Did you come for that?" The young woman standing in the driveway wore denim overalls and a gray t-shirt that I sensed must have once been white. Her blond hair was pulled back into a ponytail that brushed her shoulders, and delicate tendrils of hair framed her forehead and cheeks. I guessed her age to be mid-twenties.

"No, sorry I didn't know anything about that." I stood up and tucked the tail of my pink t-shirt back into my jeans. "You must be Ian's wife?" I would have extended my hand to her, but hers were full of baby bottles dripping foamy milk.

"Yes, I'm Ramona," she answered cautiously.

I introduced myself by letting her know which cottage we were renting. "I met Ian outside one day and he suggested I drop by to meet you."

"Well, it's nice to know a neighbor," she said with a widening grin. "Hey, want to help me feed a couple of lambs?"

At my nod, she led me toward one of the corrals. The puppies trailed behind us and two of the adult dogs wandered off. Nudging a small metal latch with her knee, Ramona opened a gate. "Catch that, will you?" she said as we walked through.

I pushed the gate shut, leaving the puppies outside. Two lambs, standing about eighteen inches high, scampered toward Ramona, eyeing the bottles in her arms. She tilted one bottle downward to the nearest baby and handed the other bottle to me. I mimicked her technique with the other lamb. His mouth latched onto the nipple and his little tail went into furious wagging. I had to laugh again.

"They're so cute," I said.

"Never worked much with farm animals?" she asked.

"Not really." I remembered one early field trip to a local dairy when I'd been in first or second grade, but the animals were so huge no one had even suggested that we get near them.

In about two minutes, both lambs drained their bottles and Ramona handed me a second one. "Just toss the empties on the ground," she said.

"Why don't their mothers feed them?" I asked.

"These two were orphaned."

"Oh? Recently?" I wanted to believe that she wouldn't lie to me, but couldn't help but remember the Dunbars just happened to have two lambs of their own missing. I ruffled the ears of my animal but didn't notice any kind of tag or brand.

"Yeah, Ian brought them in from the west pasture a few days ago. Said the mother was attacked by a big cat."

I pictured someone's tabby run amok, but she clarified. "Sometimes mountain lions come down from the hills. It's sad."

"Didn't the dogs raise a fuss?"

"Dunno'. Usually they do."

The lambs had polished off two bottles each and Ramona pushed them away, their fat little tummies bulging. "Enough for now," she said. "Off you go."

We gathered the empty bottles. "Let's go inside," she suggested. "Sorry I couldn't offer you a more proper welcome. Just can't put off these little ones when they're hungry."

We walked up a rocky path from the corral to the house, an unpainted wood and stone structure nestled into a curve in the rocky hillside. A small garden area contained some well developed vegetables—tomatoes, beans, and the leafy tops of potato plants—but the flower beds near the cottage were filled only with the bare sticks of last year's annuals.

"I've still got some coffee," Ramona said. "We could sit a minute and have a cup."

Inside, the cottage consisted of a main room with a combined living and kitchen area. Doors on the far wall presumably led to bedroom and bathroom. The cottage's dominant feature was a stone fireplace on the wall opposite the front door. Its opening was nearly large enough to garage a compact car. A battered coal scuttle sat to one side and an unruly pile of logs graced the other.

The living area contained an oak-framed sofa whose faded frame looked like it had been out in the weather for a few seasons before being brought back into service. The nubby gray fabric on the cushions showed snags and a couple of rips large enough for white stuffing to poke through. A wooden end table made of logs, a small television set, and a floor lamp with a fringed 1940s-era shade were the only other furnishings, if you didn't count the stack of magazines that held an egg-smeared plate and a dirty coffee mug.

On the kitchen side of the room, there was a folding card table with two chairs. Built-ins consisted of a metal one-piece cabinet with sink and a tiny four-burner stove. A slope-shouldered refrigerator hummed noisily in the corner. On the plus side, a window above the sink gave an unbroken view of the spectacular Highland countryside. The odor of burnt coffee filled the room.

"Oh, no," Ramona exclaimed. "Guess I left this on." She pulled a metal coffeepot from one of the stove burners. A low gas flame glowed bluely. She turned, embarrassed. "Sorry. Maybe some tea, then?"

I sensed that my accepting a cup of tea would be important to her, after the disaster with the coffee. "Sure. That would be nice."

"The place comes furnished," she explained in answer to my unasked question. "We really do have nicer stuff than this at home. But when you're renting only for a summer, it hardly seems worth the bother to bring a lot."

She rummaged through pans under the kitchen sink and came up with a small kettle.

"Where's home?" I asked, trying to stay on neutral ground.

"Near Aberdeen. We live with Ian's parents. They've got a few acres and a guesthouse out back. We've got that. But Ian's father runs his own sheep on his land and it's not really enough to support ours too. We'll do a season here, then sell them in the fall."

"Oh, I've only got tea bags," she apologized. "Hope that's okay."

"It's all I ever do at home," I answered truthfully. "Most Americans probably can't tell the difference."

She pulled out two mugs, inspected them for cleanliness and took two bags from a canister that I noticed was otherwise nearly empty. I turned away, pretending to admire the stonework on the fireplace, while she put water on to boil and discreetly stacked the dirty dishes that had covered the table.

"So what part of America are you from?" she asked, working to keep a conversation going.

I told her a bit about New Mexico and Albuquerque. I didn't

mention the private investigation business. "My husband and I are here to do some helicopter work for a friend who's—"

The door opened abruptly and Ian walked in, stomping his boots on the stone step outside first.

"Oh, hello," he said, startled at finding me in his house.

"Ian, you've met Charlie," Ramona said.

"Yes. We've met." He leaned his shepherd's crook against the wall.

"We're about to have tea," she said. "Will you have some too?"

He pulled back his sleeve and stared at his watch. "We've got the show in thirty minutes."

"Heavens, is it that late already?"

"Twelve. Is there any lunch?" His tone was surly and I felt immediate tension in the room.

"Hey, I didn't realize it was that late, either," I hastily interjected. "I better get going."

"Oh, Charlie, don't go yet," Ramona insisted. "Stay for the show. Ian's a wonder with the dogs."

I glanced toward him but he had his back to me. Ramona made a dismissive gesture. To him, she said, "Your lunch is in the fridge. I wrapped your sandwich in foil."

"I should go," I said.

"Oh, I'm sorry, Charlie. Would you like some lunch?"

"No, no. I had a big breakfast late." It wasn't true but I didn't want to put her on the spot and there was no way I'd intrude upon their rather meager supplies.

Ramona took my arm and we walked out the door together. "Charlie, don't mind Ian. He's always a bear before he gets fed. And he's got a lot on his mind recently." We walked between a dozen or so black-and-white collies who lay on the ground around the front of the cottage. They all took up the same position—head on paws, nose pointed at the door. Ramona slowed her pace once we'd cleared the dogs. "I need to put out some food for the puppies," she said. "Come along."

I followed her into the barn where large plastic bins lined one wall. She raised the lid on one and scooped dry dog food into a flat metal pan. Six puppies wiggled through cracks in the walls at the sound of the food hitting their dish.

"Just a minute." She laughed at them, then carried the dog food to a five-gallon bucket and dipped milk from it, covering the dry food and swirling the pan until the mixture was evenly distributed.

I watched in amazement as she held the pan at waist level and issued a command. "Puppies, sit!" The pups spread apart and six little bottoms went to the ground. Their bright eyes stared at Ramona as she slowly lowered the pan to the ground in their midst. Their heads followed the progress of the meal and the instant the dish hit the dirt they were all over it.

"They're not the neatest with their table manners." Ramona laughed.

Little black-and-white bodies crawled all over the large pan, into and around it.

"Luckily their mother comes along afterward and licks their bellies and paws clean."

Sure enough, the mother dog I'd noticed earlier was hovering at the edge of the barn, waiting and watching.

"Oh, I think I heard a car. Watch the pups awhile longer if you'd like." Ramona wiped her hands on her slender denim legs and headed toward the door.

Through the opening, I could see a family of four emerging from a small car. Within minutes, three more cars had arrived and a small crowd was circulating and petting the dogs, who'd abandoned their post at the cottage. Ramona greeted them all pleasantly and collected money, which I saw her shove into the pockets of her overalls. I glanced at my watch. At precisely twelve-thirty, Ian emerged from the cottage and walked down the long drive to the area where the cars had parked. His countenance had changed considerably over the past half hour.

"Good day, everyone," he greeted. "Now if you'll come just over here, we'll get started."

I left the barn and joined Ramona. "How much is the show admission?" I asked, reaching into a pocket where I'd stashed some money.

"Oh, stay, Charlie. It's on the house for you."

"No. If everyone else is paying, I will too."

"Charlie, I insist. It's not often we have a friend over. Please stay." I knew a further argument about payment would insult her, so I smiled acceptance and followed her in the direction Ian had led the others.

We stood at the back of the group, who had all taken seats on the sizeable rocks that lined the driveway. Ian stood about twenty yards away, shepherd's crook at attention, five adult dogs pacing the area with their eyes always on him.

"Each of the dogs has his own set of commands," Ian announced to the crowd after welcoming everyone. "I use whistles to single out the dog I want. He'll come to attention then I'll give him the command to go where I want him. Like this."

He called out a dog's name, then whistled a short chirpy sound. One of the dogs, who'd been up in the rocks near the spectators, dashed down the short hill and came to Ian's side. He gave another whistle, three quick chirps, and the dog raced across the open pasture to a flock of twenty or thirty sheep who were grazing about two hundred yards away. The dog circled the sheep until they gathered together in a neat little bunch.

"With each different whistle command, I can make the dog do what I want him to," Ian announced. "For instance, he'll circle to the right. Chirp-chirp."

The dog circled the flock, going to his right around them. Ian produced a different whistle sound, a three-toned ooh-ooh-ee, and the dog changed direction and circled to the left. One quick chirp and the dog stopped in his tracks and lay down.

"I'll have him bring the flock to me," Ian said. A two-toned ee-ooh and the dog was up again, maneuvering the twenty sheep across the pasture to Ian. When they reached the patch of beaten earth where he stood, the dog backed away and the sheep stopped.

"Now we'll have two dogs take them back." He shouted the names of two other dogs and they came to attention. Again, a series of whistles brought them circling the sheep and the flock retreated about a hundred yards until Ian whistled the dogs to gather them into a bunch.

I looked around at the faces of the audience, who all registered amazement as Ian continued to put the dogs through several series of moves. He called up one of the pups we'd just been feeding.

"This pup is fifteen weeks old. He's been in training since he was four weeks," Ian told the group. "He can't work with full-grown sheep yet, but he's learning his commands."

He whistled for the pup to run out to the flock and return, which the little guy did admirably before Ian commanded him to lie down with the other grown dogs. Then he ordered one of the two dogs who were still guarding the flock to bring a single sheep to him.

"The Scottish Blackface is mostly raised for its wool," he said. He grabbed the sheep unceremoniously, wrapping his arm around its chest and plopping it into a sitting position. With Ian's strong arm under its armpits, so to speak, the sheep went nearly limp and Ian picked up a pair of shears and proceeded to shear about half its body with a few deft moves.

"Anyone else want to give this a try?" he asked, looking out into the crowd.

We all became suddenly shy, no one wanting to be the guinea pig for something we all knew must be much harder than it looked when Ian did it. When no one stepped forward, he quickly finished the clipping and released the sheep. He balled up the wool, which had come off the animal as one neat pelt, and tossed it onto the ground.

"Selling wool has become a losing proposition for us here in Scotland," Ian said. "The government dictates the price we can get. My cost to raise a sheep, feed it, shear it, and ship the wool is higher than the price I sell it for. A lot of shepherds have been in the business for generations, but are having to get out now." Sparks flared in his eyes and I could tell he was just getting warmed up on the subject.

I glanced toward Ramona and caught the quick headshake

she sent toward Ian. 'Don't preach,' she seemed to be warning him.

''All right, folks,'' her perky voice said. ''Come with me to the fenced area. We have some other demonstrations and you can feed some of the animals if you'd like.''

Everyone scrambled off their rock seats and followed her, glad to avoid the sermon they'd nearly received. I lingered, watching Ian pick up his tools and the ball of wool. He stomped off toward the barn while the crowd trailed behind Ramona.

This was the second angry outburst I'd heard from Ian on the subject of the government's unfairness toward the sheep industry. Perhaps the third, considering his voice was probably one of those I'd heard outside our window Tuesday morning. Did that anger extend to a personal vendetta against one member of the Scottish parliament—Robert Dunbar?

ELEVEN

IAN APPEARED TO have shed his anger once again when he came out of the barn and joined the tourists. I stood by for a little while as he demonstrated how the youngest puppies are taught herding techniques using ducks. I had to laugh as I watched some of the little collies work around ducks that were larger than them.

Ramona mingled among the visitors, smiling and chatting, making up for some of Ian's taciturn ways. I caught up with her during a free moment. It looked like the tourists would be staying awhile. I decided I'd question Ian another time about being at the edge of the woods during the fire in the crofter's hut.

"I better be getting home," I told Ramona. "Tell Ian I really enjoyed the dog show. And do plan to come over to our place for a visit sometime."

"Sure, Charlie, I will."

Drake was still out when I returned to the cottage and I realized this was the first afternoon I'd had to myself in a couple of weeks. I stretched out on the sofa with the clan book Sarah had loaned me. Before I knew it, I was completely engrossed and began taking notes on the Davidson Clan history. Somewhere around four o'clock I must have dozed off because I came awake with a start when Drake opened the door at six.

"Hey, what's this?" he teased. "Sleeping on the job?"

"Um...no job for me today. I've taken a lazy afternoon off." I stretched and pulled myself off the sofa. "How about you? Did everything go okay at the airport?"

"I stayed in and made phone calls. We didn't have any flights scheduled out to the rig, luckily."

"Any word on Meggie?" I asked as I opened the refrigerator door and pulled out a bottle of White Zinfandel we'd opened a couple of days earlier.

"She's back at home, with her mother fussing over her. The doctors told her she had a mild concussion. They kept her overnight and let her out first thing this morning."

"They weren't worried about that long period of unconsciousness?" I asked, pouring two glasses of wine.

"I asked her that. Apparently the doctors didn't think she'd probably been out that long. We may have come back right after the intruder left."

We raised our glasses in a quick toast. I tried vainly to remember every detail about the Air-Sea office when we'd come in from our own eventful flight. Had there been any strange cars around? Anyone who didn't belong, lurking? I just couldn't pull up an image.

"Anyway," he said, "Meggie should be back at work in another day or two. Brian had called her and talked her into not quitting her job."

I scanned the contents of the refrigerator for dinner ideas while we talked. "Are we both flying tomorrow?"

"That's the plan. We'll take both ships and keep an eye on each other." He watched as I took a couple of chicken breasts out and stirred up a marinade for them.

Thirty minutes later, over dinner, I filled him in on my day with Ian and Ramona Brodie. We also mapped out our flight plans for the next day, then went to bed early.

By ten o'clock the next morning, my JetRanger was tracking about a quarter mile behind Drake in the Astar as we approached Platform 14. A total of ten rig workers rode with us, all genial fellows as far as I could tell when we'd picked them up at their dockside offices an hour earlier. I didn't get any sense of the hostility that pervaded the atmosphere on Platform 6 a couple of days ago.

Drake set his craft down at the far edge of the landing pad, leaving the more sheltered section for me. I guided the Jet-Ranger into its spot and set the skids gently on the concrete pad. My passengers waited expectantly for the thumbs-up before opening any of the doors, and I gave the signal as soon as I'd repeated instructions for correctly releasing the sometimes tricky latches.

The crew chief for this platform was a short, stocky man with a florid face and a dark fringe of hair showing beneath the rim of his hard hat. Two deep furrows between his black eyebrows testified that he was permanently mad about something. I wondered if the union problems at the other rigs extended to this one as well. I couldn't see why not. I braced myself as he stomped toward my door, clipboard under one arm, hard hat butting the air as if he were a human battering ram.

He looked up at the same moment I opened my door. "Girl pilot, eh? All right. Manifest for the return." His gravelly voice came from somewhere deep inside his compact body, probably about in the region of his navel. Each sentence came out as a short bark, the way a Rottweiler would sound if he spoke English.

He shoved a sheet of paper into my hands and backed away, his eyes on the rotor blades, which dipped lower as they slowly wound down. I watched him circle at a respectful distance and walk toward Drake's aircraft with a similar list in hand.

I pulled gently at the rotor brake and locked down my controls. Stepping out of the aircraft, I looked around at the rig. Everything appeared to be business as usual. No malevolent stares, no brandishing of weapons. None of the crew seemed to give us a second glance. So, was this a non-union rig or had these guys not yet received the word that they were at war with us?

Nevertheless, Drake and I took turns stepping inside for bathroom breaks while the other stayed outside, puttering around nonchalantly but keeping vigilant. Finally, our returnees were ready and we loaded up for the return trip. We had two more of these crew changes to do today, ferrying men from shore to the rigs and those coming off their shifts back home. A certain number of men rotated in and out each day, to keep continuity, but there were a couple of days of the week when the traffic was extra heavy and required both our aircraft.

Platform 11 proved equally unthreatening when we landed there in the early afternoon, and Platform 6, for once, was quiet too. "Maybe all the troublemakers are on the same shift," I said to Drake back at the airport after we'd made the last run at about five o'clock. "Think they all managed the same days off this week?"

"Could be. It was peaceful today, anyway." He supervised the placement of the portable tug under the skids on the Astar, and Fergus, the hangar attendant, slowly backed his machine through the huge doors, guiding the delicate aircraft to its bed for the night.

Inside the Air-Sea office there was one message on the answering machine. Drake pressed the button to retrieve it. Static fuzzed through the little speaker for several seconds before anyone spoke.

"Give up," a deep voice said. "Stay off the oil rigs."

My thoughts went immediately to the stocky crew chief, whose deep gravelly voice had been one of his most noticeable features. "Say something more," I whispered. Drake and I both bent closer to the machine, but the recording had clicked off.

"Well, I guess we know what that was about," Drake said.

"I just wonder who made the call."

"Voice makes me think of that guy today."

"My thought exactly." I twiddled a pencil between my fingers. "That guy didn't really seem angry at us though. Did you think?"

"I don't know." He'd circled the room, checking the windows. "Never can tell."

I peered out the front window, toward our car. It was alone and I didn't see another person in the vicinity. We switched off the lights and locked the deadbolt.

"I'm gonna' take one last look at the ships before we leave," Drake said, heading toward the hangar.

I tagged along, really wanting nothing more than dinner at this point. When everything looked secure and Drake had verified that the hangar doors were indeed locked for the night, we finally got away. It was completely dark out now and my whole body was buzzing from a full day at the stick. Whatever we ate for dinner wasn't terribly memorable—I think it was McDonald's food—and I fell into bed with the ominous sound of that telephone threat nagging at me.

TWELVE

THE PHONE RANG about mid-morning, just as I was finishing up the dishes and tidying the cottage.

"Charlie, it's Sarah. Sorry for such late notice. I wasn't able to reach you all day yesterday."

"Flying. Sorry, we were tied up until late."

"Oh, that's no problem, dear. We just wanted to see if you and Drake could make it for dinner tonight. I think it will just be the four of us. Richie and his friends have some sort of plans. Not that they're ever very good company, anyway. That age, you know."

I had to chuckle. "Oh, I know. I'm sure I wasn't terribly sociable at that age either. Yes, we'd be delighted to come to dinner."

"Seven, then?"

"Perfect."

I'd hung up before I remembered that I should have offered to bring something. Then again, perhaps showing up for dinner at a castle with a little bowl of salad or dessert tucked under your arm just wasn't the thing.

The clan book waited on the coffee table and I decided to finish making notes so I could return the book to Sarah that evening. I also placed a call to the Air-Sea Helicopters office, leaving a message for Drake about the dinner so he wouldn't dawdle too long in getting everything secured and coming home.

By three o'clock I'd taken pages of notes and my head felt fuzzy from too much reading. The pale blue sky beckoned and the grass around the cottage shone emerald green in the sunlight. A walk seemed to be in order. I stretched the kinks out of my legs and grabbed the front door key off the kitchen counter. Silly, probably, but years of life in a crime-ridden city had conditioned me to always lock up. I slipped the key into my jeans pocket after doing so.

The air held a strong trace of dampness after last evening's rain, but the sun had come out this morning and the lawn was dry, the flowers in the cottage's neat beds turning their heads toward the light. Maybe I would cut a small bouquet and take it with us to Dunworthy this evening.

I took a graveled path that circled behind the cottage and ran out of sight behind the orchard. Beyond that laid the burned out crofter's hut. I'd be interested to see whether the debris had been cleaned up yet, or if this would be one of those ashes-to-ashes situations where they'd simply let the old structure turn into a quaint ruin with an interesting history over time.

Apples hung heavily from the trees as I passed along their rows. The other night I hadn't realized how large the orchard was or how near to harvest time. I found a path of beaten earth down the middle of a central row and followed it to the clearing. Fifty feet away stood the blackened stone walls, all that remained of the small structure. I approached softly, mindful of the quiet of the place, with the chatter of birds in the surrounding trees the only sound. It was only when I came within five or six feet of the old walls that I heard the voices.

"...like that, man."

Male laughter rose from the far side of the cottage. It grew more raucous. Someone added something in a heavy Scottish brogue that came out sounding like, "Ya' dobbie kin wanna'—whot." More laughter, of the positively knee-slapping variety. "Aye, kinna' scob not."

I had no clue as to the words, much less where the hilarity was in them, but figured I had two choices. Either sneak away or make my presence known. Curiosity won out and I softly began humming a little tune. The laughter covered my frail efforts completely, so I finally resorted to a cough.

"Whas'ere?" one of the voices whispered.

Richie's face peered around the side of the hut. He went a shade whiter when he saw me. He dropped something small and white on the ground and covered it with his shoe.

"Oh, Richie!" I hoped I seemed appropriately startled at finding him and his friends smoking pot in their little hideout. "How are you?"

"Just fine, ma'am." Some of his previous shyness faded with the addition of the drug, I noticed.

"And are your friends here, too?"

He nudged with his boot at something behind him. "Lew, Al, come say hello," he said.

Alasdair and Lewis emerged, considerably subdued from the wildly laughing young men I'd heard moments earlier. "Ma'am." Their upper-class upbringing hadn't totally deserted them.

"Does your grandmother know you've chosen this as your hangout?" I asked Richie.

"Em'…well, not exactly, ma'am."

"We don't have to go with the ma'am stuff, Richie. I'm Charlie."

"Thanks, Charlie. Well, we uh…"

I grinned at their discomfort.

"Hey, I'm just out for a walk," I said. "Okay?"

All three boys relaxed considerably. "If ye could just…that is, maybe not…well, does Grandmother have to…"

I let Richie stammer through his attempt to beg for my silence. My eyes scanned the ground around the base of the rock walls, and I spotted the nub of another joint at the edge of the large, flat stone that served as a doorstep for the hut. I picked it up.

"Sit a minute, guys. I need to ask you something."

They perched lightly on their haunches, and I did the same. I held up the roach I'd just found. "I guess you do this a lot, huh?"

Sullen faces, ready for a lecture on the evils of drug use, stared back at me. In America, I would have gotten a comment like, ''we don't need this shit,'' and they'd have taken off. People raised in castles have a few more restraints placed on them, I guess.

''No lecture,'' I said. ''I just want to know about the other night. That fire—''

''No way,'' Lewis piped up. ''We had nothing to do with that.''

''It's true!'' It was the first time I'd heard Alasdair open his mouth and I was surprised by the maturity of the deep male voice that came out.

''They're right, ma'am—uh, Charlie. When we came out it was already going.''

Richie's back straightened as he took the lead. ''We was, uh, we were planning to hang around out here. It's a, you know, fun place just to …''

''But we came through the orchard there,'' said Lewis, ''and sudden-like, we could see the flames.''

''We didn't know what to do,'' Richie said. ''I mean, it was already so big we couldna' handle it ourselves. I ran back to the garage and got a fire extinguisher. That's when Grandmother saw me and I told her what we'd found. She brought the others to help. But we—'' He shrugged helplessly.

''It's true. Really,'' Lewis insisted.

''Okay, okay, I believe you,'' I said, kneading the roach between my fingers until it crumbled and fell away. ''Did you see anyone else out here?''

''Well, the guys who came out to help,'' Richie said. ''You mean them?''

''No, I'm thinking about anyone who might have started the fire. Your grandfather said there was no lightning that evening. I'm just wondering how the fire started.''

All three boys seemed to give it fair consideration, but no one came up with any names. Which still left me with the question of why Ian Brodie had been lurking in the orchard as everyone else worked to put out the flames.

''Okay, then,'' I finally said. ''If any of you think of anything, let me know.''

"Are you investigating it, then?" Richie asked.

I must have given him a sharp look or something at the mention of an investigation.

"It's just that Grandmother was telling us at dinner the other night that you're a private investigator back in America."

"Yes," Lewis said, "she said you were looking into the disappearance of some lambs here on the farm." His eyes glittered with enthusiasm.

"Well, I don't remember actually agreeing to that," I said.

Had Sarah really believed she'd put me on the case? And, in going to Ian Brodie's lease and looking at the lambs there, had I tacitly agreed to investigate?

I stood and brushed leaves from my jeans. "Well, I'm not getting much walking done."

The boys stood, out of habit, and shuffled their feet as I walked away. I wondered whether they'd light up again once I was out of sight.

I cut through the orchard, wanting more exercise before I headed home. At the end of a row I spotted a path leading away from the castle. I'd wanted to explore the forest a bit so I walked toward it. The wide trail led from the castle directly into the thick woods. In no time at all I stepped under the dark canopy of pines. Purple heather carpeted the ground, but the pathway was well maintained and the short, almost fluffy plants didn't intrude.

Twenty yards or so into the forest, a small clearing had been made to house a tiny gazebo. The structure looked like something out of a sleeping-beauty tale, with turned wooden columns supporting an intricately latticed cupola, all painted white. It resembled a sugar confection created for the top of a wedding cake. Under its protection stood two white stone benches, the legs faintly green with the mossy residue that clung to everything here. I walked up the two steps at the entry, enchanted by the little enclave, so different from anything I'd be likely to run across in New Mexico.

Peering out through the lattice, I could tell that there were a couple of smaller pathways leading away from the small clearing, foot trails really. The main path directly to and from the castle was definitely the one everyone used. I stepped down and decided to go farther into the forest. The trail on the left looked like it led toward our cottage and might eventually come out there. The one on the right wound out of sight around a boulder.

"What the heck," I said to the trees. "I can always trace it back if it dead-ends."

Feeling somewhat like Hansel and Gretel, I started down the narrow trail. It was only about a foot wide in the best places and deteriorated to nothing more than a smashed-down spot in the fallen pine needles in others. But it wasn't difficult to follow. I skirted boulders and worked my way over uneven ground. No wonder Sarah and Robert probably never went beyond the gazebo. In less than ten minutes I could see brighter light ahead, a clearing. I paused at the edge of it. Directly ahead of me was the back of Ian and Ramona's barn.

THIRTEEN

A FAINT BUT DISTINCT track through the grass told me that Ian regularly used this means of reaching the castle without having to take the road. The fact that this path came within a few yards of the orchard meant that he could have easily cut through there to the crofter's hut with little chance of being seen, especially in darkness. My only question was whether he'd done it the other night before or after the place caught fire. I had a sneaking suspicion that I knew the answer.

But was mere suspicion enough to warrant bringing it to the Dunbars' attention. The fact that there were bad feelings didn't mean Ian would actually start a fire. Richie and his friends could have done it accidentally and then lied to cover themselves. Without evidence I better keep quiet.

Clouds were beginning to build overhead and Drake would soon be coming in. I turned back toward home.

By six-thirty, Drake and I had showered and I put on the only semi-dressy outfit I'd brought with me, a soft, black broomstick skirt and short-sleeved burgundy silk top.

"Do I look all right to be presented at the palace?" Drake asked.

I laughed. "It's a castle, but they aren't royalty, after all. The other day when I was there we ate packaged cake and Sarah brewed the tea herself. And, yes, you look fine."

Actually, Drake's muscular body looked good in anything, from his khaki flight suit to a tuxedo to noth— I snapped myself back to the moment. "You're great, hon. Did you pick up that bottle of wine? And where's that clan book? I want to take it back.''

''In the kitchen.'' He pulled me close to him. ''You're not just a little nervous, are you?''

''Why, am I puttering around too much?''

''Well, you're ready a half hour early. Of course, I could probably think of a way to spend the time.'' He wiggled his eyebrows.

He was right—he did think of a way. I just had to rearrange all my clothing and re-comb my hair before we left.

At Dunworthy, lights shone warmly from the downstairs windows. Sarah answered the door herself.

''Ah, my dears, I'm so glad you're here. Do come in.'' She ushered us into the entry hall and draped our jackets over the same pegs we'd used before. ''Drake, it's so nice to finally *see* you.''

''It was pretty dark the other evening, wasn't it?'' He grinned and accepted her peck on his cheek.

''Charlie's told me something of your work, flying in all those exotic places. You'll have to tell Robert all—Oh, here he is now.''

Robert looked lordly in his soft wool slacks and deep blue sweater with ascot. He'd stopped short of a burgundy smoking jacket, but I could easily picture him in one. At his feet, the furry Ruffie eyed us warily. I stooped and extended a hand toward her, but she wriggled her nose and kept her distance.

''Pour you a sherry?'' Robert asked.

Receiving nods from both of us, he disappeared through the doorway from which he'd come.

''Would you like the quick tour before dinner?'' Sarah asked. ''I'd offer the long tour, but it takes nearly a full day.''

''The quick tour would be wonderful,'' I said.

Robert returned with a small tray holding four cordial glasses and we toasted briefly to everyone's health.

From the informal entry hall, Sarah led us into a more formal hall, one with a vaulted ceiling, red plush drapes, and ornate columns at the entrance.

Robert spoke up. "This is where my father greeted the queen mother on the one occasion she visited. I was only about three at the time, but I'm told she was quite taken with me. Unfortunately, I don't remember it."

"I'm sure you were quite charming in your short pants and small necktie, dear." Sarah indicated a staircase that gracefully arched around the curved wall. "Upstairs, the nursery is probably the most charming of the rooms," she said. "Since our children moved away, more than twenty years ago now, I brought a lot of the antique toys out of storage and did a little decorating."

The cheerful yellow and white room contained two hand-carved cradles, along with an ornate crib and shelves full of elaborately clothed dolls that must be worth a fortune today.

"There's a second library up here," Sarah continued. "Mostly it's been used as a study room for the little ones. Robert did his schoolwork in here, as did our children. Nowadays, I seem to keep one project or another spread out on the table."

Stacks of cards and envelopes covered the carved mahogany table in the center of the room. Shelves of books, mainly references, covered one wall while the exterior wall had a window that I assumed looked over the rose garden.

"Bedrooms—four along this corridor." Sarah led us by them with a quick peek in each. "Each now has its own bath, which took no small amount of effort, converting spare closets and such. Luckily that was all done before my time."

Robert waved toward a smaller staircase, leading up. "Third floor has more bedrooms. Our two live-in staff people are using a couple of them right now, and guests use some of them when we have a large crowd in. Fourth floor was designed for defense. That's where the really narrow passages are and the stone steps up into the turrets. You can see a large part of the grounds from there, but the steps are very tricky. Have to take you up there sometime during the day."

At the far end of the corridor we descended a flight of stairs, steeper and less spacious than the curved ones off the main hall. We found ourselves near the library Sarah and I had visited the other day. She deposited the clan book, which she'd been carrying all this time, onto the table.

"On to the dining room," Sarah said. "Surely Molly must have the soup ready by now."

We followed her through the library and drawing room, down a short corridor and past the hall. Carved double doors stood open into a dining room that surprised me with its intimacy. An oval cherry table was set for four, with a centerpiece of roses in a silver bowl in the center and two pink tapers in silver candlesticks flanking the flowers. The room itself was not large, about fourteen-feet square, with gleaming wood paneling and an angelic mural painted on the ceiling in pastels.

"This is the family dining room," Sarah said, reading my expression. "It's the one we use nearly all the time. There's a formal dining room, but it's a monstrosity."

Robert sputtered.

"You know what I mean, dear," she said, waving off his objection. "It's huge. Must seat twenty-four or more. Can't remember the last time we had that many for dinner."

"Right about that. Here, let's sit." Robert indicated our chairs, while Sarah rang a tiny silver bell beside her plate.

The soup Molly brought was excellent, a hearty broth with bits of potato and mushrooms. No one spoke for the first few minutes.

"So, Charlie," Robert finally said, "any leads on those missing lambs?"

I swallowed a spoonful of the hot soup a bit too quickly. "Well, not really. I don't have any expertise in livestock."

"Oh, nonsense. What's there to know? About like finding a missing child, I'd expect." He winked in Drake's direction and sipped slowly at his soup. "Check out that Ian Brodie fellow. Bet that's where they've gone."

"Actually, I did go over there a couple of days ago," I said.

"See? Bet they were right there, eh?"

"I have no idea. There are sheep and lambs all over the place. I can't tell one from the other."

"Ours are tagged. Do 'em right after they're born. Little tag on the ear."

"I didn't see any tagged ones," I said truthfully.

"Hmph. Probably got 'em hidden somewhere." He muttered the words to his empty bowl.

I didn't mention the path I'd found through the forest. Undoubtedly, Robert must know that there was a direct way from the castle to the Brodie cottage. I didn't need to remind him.

"There's pheasant tonight," Sarah said, ringing the tiny bell again. "From right here on the estate. Our daughter's become such an environmentalist that she lectures me every time we kill one, but heavens, we've got thousands. Can't see that it hurts to eat one now and then."

"Elizabeth's a twit," Robert said. "Couldn't manage an estate this size if you handed it to her."

"Elizabeth is very successful at managing her many charity events." Sarah closed her mouth in a straight line as Molly walked in, carrying a platter with the golden-brown pheasant on it. Molly set the platter in front of Robert and retreated.

He stood up and picked up the carving knife and fork. "Charity events, pah!" He stabbed the fork into the pheasant's breast. "Get a bunch of Edward's nouveau-riche friends to feel important by paying a thousand pounds each for dinner. She manages to do that, all right."

He sliced viciously at the bird. "Just hope Richie turns out to have some business sense."

"Well." Sarah closed the subject by passing the bowls of potatoes and vegetables Molly had brought in during Robert's tirade.

Drake looked a little uncomfortable at their arguing but I, frankly, was glad the subject had turned away from my assignment to find the lost lambs. I searched for a non-controversial topic.

"Drake and I have been getting to see quite a lot of the countryside with all the flying we're doing these days."

Both Sarah and Robert seemed happy to talk about something different, so the conversation turned toward helicopters.

Soon, Drake was sharing a few of his adventures in Hawaii, with tourists who invariably do predictable things like sticking their cameras out the windows in flight, immediately after being told how dangerous it is.

By the time dessert arrived the air had lightened considerably and we were all laughing. The two bottles of wine with dinner and extra glasses of port afterward probably hadn't hurt, either. I was surprised to notice that it was nearly ten o'clock. Then I heard a scream from another room.

FOURTEEN

SARAH TURNED startled eyes to Robert. We'd all frozen in our spots.

Molly burst through the doorway from the hall, her round face flushed, carrying a portable phone. She thrust it at Robert. Puzzled, he took it from her.

"Hello? Who's that?" The blood drained from his face as he listened. "Kidnapped! Whatever—"

He held the receiver out and stared at it.

"Robert!" Sarah nearly screamed his name.

He looked up blankly. "Bloody bastard hung up." His voice trailed away.

"What is it, Robert? Who's been kidnapped?" I couldn't stand the suspense any more than Sarah could.

"Richie," his dead voice replied.

Drake had risen from his chair. "Any way of knowing who it was?" He took the receiver from Robert. "Do you have caller ID or something like that?"

"No..." Robert looked like he was about to go into shock. His eyes had a glassy look and his lips were nearly white. Sarah's pulse showed as a fluttery beat in her temple.

"Listen to me, Robert," I said. "Tell us exactly what they said."

"Said Richie's been kidnapped."

I looked up at Drake. He clearly didn't want two medical emergencies on his hands either. I stood up and went to Robert. I placed my hands on each side of his face, making him look directly into my eyes.

"Okay, we need to get this before it fades away," I told him. "First, was the voice a man or a woman?"

"Man. I think it was. Deep. Lot of static, though."

Drake came up with a pen and small piece of paper from a pocket. I took them and prepared to write it all down. Chances were that Robert's recollection would soon blur. Drake pulled his chair near Sarah's and she gripped his hand.

"Okay. A man's voice. Now, tell me what he said. Exactly."

"He said, 'I'm only sayin' this once more. We've got Richie Campbell. If you want him back alive, you'll pay fifty-thousand pounds.' That's all he said."

I looked at Molly, who was still hovering at the edge of the room. She nodded. "That's right. He said that to me, too, ma'am."

Robert's color had improved and he seemed to be more in control. Sarah was sobbing quietly, still clinging to Drake's forearm.

"Let's all go somewhere more comfortable," I said. "Molly, could you bring tea to the library?"

"There's a fire in the drawing room already," she suggested.

"Good. We'll be in there." I took Robert's elbow and helped him up. Drake guided Sarah and we all went to the drawing room, where indeed a cozy fire and overstuffed chairs waited.

"We should first call the police," I said. "Then may—"

"No! That's the other thing the voice said. 'Don't call the police.'" Robert spun toward me. "We can't do that."

"But it only makes sense," I said. "They know how to handle these situations. We don't."

"Charlie, you can investigate it," Sarah said. Her eyes were too eager.

"Sarah, Robert, *please* don't put this on me. Richie's life is at stake and I don't want to be responsible. And what about the other two boys? Lewis and Alasdair haven't turned up either."

"Let's all sit down," Drake said. "Maybe we can think of something."

Molly came in with a tray holding a silver tea service, delicate porcelain cups and saucers, and pots of sugar and cream.

"Stay a minute, Molly," I said. "You heard the voice too. Did either of you recognize it? Take a minute and think very hard. Have you ever heard that voice before?"

"It sounded like that American actor, Robert DeNiro," Molly said.

A tiny smile flickered across Sarah's face.

"Um... I don't think Robert DeNiro kidnapped Richie." I looked at her hopeful face. "But thanks for offering that, Molly. Every detail helps."

"I can't place the voice," Robert said. "It sounded like someone trying to disguise his voice. You know, make himself sound more gruff."

I tried to visualize DeNiro's soft voice sounding gruff. It didn't give me much to go on.

"We better call Elizabeth and Edward," Sarah said. "They'll be worried sick."

"They'll be asleep," Robert said. "It's going on eleven."

"True, they don't know anything's happened yet." I wasn't sure the best way to handle this.

Sarah straightened in her chair. "If my child were missing, I'd want to know it immediately. Elizabeth will be very angry if she learns this hours after the fact."

I nodded and Drake handed her the phone.

After what must have been at least five or six rings, someone picked up. "Edward," Sarah began, "I'm afraid..." Her voice broke and a sob escaped.

"I'd better—" Robert snatched up the receiver. "Edward. Well, not good, I'm afraid. Richie's missing."

I noticed that he took the more gentle way of saying it.

"No, there's been a call. We just learned of it. No, they said *no* police."

I could hear a demanding voice coming through the phone.

"Look, no sense in driving through the night. Take the first train in the morning. Someone will pick you up." He listened for a minute. "All right, then, the airport. Seven-thirty? Hold a second.'' He put his hand over the mouthpiece and turned to Drake. ''Could you meet their plane and fly them out here in your helicopter, by chance?''

''I'll have to rearrange some things, but yes. Tell him one of us will be there.''

Robert turned back to his call and Drake and I hastily conferred about our flight schedule for the next morning.

''Here's what we'll do,'' Drake said, the minute Robert clicked off the call. ''I have to meet some people out on one of the rigs early. So Charlie will take the JetRanger and meet Edward's flight. She can have them here within five minutes.''

''Tonight, if it's okay with you, I'd like to look through Richie's bedroom. See if I can spot anything that would give us any ideas.''

Robert and Sarah both looked relieved that someone was taking charge.

I set my cup and saucer on the tray. ''Earlier today, Sarah, you said the boys were going out tonight. Do you know where?''

Her smooth brow wrinkled in thought. ''A club in Inverness. I can't remember if they told me the name of it. Surely they did, but I can't think of it.''

She turned to Robert, looking helplessly at him. He shrugged. ''Don't know as they ever mentioned it me,'' he said. ''Then again, I've been in Edinburgh the past couple of days. Didn't keep up with the boys much.''

''There is a girl Richie's been seeing in Inverness,'' Sarah said. ''Janie…Janie something… Oh, rats, why can't I remember it.'' She looked ready to cry.

''Don't worry about it for now,'' I said. ''Maybe I'll come across it in his room. Show me the way?''

Robert stepped forward.

''I still think this is a police matter,'' I said.

They both flinched.

''Please consider it.'' I tried for a gentler tone. ''I feel very inadequate here. I might overlook something important.''

''For now, Charlie, this is what we should do. We should

find out what their demands are and try to get Richie back ourselves.'' The firmness in Robert's voice left no room for argument. I followed him up the stairs.

Richie's bedroom looked like just about any other teen's room I could imagine—if that kid lived in a castle. Beneath the scatter of dirty clothing and rock music magazines was a room with high ceilings, elaborate crown moldings, a fireplace, and an oriental carpet that must be priceless. The décor was clearly guest-room—twin beds with flowered spreads (now puddled haphazardly, half on and half off), good antiques, and filmy drapes. A third bed had been set up and things shuffled a bit to accommodate the three boys. My guess was that Richie had no permanently assigned bedroom here, just chose one whenever he came to visit the grandparents.

I picked through the visible clutter, not finding anything notable, then delved under the mattresses and into the bedding. A baggie of marijuana in the pillowcase of the third bed probably meant that one of the visitors had brought the stash for all of them. My guess would be Alasdair. He'd seemed the more defensive toward me earlier, but you never knew.

A feminine dressing table with all the decorative items shoved to one side contained an assortment of boy-clutter. A walkman CD player, stacks of music CDs by heavy metal groups, a car magazine, and a handful of pocket junk—coins, a shiny rock, some lint, and a wrapped condom. This last lay covered by the magazine, not readily apparent had Grandma peeked into the room.

Jammed into the pages of the magazine, an envelope peeked out. I pulled it free. There was nothing inside but the envelope itself was interesting. The paper was wispy lavender, scented with some cloying perfume, addressed to Richie at school. The return address was from Janie Grahame, with an Inverness address. We now knew where to find the mysterious Janie.

I kept the envelope and turned my attention back to the rest of the room. At the foot of the temporary bed lay a large green duffle bag, the floppy kind you see traveling kids wrestling with in airports. Its contents revealed nothing more than wadded clothing with a dirt-caked pair of boots in the midst. A large backpack stood propped against a delicate inlaid table. I pulled it over to one of the beds and went through it, too, with about the same results. I couldn't put my finger on it but something was out of place.

I wondered where the two other boys were right now. Had their families also received ransom calls? Were they witness to Richie's abduction and talking to the police now? The questions just kept coming.

FIFTEEN

I SCANNED THE ROOM one more time, lifted bed skirts to look under. The room had no closet, and the large armoire was completely empty. The lavender envelope crinkled in my hand. How deeply was Richie involved with this girl? Did Janie Grahame have something to do with this?

"Sorry to disturb, Charlie."

I must have jumped because Robert apologized a second time.

"It's okay. Sorry I've been taking so long."

"Just wanted to let you know that Sarah remembered that girl's name. Janie Grahame, it is."

"I just discovered that," I said. I showed him the envelope.

"Ah, and an address too. You are a fine detective." He managed a smile.

"When the boys arrived, did they each have their own bags?"

"Hmm...I assume so." His eyes darted around the room, puzzled.

"I'm only finding two in here."

"Ah, well, I remember Sarah saying last week that the boys were taking an overnight jaunt to see another friend in Fort Augustus. That's at the tip end of Loch Ness. Probably stuffed a few things into someone's bag and took it."

"But they would have brought it back."

"Probably still in the boot. Boys never bring things in and put them away." He shrugged.

That was probably true. "Did anyone remember the name of the club where the boys went tonight?"

"Afraid not."

"I think we should call Janie's family and see if they know. Shall we see if there's a phone listing for them?"

We trooped back down to the drawing room, where Sarah paced and Drake concealed a yawn. I patted him on the shoulder. "One more thing tonight, and then we'll get you to bed."

"Oh, yes, certainly," Sarah said. "You've both got to fly in the morning and we're keeping you up awfully late."

"You wouldn't happen to know a phone number for Janie Grahame, would you?" I showed Sarah the envelope I'd found.

"No, but let's check the directory." She headed toward the library and came back in a couple of minutes. "Here, let's see…"

Robert stood by with the phone in hand. He punched the numbers as she read them out. I jotted them on the back of the lavender envelope as well.

Again, he waited as the ringing telephone woke up another sleeping family. Finally, someone picked up. "Hello, is that Mr. Grahame? Uh, Hugh Grahame?" He introduced himself and explained that we were trying to learn Richie's whereabouts earlier this evening.

"Did your daughter go out with Richie last night?" Robert asked. "Is it possible to bring her to the phone? We've got an American private detective on the case…"

Oh, god.

"…and she'd like to ask Janie some questions."

There seemed to be a bit of arguing back and forth, followed by a five-minute wait while Robert held the phone. "He's going to get her," he stage-whispered to the room.

"Ah! Janie, dear, did your father tell you, this is Richie's grandfather calling?" He nodded twice. "I'm going to put a lady on to talk to you."

"Janie, hi. My name's Charlie. We need to find Richie, and no one remembers the name of that club he and his friends were going to tonight. Can you help me?"

A teen girl voice came through, fuzzy and nasal sounding. "Em...Richie? It's about Richie?"

"Yes, Janie. Did you go out with him to a club tonight?"

"Uh, no. I didn't go out tonight." I thought I heard her rubbing a hand over her face. "I think Richie and some friends were going out. Two guys from his school."

"Yes, that would be right. Lewis and Alasdair are their names."

"Yes, I think so." Her voice was slowly becoming more alert.

"So, do you know what club they went to?"

"Club? It could've been Mike's. We go there sometimes." She sounded genuinely confused.

"Mike's," I said. Sarah shook her head, mouthing "I don't think so."

"Any others?" I asked.

"The Pelican. I know he likes that one."

Again, I repeated the name aloud. Sarah shrugged.

"More?" I said to Janie.

"Waldo Green's. We go there a lot."

"Waldo Green's?" Sarah brightened a bit as I said it.

"Janie, I'll let you get back to sleep now," I said. "Please call one of us if you hear anything from Richie. We're all pretty worried." I gave the phone numbers to our cottage and the Dunbars. She mumbled a sleepy goodnight and I wondered whether she'd remember the conversation at all by morning.

"Do you think any of these places would be open right now?" I asked, handing the phone back to Robert.

"Doubt it. They're all teen clubs, underage crowd, no liquor. Closed before midnight, most of 'em." His eyes were weary. "You've done what you can for now. Go get some rest and be ready to get my daughter at the airport in the morning, eh."

Drake rose from the overstuffed chair where he'd become way too comfortable.

"You're right, Robert. I better get this guy to bed or he won't be fit to fly out to that rig in the morning."

Despite the fact that I was worried about Richie and wondered why the two other boys hadn't returned, I fell asleep the minute my head hit the pillow. The alarm rang at five-thirty and Drake dragged himself from the warmth of the bed, but I rolled over for another half-hour. By the time he'd finished showering I'd made myself sit up.

We opted to take two cars to the airport, since there was no way of knowing where either of us would be by the end of this day. I saw Drake off on his flight about seven then I radioed Inverness tower to be sure there wouldn't be any problem with my landing the JetRanger next to the British Air 767 after it came in at gate four. The controller seemed hesitant about it until I mentioned the name Dunbar.

Today would be Meggie's first day back in the office after her ordeal and I'd really wanted to be there to lend a hand if she needed help getting things back in order. I could also be a second person in the office in case she felt uneasy about being alone at first. But it looked like that was not to be, at least for the first few hours. Maybe I'd be able to get back soon if there were some miraculous break in the Dunbar situation.

Precisely at seven twenty-eight the British Air flight from London touched down and rolled down the taxiway to Gate 4. The entire Inverness airport consists of one long terminal building with four doors, where passengers walk outside to climb portable steps to their planes. I watched through field glasses from my seat in the helicopter, two hundred yards and two fences away.

As soon as the ground crew wheeled the stairway toward the plane, I brought my engine up to speed and pulled pitch. Setting the ship down fifty feet away from the jet, in my pre-cleared spot, I tightened down my controls and waited.

Edward and Elizabeth Campbell weren't hard to spot. Evidently they'd been in first class because they were among the first ten people off the plane. Edward was scanning the area and he nudged his wife and pointed toward the helicopter. I climbed down from my seat and unplugged my headset, leaving it on to muffle some of the turbine whine that filled the area. I reached them by the time they hit the bottom of the steps.

Edward wore a charcoal business suit, white shirt, and light gray tie with tiny black dots. His thinning brown hair was trimmed short and his smooth-shaven face had not quite become jowly, yet. His mouth was pulled into a somber expression. He moved with the authority of a man accustomed to getting his way.

"Hi, I'm Charlie." I held out my hand and noticed that Edward looked at it before he shook it. His eyes skimmed the black slacks and cotton sweater I'd purposely chosen instead of my usual jeans.

Elizabeth bore her worry directly on her face. Physically, she was a replica of her mother—slim and blond, with gray eyes. They were puffy from a night without sleep and red-rimmed to the point that makeup couldn't disguise it. But where Sarah's manner was soft and friendly, her daughter had a veneer of big city on her. Her black pantsuit, trimmed in satin piping, was clearly expensive and I recognized the sunglasses she slipped out of her bag as being a brand that sold for $450 at home. She wore her hair in a style that was currently popular with twenty-somethings, a gelled piece of work that was meant to look like she'd just had a good tumble in the hay. She thrust a carry-on bag at me without a word.

Okay.

I turned and ushered them toward the helicopter with my teeth firmly in a demure smile. I made them stand aside while I stowed their two bags into the cargo compartment. Elizabeth stood with both hands firmly holding her blond hair against the tremendous wind whipped up by the blades. Edward didn't have enough hair to worry about.

"Front seat? Back? Who wants to ride where?" I shouted.

He instinctively moved toward the front, so I opened the back door for Elizabeth. She had a little trouble figuring out that she would need to put her left foot on the skid step before she could swing herself up into the seat, but she finally got it. Luckily, she'd worn the slacks. The whole maneuver can be truly awkward in a dress. I reached across her and snapped her seat belt in place, then handed her a headset from the shelf behind her. She wore it gingerly, high on her head, cautious about her "do."

Edward had opened his door and gotten into his seat while all this was going on, but the seat belt confounded him, since those in the front were a combination belt and shoulder harness. I could tell the harnesses crisscrossing his charcoal business suit didn't please him. I clicked them into place and cinched them tightly.

Circling the nose of the aircraft and taking my own seat, I adjusted my mouthpiece and flicked the switch for the intercom.

"Everyone comfortable?" I glanced back at Elizabeth but she was checking her nail polish for chips. Edward merely nodded.

I switched back to the tower frequency and transmitted my intention to take off, cross the active runway and take a heading to the south-southeast. Once the controller confirmed it, I pulled pitch and lifted the ship slowly off the tarmac. Edward looked back to be sure all the other passengers from the plane had noticed that they were being picked up by a private helicopter. I stifled the smile that twitched at my mouth.

"We should be there in just a few minutes," I told them. "In a straight line, Dunworthy is only about twelve miles from here."

Open fields gave way to dense forest after we'd cleared the airport, but the bold patches of new green were clearly visible in all directions. I spotted the high turrets of Dunworthy Castle in the distance. They made excellent reference points—far easier than finding an oil rig in the middle of a gray, swelling sea. I guided the aircraft in and saw Sarah and Robert come out the front door as we approached. With acres of smooth green lawn available, I chose a spot about fifty yards away from the castle and set the JetRanger down softly.

The Dunbars walked toward us as I let the turbine engine wind down and slowed the rotor blades gently with the brake.

Sarah greeted me with a hug when I'd climbed out of my seat. She shook her head softly when I asked whether there had been any more news.

I walked around to release Edward first from his seat, then Elizabeth, then I opened the cargo door and placed each of their bags firmly in their hands while I closed the compartments. I joined the other four as they stood back from the helicopter. They'd exchanged quick hugs. Now Robert held out an arm, which he slipped around my shoulders.

"You've met Charlie, our private detective," he announced. "Come inside, everyone. Sarah's got coffee on and a coffeecake that looks scrumptious."

The two newcomers sent some daggers my way as Robert steered me toward the castle like a family member.

"Mother, surely you've decided to call the police into this by now," Elizabeth said, dropping her bag in the entry hall. She shed her jacket and draped it over the bag on the floor. "I mean…" she glanced at me to emphasize her opinion of my capabilities.

"No, dear," Sarah said. "Absolutely not. The caller was quite firm. Your father and I feel that we have to follow instructions on this." She led us toward the spacious kitchen where she'd made tea for me the first time I'd been here. Ruffie lay on the floor like a dustmop someone had left out. She flapped her tail once at the sight of us.

"Charlie is absolutely qualified," Robert said.

I started to interrupt with a denial, until I caught the look on Edward's face.

"I also suggested they call the police," I said. "Just so you understand that this wasn't my idea."

"Father has always been stubborn as a rock," Elizabeth murmured to me as Sarah and Robert clattered plates and cups on the far side of the room. I got the feeling she was loosening up toward me a bit.

"I still don't like it," Edward said. "What's been done so far?"

I told him briefly what we'd learned the previous night,

while Sarah passed plates of coffeecake covered in a crumbly cinnamon topping. I noticed that neither Elizabeth nor Robert picked up their forks.

"Have you talked to either of the other boys' families?" I asked the Dunbars. They both shook their heads.

"Then we have to do that. Surely, if they'd received ransom calls they would have already called you, but we have to be sure."

Dread showed clearly on Sarah's face.

"If they have received calls, I'm afraid I have to insist that we call the police into it immediately. All three boys are clearly in danger. If they haven't, and *if* the boys haven't turned up somewhere else, we're really looking for all three."

Mumbled conversations ran through the room. "I guess you're right, Charlie," Robert finally said.

"Wherever they are, I hope they're together," Elizabeth said.

SIXTEEN

THEY ALL VOTED that Robert, with his diplomatic experience, should be the one to make the calls. We all hovered shamelessly as he got Lewis's mother on the line. He queried politely as to her well being. We tapped our toes. He finally got around to asking whether the boys might have come to their place. A series of nods and one-syllable responses convinced us that Lewis's family hadn't heard from the boys. Robert told her that they'd gone to a teen club last night and hadn't come home. He didn't mention the phone call about Richie's ransom.

"I'll call Alasdair's family, then," he said, ending the call.

"You didn't tell that woman her son might have been kidnapped!" Edward demanded.

"We don't know that." Robert's face remained calm. "We only know that we received a call about Richie. What's the sense in frightening the poor woman to death if it turns out Lewis is perfectly safe somewhere?"

Elizabeth laid a hand on her husband's arm. He stared at it a moment before crossing the room to pour himself another cup of coffee.

The second call, to Alasdair's home, netted much the same. The boy's father hadn't heard from him.

"Unfortunate lad is one of those who's been shipped off to boarding school to get him out from underfoot," Robert reported when he hung up. "Shame when parents don't want their own children around."

"Now, father, if that's a remark—" Elizabeth rose from her stool indignantly.

Robert held out one palm to her. "I meant nothing by it."

"Richie's attending Greenbriar because it offers the finest education for a young man of his class and standing," Edward said.

"Look, everyone, I think we need to focus on what to do about this right now," I said. I certainly had other things to do besides listen to them quibble about old family sore spots. "With your permission, Robert, I'll go talk to Janie again, and I'll see if I can get any information at those clubs."

"Certainly, Charlie. Do what you need to."

"First, I need to get this aircraft back." I carried my cup to the sink and left them all sitting in the kitchen. In the hall, I noticed that the Campbells' bags had been removed. I wondered briefly what it would be like to go through life with others toting and carrying for me.

At the helicopter, I quickly checked hatches and doors and did a mini pre-flight inspection. I glanced up to see Edward crossing the lawn toward me. Sarah had told me he was a successful real estate developer and I could believe it. His purposeful stride and pushy manner showed his take-charge attitude. I wondered if he thought he would come out here and take charge of me.

"Edward." I kept my tone cool.

"Charlie, a word?" He glanced back at the castle.

"Certainly."

He shoved his hands into his pockets and tamped a small patch of grass with his toe. "I'm not sure how much credence I'd give to Richie's disappearing act."

"Act? Is that what you think this is?" My mind flashed back to the absolute horror Robert and Sarah had felt after the phone call.

He smiled in a conciliatory, almost oily, way. "He's done this before."

"What! Tried to demand a ransom?"

"No, not that part. But he's taken off before. Disappeared without a word. Shows up a few days later after we've been sick out of our wits."

"So, what are you saying? That we shouldn't worry? That we shouldn't attempt to find him?" I felt my blood pressure rise a notch.

He studied the perfect shine on his shoes.

"I can't believe you'd take the risk," I said. "How can you take the chance that the ransom call wasn't real?"

He shrugged. "Talk to that girlfriend of his. I'd bet she knows more than she's said."

"I'll do that. Now if you'll excuse me." I stepped up into my seat and put on my headset, effectively cutting off anything more he might want to say. I forced myself to blank out Edward and the whole situation with the Campbells and the Dunbars so I wouldn't miss a crucial step in my flight procedures. Once I was airborne, I allowed myself to ponder. What had I gotten myself into here?

Back at the airport I saw Meggie's familiar tiny white car parked by the office. Good. I landed in my usual spot and shut down.

"Glad to see you're back," I greeted as I walked into the office.

"Hi, Charlie! I'm glad to be back." Meggie's dimples showed once again, and I noticed that she'd combed her bangs down to conceal the small bandage covering the two stitches in her forehead.

Stacks of papers still covered the top of the desk and two of the file drawers gaped open.

"I'm sorry we left such a mess for you," I said. "I had no idea how to put all this back together."

"It's okay. Looks better than when I left."

I was amazed that she was taking the whole incident with such calm.

"Drake still out?"

"Yeah. But he's left a message for you." She rummaged through papers on the desk. "I know I wrote it down."

"What was it about?"

"You're needed at one of the rigs. He said it was urgent. But I can't—"

''What time did he call?''

''Oh, it was maybe an hour—oh, here's the note.'' She shoved a yellow slip of paper at me.

''He wants me to go to Platform 6?'' My least favorite of all the rigs. I wondered if Brankin was on duty today. ''Did he say why it was urgent?''

''No…I should have asked.''

''It's okay. Get me refueled while I get dressed.''

With her usual efficiency, Meggie called Fergus to bring out the fuel truck. I made a quick visit to the restroom then slipped my survival suit on over my regular clothes. As usual, donning the gear reminded me of the dunk test I'd undergone before being allowed to fly over the sea. The sheer terror of being submerged in icy water always floated just below the surface of my consciousness.

Fergus finished topping off the tank as I emerged from the office. Thirty minutes later I was over open water, a deep blue today, reflecting the clear sky. Moving along in level flight with my GPS pointing the course, I found my mind flitting back and forth from the situation with Richie Campbell to the battle between the boat operators, the helicopter companies, and the oil company. I couldn't get my thoughts to settle.

I spotted the rig in the distance and slowed my airspeed as I approached it. I circled it once before bringing the JetRanger in beside the Eurocopter on the pad. Drake met me before I'd even brought the rotor speed down. His lean face showed worry lines.

''Problems?'' I shouted over the noise of the turbine engine and the whopping blades.

''Yeah. A breakdown. We're gonna' have to leave the other ship here overnight.''

Uh-oh. Unguarded, and on the unfriendliest rig in the North Atlantic.

''Exactly,'' he said, reading my mind. ''I need you to fly me back to the office. I've been on the phone with the mechanic and he thinks the problem is in the fuel injection system.''

We've ordered a part, overnight from London, and I'll have to bring him out with me to install it.''

"So, are you ready to leave now?''

"In a minute. I'll grab my gear and lock things up. Stay running.'' He ducked around the nose of the JetRanger and walked to the other ship.

Colin Finnie, the crew chief, came out of his office and I immediately saw Brankin approach him. Brankin turned away from me, but his gestures and body language pretty well said it. He was making his point that the helicopter service was unreliable. Barrie and Tolliver stood by, a solid little group. Finnie looked down at Brankin and took it in. His face remained placid. He let Brankin go on for a couple of minutes, then dismissed him. The three men stomped back to the elevator.

Finnie crossed to Drake, who had just finished locking the doors and compartments on the Astar. He listened as Drake talked, that same unruffled look on his face. After a short exchange, he gave me a small salute and headed toward his office. Drake came over and stowed his survival gear and flight bag in the cargo compartment.

"Finnie says he'll do his best to keep his eye on things until I can get back," Drake said, once he'd fastened his harness and put on his headset. "He's not happy about this breakdown.''

I re-checked my instruments and brought the engine up to speed again.

"I guess Brankin gave Finnie an earful about how unreliable we were," Drake said. "He's really putting the pressure on the oil company to cancel their contract with us and to let the boat operators handle all the work.''

I concentrated for a minute on getting safely off the platform and onto the correct heading for the airport. "Do you think the union men had anything to do with your breakdown?''

"Probably not. Well, if the problem is what the mechanic thinks it is, they didn't. But you can bet I'll have the guy go over the ship with a fine tooth comb before I head out over open water again.'' He fidgeted in his seat, then rubbed his hands briskly along his pant legs. ''Damn.''

''You know, hon,'' I said, ever the voice of reason, ''this really isn't our problem. Maybe you should tell Brian he needs to get back here and run his own business.''

''I would. In a heartbeat.''

''But, his mother's dying and you just don't have the heart to do it.''

The side of his mouth quirked upward in a little grimace.

''No more than I have the heart to tell the Dunbars that I want nothing to do with tracking down Richie.'' I filled him in on the arrival of Edward and Elizabeth, the calls to the other boys' families, and Edward's revelation that Richie had run off before.

''Do you think that's what happened?'' he asked.

''I don't know what to think at this point. That ransom call certainly convinced Robert. And Edward admitted that the scare tactics didn't sound like Richie. I'm going to talk to his girlfriend this afternoon and try to locate someone at one of those clubs who may have seen the boys last night.'' I paused to make a brief course correction. ''That is, if you don't need me.''

''No, nothing you can do at this point about the Astar. I'll take this ship and finish shuttling the crews out and back today, and I want to talk to the mechanic. Just to be sure he brings enough diagnostic equipment to test the aircraft thoroughly.''

We made an uneventful landing and he took over the controls. ''Be careful,'' I said as I got out.

I stood at the edge of the tarmac, an uneasy feeling hanging over me as I watched him become a speck in the distance.

SEVENTEEN

INSIDE, I PEELED OFF my survival suit and asked Meggie if there were any messages. None. She'd done an impressive job of organizing her files, and the place was nearly neat again. I picked up the phone and dialed Dunworthy. Sarah answered.

"Any news?" I asked.

"Not a thing. The men have gone out to practice their putting on the lawn. Edward reminded us that Richie has run off before and I think that put Robert's mind at ease quite a bit."

"But the ransom call? Richie wouldn't do that, would he?"

"Oh, heavens no," she said. "But I just don't know...I mean, what else is there to think?"

Only the unthinkable.

I told her my afternoon plans and gave her a cell phone number in case there were any developments. Instructing Meggie to call me if Drake encountered any problems, I got into the rental car and headed toward town.

The Grahame's neat stone house wasn't too hard to find. With my trusty map of Inverness's winding residential streets, and my learning to drive on the opposite side of them, I only missed it twice before I negotiated the one-ways correctly and pulled up in exactly the right place.

"Janie? She's at work," a short, round man with bristly light brown hair told me. He'd answered the door wearing wrinkled khaki pants and a dingy sleeveless undershirt. "Up Beat, at the mall. It's a music store. Be there till six."

I thanked him for the information and declined the beer he offered me.

I knew where the mall was—I'd passed it twice on my way. The only trick would be negotiating the one-way streets until I actually got to it. Chin up, Charlie. You can do this.

Actually, it only took about ten minutes. I rode the elevator from the parking garage to the second level and emerged onto the shopping level. Aside from the Celtic patterns in the floor tile, the shiny, bright, fluorescent-lit shops filled with jewelry, clothing, and electronics could be in any mall in the world. I spotted Up Beat about halfway down the main corridor.

When I asked for Janie Grahame, the clerk at the front of the store pointed to a desk at the back. "The girl on the telephone," he said.

I browsed through CDs by everyone from Tim McGraw to the Rolling Stones before Janie ended the call. When she finally appeared to be free, I approached her.

"Janie, hi. My name's Charlie Parker. I was with Mr. and Mrs. Dunbar last night when they called you."

Her pretty face went blank.

"It's about Richie," I explained. I could see where the attraction would be for the gangly, sixteen-year-old boy. Janie's blond hair had the texture of silk and hung midway down her back. Her body was willowy, although she stood only about five-three. Her skin was flawless and her makeup tastefully done.

"Oh! There was a phone call during the night, wasn't there?" She automatically straightened racks of CDs while we talked.

"Richie never did come home last night," I said. "His parents and grandparents are awfully worried. Have you heard from him?"

Her Wedgwood blue eyes widened.

"Look, I have a break in fifteen minutes." She checked a chunky blue plastic watch that looked huge on her delicate wrist.

"If there's somewhere we can sit down, maybe grab a Coke or something...? I can meet you there."

She suggested an ice cream place in the mall and pointed the way.

I located it, two doors away from the music store, and remembered I'd only eaten half a slice of coffeecake all day. The smell of grilling hot dogs suddenly turned me ravenous. I ordered one, along with chips and a large Coke. My request for ice branded me immediately as an American, I felt sure, but I didn't think I could handle another lukewarm soda.

I stuffed the last bite of hot dog into my mouth and checked my watch. Fifteen minutes had passed and no Janie. I stepped to the door just in time to see her leave the music store and turn the opposite direction.

"Oh, Janie!" I shouted. "Over here!"

She spun around like she'd been nipped in the flank.

I waved her toward me.

A look of something between despair and dread crossed her face. Her feet dragged her to the ice cream shop, but she clearly didn't want to come. Only an ingrained sense of obligation to obey adults propelled her. Adults. I realized with a mild shock that I was nearly old enough to be her mother.

"Can I get you an ice cream or a drink?" I offered, making my voice as gentle as possible. I certainly wasn't going to get any useful information out of her if she was afraid of me.

She shook her head. I pushed my fries toward her but she ignored them.

"Janie, this is really important or I wouldn't be asking."

She nodded, but her eyes wouldn't meet mine.

"Something may have happened to Richie. We need to know anything you can tell us about where he might be."

"I told you the names of the clubs where he hangs out."

"I know, and I'm going to check them out. But did you see him last night at all?"

Her drooping head went back and forth slowly. A tear rolled down one cheek.

I glanced around. We were at a corner table and no one was paying any attention to us. "Janie? What's the matter?" I reached out to stroke her upper arm, but she flinched away from me. "Do you know what's happened to Richie?"

A second tear began its trek down her other cheek.

"Janie, I need to know anything that might help us find him." No movement whatsoever. "Now." The single word came out more firmly than I'd intended, but it had its effect. A sob escaped beneath the curtain of golden hair that shielded her face.

"You can't tell anyone."

"Janie, that depends on what it is. If this has to do with Richie's safety, I may have to."

"It doesn't."

"Just tell me." I wanted to shake her.

"I'm preg—"

"Oh, boy." I didn't mean to make it sound so fateful, but it did. "Does Richie know?"

"Yes. I told him last week." She picked up one of the fries.

I pushed a paper napkin toward her and she dabbed discreetly at her eyes. She took another fry. Now that the big secret was out, her appetite returned with a vengeance. I let her go at them while I formulated my next few questions. A sixteen-year-old boy who's just learned he's going to be a father might have reason to think he could avoid the problem by simply running away. I had to admit that I didn't know Richie well at all, but his respectful attitude and demeanor toward me made me think he'd be likely to have a sense of honor about this too.

"Do your parents know?" I asked.

Her eyes grew wide. "No! And I can't face them alone, I can't. Richie said he'd be here with me. Stand by my side. All that."

She reached for another potato but a tear rolled toward her mouth. "He said he loved me. I thought we'd be married."

"Janie, we're doing everything we can to find him." I reached out to pat her hand and this time she let me. "When we do, I promise you, I'll—" My cell phone began to chirp away down inside my purse.

Drake and Sarah were the only people with the number, and either way, I wasn't sure the news would be good. I answered it with a twist of trepidation in my gut.

"Charlie, it's Sarah. Alasdair and Lewis have just come back."

EIGHTEEN

"DON'T LET THEM get away. I'll be there in twenty minutes."
I clicked off and jammed the phone down into my bag.

Janie's china blue eyes watched me, a mix of hope and fear
running across her face.

"Sorry, it's not Richie. Not yet. But it's a good lead." I
pulled out my keys and stood up. "I'll let you know what I
find out." I'd started to leave, but turned back to her. "Hang
in there, okay?"

She nodded, her full lower lip quivering.

I dashed through the procedure of feeding my parking ticket
into the automated payment machine on the wall near the el-
evators and giving it a few coins, then practically ran through
the garage to the car. Now, if I could just get out of town
without getting completely turned around. My mind was whirling as I negotiated the roundabout at the edge of town and
headed toward Dunworthy.

"Everyone's in the kitchen," Molly said, letting me in.

Kitchens must be the gathering place in every culture, I decided. Three boys sat on stools at the counter and for a second
the happy thought hit me that Richie had also come back. But
the third young man was a stranger to me.

The four adults hovered over them and it seemed that everyone was talking at once, most of it a fast Scottish brogue that
I couldn't follow. Ruffie stayed near Sarah's heels.

"Ah, here's Charlie," Robert said, motioning me in. "Let's
let her handle the interrogation."

I wished he hadn't put it that way.

"Tea, Charlie?" Sarah asked, clearly looking for a way to stay busy.

I declined and turned to the boys. Alasdair and Lewis were wearing the same clothes they must have worn the previous night. Over-large black jeans and shirts, a single gold earring each, and an assortment of chains and other little decorator items. The third boy was dressed in everyday jeans and a big Benetton t-shirt. His flame-red hair was gelled into carefully disarranged spikes.

"Guys?" I interrupted their lively exchange of heavy brogue interspersed with doses of Scots Gaelic. "Can we take a deep breath here? I need you to tell me where Richie is."

"We don't know, ma'am." Alasdair, by default, became the spokesman for the group. "Swear. We lost him last night and thought he'd come home."

"Tell me everything that happened last night. From the start."

They'd already covered this ground, I could tell, but I made them go through it again.

"We left here about six. Went to Waldo Green's."

"No—" Lewis interrupted. "The Pelican first."

"Right," Alasdair said. "The Pelican first. Not much happening there, so we went to Waldo Green's. It was just a short time later. Richie was driving."

"I'd let the boys take my car. The white Range Rover," Robert interrupted.

"Okay." I turned back to the boys. "Then?"

"Then, well, we danced with some girls we met there. Place was really jumping." He fidgeted on his seat. "Then, I guess we'd been there a couple hours, Lewis and I went out back for a smoke."

His eyes told me that he really didn't want me to ask what kind of smoke. I didn't.

"We came back in and danced some more. After a bit I realized we hadn't seen Richie in a while. It's after nine now and the place closes at ten. I figure he's maybe in the loo, maybe taken some girl outside.'' He shrugged. ''No big deal. I have another smoke, and I'm feeling kind of tired.''

Mellow, you mean.

''So, like, around a quarter of ten, we get together and really start looking for him. And he's nowhere. I mean, the place is packed, his car's still outside, but he's *not there*.''

''And?''

''So we still don't find him by the time they announce the last dance. Lewis remembers Billy lives pretty close. So we get some chap to give us a ride and we crash there. Pissed at Richie, I was. Leaving us like that.''

Billy spoke up for the first time. ''And I drive 'em all the way out here this morning and ain't even got me petrol money yet. Old man's gotta' be after me by now. Supposed to be workin' for him today.''

Lewis fished out a five-pound note and slapped it into Billy's hand.

''I think that's all Billy knows,'' Robert said. ''Ought to let the lad get back to his work.''

Billy threw a sharp glance back at the room as he left.

''So, you never did see Richie again the rest of the evening?'' I asked.

''Told you. He left us there, stuck.''

I sensed there was something else they weren't saying, but it was more likely to do with smoking pot or chasing girls. Richie had apparently disappeared from a crowded club without a word to his friends.

I caught myself chewing on my lip as I tried to imagine what might have happened to him.

Edward, who'd been remarkably quiet since my arrival, pushed his way toward the counter. ''Look, you two, if there's anything you're not telling us…''

Elizabeth pulled at his arm. Edward's clenched fists relaxed, but only a little.

''Threatening them won't solve anything,'' Sarah said. ''Now, lads, first I think you better call your parents and let them know you're back. We'd called them earlier and told them you'd not been home during the night. You'll have some explaining to do."

Lewis looked like he didn't relish making his call at all, while Alasdair's face remained passive.

"After your calls, you'll want to go up and take showers. Then we can decide whether you're going home or staying here." Sarah's grandmotherly firmness brought no argument and the boys shuffled off to do their duties.

"I'd like Charlie to drive me down to this place and we'll retrieve the car," Robert said. "First, I'd better call my assistant in Edinburgh. We're supposed to be in session this morning and it looks like I'm going to miss my vote on the farm bill." He scrubbed at his temples with his fingertips. "Well, not much to be done about it."

"If I could make a suggestion?" I said.

All eyes turned toward me.

"Um, I don't think it's a good idea to simply take the car and bring it back."

Robert gave me a look that said, "why not, it's my car."

"There could be evidence. Fingerprints…"

"Nonsense. My own prints are all over the thing anyway. Adding one more batch won't change anything. I'm not having my vehicle sit there in that part of town, unguarded, subject to vandalism."

"The police…" I meant to say that the police wouldn't look kindly on us removing the vehicle from the scene of the crime, but Edward interrupted me.

"No police. That's been decided," he said.

So, that was that. I continued to argue with Robert as we drove into downtown Inverness, but nothing would change his mind. He seemed to feel that we would get Richie back without having to call the police, but if they came into it he could deal with them. Apparently politicians here don't have to abide by the rules either.

We drove past Waldo Green's. It was in a basement slot on Derryvale Close, a block off the main street and three or four blocks away from the train station. It was still early for a club, only a little past noon, but I thought I'd come back and see if I could catch someone who worked there.

We found the white Range Rover parked curbside two blocks away with two parking tickets under its wipers. Probably the only thing that had saved it from being towed was Robert's special Member Scottish Parliament plates.

"I'll have to let you out here," I told Robert. There were no empty parking slots on the whole street. "I'm going to stay and ask a few questions, then I better check in with Drake."

"Right. See you back at the house later," he said. "Come for dinner."

Truthfully, I would have preferred a little time alone and dinner with Drake at our own place. "We'll see how things go. I'll call you in a while," I said.

I watched him unlock the Range Rover and open the door. He crumpled the two tickets and jammed them into his pocket. I'd wanted to take a look inside the car before he drove it, but wasn't going to get the chance. Already traffic was stacking up behind me and the occasional horn toot reminded me that I needed to get out of the way. I circled the area but didn't find an open parking spot anywhere. The mall's big parking garage was only about three blocks away so I opted for that.

Walking the streets of Inverness gave me a better idea of the layout of the town anyway, taking my time rather than being pushed along by traffic. I passed in front of the train station and Victorian Market, and located Derryvale Close again without difficulty. Descending the few steps to Waldo Green's, as expected, I found the place locked. The two narrow windows had been painted black on the inside so there was no way to tell whether anyone was working. I pounded on the door a couple of times but wasn't terribly surprised when no one answered.

Upstairs, a small jewelry shop was open. One bored-looking middle-aged clerk sat behind the counter, reading a paperback romance. She hastily shoved it into a drawer when she spotted me.

"Actually, I was wondering about the club downstairs," I

told her, in reply to her friendly may-I-help-you. "I need to talk to the owner or manager. What time does someone usually come in?"

"Oh, Bruce comes in about five, getting ready for the night."

Nearly two hours away.

"But sometimes Tommy's there early. I thought I saw him a little while ago."

"I knocked at the door but no one answered."

"No, Tommy wouldn't. He'd think it was kids, wondering if the club was open. He'd be in the back, doing paperwork."

I fidgeted, impatient with the time I was wasting.

"Want me to give him a shout?" the lady offered.

I assumed she meant picking up the telephone, something I could have thought to do, but she literally intended to shout. She motioned me to follow her into a back room of the store, where she stomped a heel loudly three times on the wooden floor. She opened the back door, which led to a stone step in the alley behind. A man poked his head out the basement door and looked up.

"Hey, Tommy," she said. "Lady here's wanting to talk to you."

"Yeah? What about?" His dark eyes narrowed, the heavy brows pulling together. He was tall, over six feet, I'd guess, with dark brown hair that had receded beyond the halfway mark.

"I'll just take a minute," I said. "My name's Charlie Parker. Can I come down?"

He fished in his pocket and pulled out a key that unlocked a padlock on the iron gate to the basement's narrow cubbyhole. I followed the steps downward to the back porch, trying to size him up. He didn't look terribly happy to have me interrupting his work, but I didn't sense outright hostility. He instinctively ducked to clear the short doorway and I followed him into the dimness of a narrow hall. I caught a glimpse of four doors lining the hall before the space opened up into a large room, which I assumed was the dance floor.

Tommy turned to the first door on the right, a closet of a space that held a battered wooden desk, a four-drawer file, and a swivel chair. Stacks of credit card receipts and bills littered the top of the desk. He dropped the bundle he'd been carrying into the fray.

"Now, what can I do for you?" he asked.

"I'm looking for a sixteen-year-old boy who disappeared from this club last night. Two friends were with him and they lost sight of him about nine or nine-thirty. He never made it home." I planned to avoid mention of the ransom call unless I absolutely had to bring it up. "His car was parked on the street all night. We just located it."

"And this is unusual?" he asked with a grin.

"His family is awfully worried."

"Sorry, ma'am, but kids come and go as they please from here. We don't allow any alcohol or drugs, and that's about as far as we can go to keep them safe."

"I know this boy. Richie Campbell is his name. His grandparents are the Dunbars at Dunworthy." Maybe I could use their wealth and privilege to my advantage too. "Richie just doesn't seem like the kind of kid who would do something so irresponsible."

"He got a girlfriend?" Tommy asked.

Point taken. Richie hadn't acted so responsibly there.

"He didn't go off with her," I said. "We've already confirmed that."

"Don't know what I can tell you," he said. "A Friday or Saturday night in here, we've got about two hundred kids. Boys all wearing black, most with an earring or two and their hair spiked out every which way. Girls wearing those wee short tops that leave their fat little tummies hanging out, and a skirt that looks like they pulled a wide rubber band around their hips. Whoever decreed that that look is attractive should be shot."

I had to stifle a grin because Drake had said nearly the same thing on more than one occasion back at home.

"So you don't know Richie Campbell personally?" I asked.

"They all look alike to me."

"And you didn't notice a boy who looked like he might have been leaving against his will? Someone forcing him along?"

"Sorry."

I turned to leave and he followed. At the top of the steps, he reached to relock the iron gate.

"Is this gate unlocked when the club is open?" I remembered Alasdair saying that he and Lewis had come out back for a smoke.

"Definitely. Fire code. We have to keep both front and back unlocked."

"So, a person could leave from either door?" I asked, looking toward each end of the alley, which curved out of sight.

"Oh, yeah. The wynd here leads out. That way takes you to High Street." He pointed. "The other way and you'll come out on Union."

I opted for High Street and followed the winding, cobbled roadway out. Like many European cities that had been walled fortresses at one time, the modern day towns included many narrow and secretive-looking places that actually teemed with business. I noticed a dental office and two boutiques whose main entrances opened onto the narrow wynd.

Eventually, I emerged on a road that had been blocked off into a walking mall and I found myself suddenly wanting a break. Alone for the first time in days, I couldn't resist finding a place to sit. I purchased an ice cream cone at a tiny stand and located an unoccupied bench. The cool chocolate slid down my throat and I allowed myself to forget entirely about everything—no stolen lambs, no burning huts, no missing teens, no irate union workers, no mechanical problems. I wanted nothing more than to enjoy the hanging pots of bright pink and purple petunias and snatches of conversation from passersby.

At the far end of the mall, a kilted piper played the traditional "Scotland the Brave" on a nasal set of bagpipes, the sound wafting down the road and bouncing off the glass-fronted shops. Beyond him, I caught a glimpse of the red sandstone towers of Inverness Castle. I turned my face toward the sun and wished all the problems would go away so Drake and I could simply play tourist, visiting castles and museums and eating out in fine seafood restaurants.

"Charlie?"

The voice snapped me back into the present. I whipped my head toward it and opened my eyes.

NINETEEN

"JANIE! What are you doing here?"

"Just got off work." She tipped her head toward the far end of the walkway. "It's just up there."

"Oh." Belatedly, I realized that the indoor mall was just at the end of this street.

"Is there any word about Richie?" Her lip quivered slightly as she spoke his name.

"Nothing yet, I'm afraid." I watched her shuffle from one foot to the other. "Here," I said. "Sit down."

"I really don't have time," she said. But she sat anyway. "My parents will be wanting me home soon. I watch my younger brother when mum works."

"I meant to ask you how long you've known Richie," I said.

"Oh, since primary school. When his parents lived here, that is."

"I thought they lived in London."

"Last few years, yeah. When Richie and I were little, they lived at Dunworthy and he attended school here in town. We happened to be in the same class, fourth year, I think it was. Then they moved away."

"And you and Richie stayed in touch all that time?"

"Oh, no. Boys don't write letters all that well. But I'd see him now and again, during the summers. We met again this spring at The Pelican. That's when the magic happened. We fell in love." She cast her eyes downward, suddenly shy about having told me all this.

"Did your two families know you were getting this serious?"

"Oh, I don't think so. I didn't tell mine, anyway." She glanced at the chunky watch on her wrist. "I really better…"

"Sure. Let his family know if you hear from him."

She strode away, her shapely legs under the short skirt drawing admiring looks from males along the way.

I had a sudden vision of her in five years—alone, with two or three kids from various fathers, struggling to earn a living because she'd never finished high school. The legs would still be shapely but the body would be twenty pounds heavier. I shook off the image, hoping Janie would make better choices than that.

Foot traffic was clearing and I realized that many of the shops were beginning to close. I pulled my cell phone from my bag and punched in the speed-dial number for Air-Sea Helicopters. Meggie answered on the first ring, sounding chipper.

"Oh, hi, Charlie! Yes, things are going great," she said. "Just about have all the files back in order."

"What's Drake up to? Is he in yet?"

"Radioed in his last flight a few minutes ago, so he should be here in about thirty, forty-five minutes."

"Tell him I'm heading home and will see him there. He doesn't need to call me unless he's going to be delayed." By the time Drake landed, got the aircraft ready for the night, filled out his logbooks, and drove to the cottage, I figured I had close to two hours on my own yet.

I placed a quick call to Dunworthy and learned that there were no new developments. I told Sarah what I had, or rather hadn't, learned at Waldo Green's. I didn't mention running into Janie again. I figured the shit was really going to hit the fan when that little secret came out.

I walked the length of Church Street and circled Inverness Castle. As castles go, it wasn't a huge one—probably no bigger than Dunworthy, for that matter. An adjacent museum was just closing and I made a mental note to come back to it someday. I stood on the high ground at the edge of the River Ness and let my eyes travel its length. The water reflected the deep blue of the sky, while the sun—now working its way lower in the west—brought the town's stone buildings into sharp focus.

A bridge crossed the river near me, and another, more ornate, crossed a few blocks down. I walked across the near one. At the other end, on a street lined with stone buildings from various periods, a small kilt shop was still open. I ducked inside.

The walls were lined with bolts of tartan, in the myriad color combinations representing each clan. Mannequins modeled traditional Scottish wear, from everyday to formal. But the thing that drew my eye was the glass display cases of knives. From long broadswords to the tiny dirks that Highland men wore in the tops of their knee-high socks, the array was dazzling. I'd seen Drake admiring them in shop windows. I made a spot decision to get him one as a gift.

The shop's one clerk was bustling about, getting ready to close for the night so I quickly chose one of the dirks. Its four-inch blade had a delicate thistle pattern engraved on it and was sheathed in black leather that matched the woven leather pattern on the knife's handle. The girl wrapped my purchase in tissue and bagged it while I admired their display of small jewelry items made from heather wood. I chose a brooch with an intricate heather wood center and an arrangement of silver thistles circling it. Five minutes later, transactions complete, I was back out on the street, following the river until I came to the second bridge.

Its smooth stone abutments rose, forming a tall square tower at each end. Cables draped in elegant suspension between them, holding the bridge with their strength. A two-lane road, busy with cars, ran down the center of it, with a sidewalk on one side. As I reached the center of it, I felt the entire bridge vibrate slightly with each passing car. I picked up my pace.

By the time I'd retrieved the car and driven back to the cottage, it was nearly time for Drake to be home. I pulled two steaks from the freezer and put the microwave to work defrosting them. He walked in while I was figuring out how to use the small gas grill on the veranda.

"Well, helluva' day, huh?" he said. He twisted two knobs on the grill, pressed an igniter button, and a blue flame came to life.

"Did your mechanic get there?"

"First thing in the morning," he said. "I'll fly him out to the rig and see if I can lend a hand while he works on the problem. I'll need you to bring the JetRanger back, once we know we have the Astar running."

I handed him a glass of wine. "Sure. For now, let's hope for a few uneventful hours."

Over dinner, I filled him in on the return of Alasdair and Lewis, my visit to the teen club where Richie had last been seen, and the little secret Janie was carrying. Drake did the dishes while I took a shower, and we blissfully fell into bed early after watching only a little TV.

The alarm went off much too early. Drake moaned and draped his arm over me. "Five more minutes," he mumbled into my shoulder. When the snooze timer went off again, he dragged himself away.

"Am I coming with you now?" I asked.

"Let's wait. You can stay here until we assess the problem and find out how long it'll take to fix it."

"Um, I love you," I murmured, burrowing into the covers again.

I heard the shower go on, then off, heard the bee-like buzz of his electric razor. And somewhere in the background, a persistent ringing. I raised my head to get my bearings. The telephone downstairs.

A phone ringing before daybreak is never a good thing. I tugged a huge t-shirt on over my head and snatched up the pair of socks I'd worn the day before. The light on the landing nearly blinded me and it took another full ring for me to stumble down the stairs. Another while I sprinted across the living room, jamming my little toe against a table leg, and grabbed for the phone on the kitchen counter.

"What!" Short for what-the-hell-do-you-want-at-this-hour. "Sorry, I meant 'hello'."

"Charlie, I'm sorry. This is terribly rude of me, calling so early." Sarah's voice sounded genuinely contrite, but a tiny sob quietly escaped.

"No, Sarah, that's okay." I pulled the phone off the counter and sat on the floor, squeezing my throbbing toe with my free hand. "What's going on?"

"We've received a ransom note."

"Oh my god." Richie's disappearance suddenly seemed so much more ominous again. "What does it say? How did it arrive?"

"It was placed under our front door," she said. "I can't believe it! These evil people have actually come right up to our home."

TWENTY

"SARAH, HOLD TIGHT," I said. "I'll be right there."

I switched on the kitchen light and examined my little toe, whose severe pain had dulled to merely an aching throb. The nail was split but otherwise the tiny digit looked fine. I limped back up the stairs to find Drake dressed and heading down.

"What was that?" he asked.

"A note about Richie," I said. "I told Sarah I'd go right over there."

"Why are you limping?" He nearly smiled, but avoided it judiciously at the last second. My ability to bump, bruise, scrape, or sprain things frequently meets with admonitions from him to slow down.

"Oh, it's nothing."

"Um hmm. I'll make coffee while you get dressed," he offered.

Determined not to let him make an issue of the toe, I trimmed the nail and bundled my feet into thick cotton socks and walking shoes. Five minutes later, dressed and combed, I poured coffee into a travel mug and kissed my hubby goodbye in the driveway.

He promised to call my cell phone when the repairs to the Astar were finished and he needed me to fly the JetRanger back.

Things were aflutter at Dunworthy. As I drove up the lane to the castle I saw Robert and Edward circling the white Range Rover. Edward held a phone up to his ear, looked impatiently at it, then jammed it into his inside pocket.

In the front hall, Sarah paced, a sheet of rumpled paper in her hand. Elizabeth barked an order at Molly, who looked like she was about to cry. She skittered from the room as I turned to close the door. Robert and Edward followed close on my heels.

"Can't raise anyone at the bank," Edward grumbled to his wife.

Elizabeth looked at a delicate diamond watch on her wrist. "It's only going on seven o'clock." "You twit" seemed to be the unspoken ending.

"Charlie! I'm so glad you're here," Sarah said. Her chenille robe covered a utilitarian cotton gown—no lace or ruffles for this sturdy country woman.

Elizabeth, on the other hand, wore a pair of elegant gray slacks—expensive by the cut of them—and a yellow sweater so fluffy it might have been made of baby chicks. Her hair, makeup, nails, and jewelry were all perfect. I was willing to bet she never emerged from her bedroom looking otherwise.

"Is that the note?" I asked, indicating the paper in Sarah's hand.

"Oh. Yes." She smoothed the page against her chenilled thigh with both hands.

I cringed as I watched any potential evidence being wiped away. Undoubtedly, Robert and Edward had obliterated any footprints that might have been left near the door, and now Sarah had handled our only other clue until it was probably useless too. Didn't these people ever watch crime shows on TV?

I took the note. The paper was standard letter size, plain white, probably the stuff that everyone who owns a computer buys by the ream. The lettering was in black ballpoint ink, a deliberate block print, faintly wavy like it was done by a right-handed person with their left hand: *Gather :bp50,000. We will call at 12:00 with delivery instructions. No police or he is dead.*

It was signed with a reddish-brown X. Blood? It certainly looked like it.

"This was slipped under your front door?" I asked.

"Yes," Robert said. "I'd gotten up. Planned to meet our foreman at the dairy barn."

I noticed for the first time that he wore a quilted, plaid shirt-jacket and brown utilitarian twill pants tucked into rubber boots.

"We were planning to go over the milk production figures."

Elizabeth shot her father a look that said, "how can you think of business when your grandson is missing."

"Don't you think it's time to bring the police into it now?" I asked.

"No!" Four voices shouted at me at once.

"You read the note, Charlie." Sarah's no-nonsense tone told me there would be no arguing this point. "That X is made in blood, isn't it?"

I nodded.

"I'd say that means someone is very serious about this, then."

"So, what do you plan to do?" I asked.

Edward spoke up. "As soon as I can reach my banker, we'll have the money transferred to Robert's bank here. We'll get the cash and await instructions. Just as the note says."

A clock in the hall chimed the half-hour. Seven-thirty.

"Until then, I think we should all have something to eat," Sarah said. "It's likely to be a very long day."

"I couldn't—" Elizabeth began.

"Molly has something set up in the small dining room."

We all dutifully followed Sarah. She shot Robert a look, and he shed the rubber outdoor boots and slipped into soft leather house shoes before coming into the dining room.

Molly had laid out covered chafing dishes of scrambled eggs, bacon, sausage, and broiled tomatoes, buffet style. There were racks of toast and crockery pots of jam, plus a couple of large bowls of fruit and assorted pastries. I'd forgotten that when the Scots say breakfast, they mean breakfast. It was obvious that the people of Dunworthy were accustomed to feeding people on a large scale and on short notice.

Despite my trepidation about the day and its potential outcome, I found myself filling a plate and eating way too well. Everyone else did, too, except Elizabeth who stuck with her original objection and only managed a few pieces of fruit and some dry toast. It was easy to see where her stick-like figure came from.

Edward kept looking at his watch. At eight, he announced that he would try calling the bank again. Apparently he had a private number to an important person's office because he reached someone and made arrangements for the £50,000 transfer to happen precisely at nine o'clock.

"That should give us ample time to collect the money and arrive back here by noon for the telephone call," he told Robert, once he'd stashed his cell phone.

"Well, it sounds like you have things well in hand," I said. "Maybe I better—"

"Oh, don't go, Charlie," Sarah insisted. "I'd feel so much better if you were here to help us rescue Richie."

Privately, I thought they were going to do things their own way, no matter what I said. I couldn't see that they'd taken a bit of my advice yet. I told her I'd stay, unless Drake called and needed me on business. His safety was of more value to me than Richie's. I didn't tell her that part.

I chewed on one last piece of toast while the rest of them chattered away, hashing and rehashing plans for collecting the money.

At 8:40 Robert and Edward decided it was time to go to the bank. I said I'd wait behind with the ladies. Within fifteen minutes, though, I was beginning to wish I'd gone along on the ride to town. Elizabeth's constant fretting over Richie's safety and Sarah's pacing were driving me nuts. I longed for a crew of police and Scotland Yard agents to be here, tapping phones or dusting for fingerprints, just to be doing something useful.

"I think I'll take a walk and look around," I told Sarah, finally. "My phone's in my pocket if there's an emergency." I pointed to it.

Outside, the air was damp. There had been rain during the

night and high clouds remained, sealing the area in a cocoon of gray. I went out by way of the main entry and scanned the ground for signs of footprints leading toward or away from it. The graveled area immediately outside the door showed nothing, and the damp grass farther out had been trampled by several sets of feet, my own included as I'd arrived at daybreak.

Down by the parking area, the ground was muddy but, again, too many sets of prints made any type of identification impossible. Then I spotted them—a single set of prints pressed into the wet grass, coming from the orchard.

TWENTY-ONE

I PICKED UP the tracks at the edge of the smooth, green lawn. Following them with any precision became impossible because as I stood directly over them they disappeared. It was only from the angle at a distance that I was able to pick them out over the glistening moisture on the grass. I headed toward the orchard.

Under the trees I picked out the occasional clear print where the damp ground was free of grass and leaves. There was no way to identify a pattern to the prints, but I could tell that they were somewhat larger and quite a lot wider than my own size eights. Most likely a man's print, or a woman wearing heavy boots.

The burned-out crofter's hut immediately came to mind, since this was the same way I'd taken to it before. If the person leaving the note had hidden there before approaching the castle, this is most likely the way they would have come. Only a few people knew of the existence of the hut—someone in the family or those who worked on the grounds—which shot down theories of random strangers abducting Richie from Waldo Green's and spiriting him away to their evil lair.

The amount of the ransom demand told me that we weren't dealing with big-time operators, either. Fifty thousand pounds just wasn't that much money, especially to anyone who perceived the Campbells or the Dunbars as wealthy.

Ahead stood the blackened stone walls of the crofter's hut. I paused, wondering briefly whether I should be armed, if someone were hiding inside…I listened intently and heard nothing but a few birds twittering in the trees and the occasional drip-drip of water from the leaves.

Paying attention to my own footfalls, I approached the small building cautiously. As I'd expected, it was deserted. There were a few partial footprints on the damp, hard-packed earth. They looked relatively fresh, considering last night's rain, but the indentions were fairly plain and I certainly couldn't make out any identifiable tread marks.

I circled the hut, keeping to the grass, finding that the prints went all around the place, inside and out. Could Richie and his friends have made them? I stared toward the castle. I didn't think so. They'd not been here for nearly forty-eight hours now, and the overnight rains would have surely done away with traces that old. My eyes fell on the forest to the south. The other path…

I cut back into the orchard looking for the route I'd taken the other day. At the southern edge of the fruit trees I spotted it. Plenty of dips and disturbances showed in the gravel but nothing that could be called a footprint. I walked it slowly. Under the cover of the tall pines, water dripped from a million needles causing a shower in a microcosm. I hadn't brought an umbrella and my light jacket certainly wasn't waterproof, and I was quickly becoming damp. I picked up my pace.

At the gazebo I decided to duck under cover for a minute. I shook some of the water off my hair and sleeves. There, at the foot of one of the concrete benches, lay a cigarette butt. Had it been there before? I was virtually certain it had not. Instinct told me that the police would view any little scrap as possible evidence until proven otherwise, but I didn't know if it was up to me to decide that. I glanced around the area.

I wished I knew more about the habits of the family. It could be that Robert came out here all the time to sneak a smoke. Richie or his friends certainly could have. But those footprints leading across the wet grass this morning made me think that someone outside the family had been around. Someone who could have also left this tiny bit that might turn out to be an important lead. And what was I supposed to do about it? Pick it up? Leave it? Report it?

In one pocket of my jacket I found a tissue, wadded but clean. I used it to pick up the stump of filter. It was plain white, with a gold-stamped brand name I didn't recognize. I loosely cradled it into the tissue and put it in my pocket. Depending on how this all turned out, surely it would potentially be more useful by my picking it up than one of the gardeners discarding it. I scanned the gazebo, inside and out, but didn't see anything else out of place.

Noticing the smaller path, the one that trailed off and eventually came out at the Brodies's rented place, I wondered if Ian ever came up here to the gazebo for a little relaxation. I found myself looking for footprints as I followed it, but the trail was so rocky that nothing showed. It was a relief from the constant dripping water when I finally looked down into the clearing behind their cottage. Ramona was coming out of the barn, some fifty yards away. I negotiated my way around the rugged hillside boulders until I was on more level ground. She carried a bucket full of nursing bottles and the two lambs and a calf were trailing hopefully behind her. I gave a shout and she looked in my direction. The hungry babies never took their eyes off the bucket.

"Hi, Charlie," she said. "I was hoping you'd come by."

"You were?"

"Sure. Things get lonely out here sometimes. Ian's been gone for two days and I've run myself ragged keeping the wee ones fed and the others under control."

She set the bucket down and handed me two bottles. The lambs switched loyalties in a flash and I had to brace myself as they attacked their breakfast. Ramona held a bottle out to the calf, who flicked its tail in the faces of two puppies who tried to get in on the action too.

"Where's Ian gone?" I asked.

"Ah, well his father's taken ill. They've put him in hospital in Aberdeen."

"I hope it's not serious."

"Heart attack." She grabbed up another bottle for the calf and tossed the first one aside. "Here, get some more. They'll each take two."

I made the switch, but not as neatly as she had. I ended up with two good-sized smears of lamb slobber on my leg in the process.

"At least he survived it," Ramona said. "He'll probably be in hospital a few more days before he can go home. It's after that we're uncertain about. He'll have to slow down, an' that's for sure."

"No doubt. So, that's left you running everything here."

"Yeah." She rolled her blue eyes skyward. "And it's usually a full-time job for two."

The two lambs had slowed their aggressive sucking and were now wagging their tails contentedly. I watched their little heads bob happily with the ritual of feeding. I didn't see any tags on their ears. It didn't seem likely that these were the missing lambs from Dunworthy—after all, I doubted the Brodies would want me this close to stolen merchandise. But a nagging doubt lingered. What if Ian had somehow removed their Dunworthy ID tags and brought them up from the fields with the story for Ramona that their mother had been killed. She probably wouldn't know any differently.

"I've had to suspend the dog shows," Ramona said. "I can't put them through the paces the way Ian does. I put a sign down on the gate, let the tourists know we're off for a few days."

We gathered the empty bottles and put them back in the bucket.

"What about the other sheep in the pasture?" I asked.

"Oh, they do fine. Eat and sleep. That's about all sheep do anyway." She laughed, a sound that was somehow unfamiliar to her normally serious nature. "The dogs go out with 'em. Especially at night, it's good to have them guarding for wolves. I've got a shotgun in case there was a ruckus, but I don't know as I'd want to be using it."

We'd reached the barn now and the puppies were becoming increasingly vocal. "Think you could get them some food, while I run down to the pasture and check on things?'' she asked.

Before I could answer, she thrust the dogs' large, flat feeding pan into my hands. She pulled a small plastic whistle on a cord from the neck of her shirt. Giving two quick bursts with it, she grabbed the attention of three adult dogs who trotted with her toward the pasture.

I carried the puppies' dish into the barn, where I set the bucket full of empty nursing bottles on a shelf. Seven tiny black-and-white bodies swarmed around my feet.

''Okay, you guys, now where was that food?''

I remembered the large bins against the wall and fumbled through them until I found the one with the small nuggets. Adding milk, as I'd seen Ramona do, I swirled the mixture and set it down. I couldn't help but smile as all seven of them crowded around and into the pan.

I glanced around, wondering if there was something else I could be doing to help Ramona. Against one wall of the barn I noticed a large deep-sink, so I carried the used milk bottles to it and ran water over them. There was just a single cold-water tap, but if Ramona wanted them taken into the house for a better cleaning, she could let me know.

A couple of the feed bins stood open, so I closed the lids and stacked some buckets, attempted to tidy the place a bit. The puppies were now wandering away, except for one who still sprawled inside the food pan, licking furiously at the corners, and another who pawed at the edge of the pan, wanting to tip it over and dislodge his smaller brother.

''Okay, you guys are done, I think,'' I said. ''Let's pick this up now.''

I'd just reached for the metal dish when a bright fleck of white caught my eye near the wheel of an old wooden wagon that sat jammed into a corner of the big wooden structure. Letting the puppies have their fun a little longer, I walked toward the wagon. The white fleck was a cigarette butt. I knelt down to get a closer look. It looked identical to the one I'd just picked up at the gazebo.

I was pretty sure Ramona didn't smoke; I'd never smelled it on her. But Ian did. Were these the same brand, and did that mean he'd been out at the Dunbar's gazebo recently? Why?

I reached for the little stub of filter and picked it up gingerly. I slipped it into my pocket just as the door to the barn opened.

TWENTY-TWO

"WELL, THINGS LOOK all right out there," Ramona said. She gave me a questioning look, clearly wondering what I was doing kneeling on the ground near the old wagon.

"This looks like an interesting antique," I sputtered. "Is it yours?"

"No, it was here in the barn," she said, still looking at me crossways.

Had she seen me stick my hand in my pocket? I almost got the feeling she'd caught me stealing.

"Oh, look at these guys. They're all finished," I said. "I put the other milk bottles in that sink over there. I hope that was the right thing."

Ramona relaxed a bit. "Yes. Oh, thanks for doing that. Here, I'll just add the puppy bowl to the stack and I'll wash them up later."

She carried the pan to the sink, losing her wariness as she slipped back into doing the familiar.

"Want to come in for tea?" she asked. "I think I'm due a break by now."

"I'd love to," I said, "but I really should be getting back. Drake has a mechanic out working on one of the helicopters right now, and he'll probably be calling me soon to come out and do my share of the flying."

"Ah, well, then. That must be pretty exciting work."

"It has its moments," I had to admit. "Not all of them fun."

She looked like she was about to say something sympathetic.

"But most of them are. And like you, I enjoy working with my husband."

"Ian can be..." Her voice trailed off and I wondered what she was about to say. Something she decided against, since her face clicked into another mode almost immediately. "But I love him. He's got big plans, you know. Says we'll make a lot more money this season. More than we ever have."

Like £50,000 more? Was Ian that angry at the Dunbars? I felt a rock thud to the pit of my stomach.

"Charlie? Are you all right?"

I gave myself a little mental shake and willed the blood to flow back into my lips. "Oh, yeah, fine. You know, that tea does sound good."

"All right, then." She led the way toward the cottage. "I get those little mid-morning sinking spells myself. Tea'll be just the thing."

I walked behind her, letting her chatter on. A hundred questions raced through my mind. If Ian had indeed kidnapped Richie, where had he taken the boy? Ramona seemed genuine. I couldn't imagine her being in on it and staying this calm toward me. Surely she wouldn't be inviting me inside. Unless...I made myself stop. Just keep your eyes and ears open, Charlie.

"...sometime?" Ramona turned to me. Apparently she had just asked a question.

I jerked back to reality. "I'm sorry, I got a little ways behind you and didn't hear that last part," I said.

"I was just asking whether you'd like to go into town for some shopping sometime. I guess women who don't work on farms do that—girl's day out, that sort of thing."

"Sure." I forced a smile. "That'd be nice."

If I haven't found enough evidence by then to throw your husband in the slammer.

I followed her into the cottage, my eyes darting to every spot inside while she went directly into the kitchen and filled the kettle.

"Can I use your bathroom?" I asked.

"Oh, sure. The door on the left," she said, indicating the two closed doors beyond the living room.

I purposely went to the door on the right and opened it. In one quick glance I could tell that it was a bedroom, bed neatly made, dresser top covered with framed photos, and a few items of clothing draped over a chair. No teenage boy, bound and gagged.

"Oops! The other left," I said, quickly backing out and heading toward the real bathroom door. I closed it behind me and pondered what, if anything, I should do next. If Ian were involved, I didn't think Ramona knew it. The way she'd talked about his great plan for making more money than ever before, I didn't get the sense that she knew anything about the plan herself. If Ian had given his father's heart attack as his reason for being gone awhile, then I imagined that was all she knew. He was operating on his own, or at least without his wife's help, I felt sure. The heart attack story would be easy enough to verify. For now, I'd see if I could get any more information from Ramona.

I flushed the toilet for authenticity and rinsed my hands at the sink.

"That was quite a rain we had last night," I said, striving for a topic that wouldn't allow my face to give away my inner thoughts.

"Yes, it was. Here, the tea's just about ready. I'm afraid I don't have anything much to offer with it. Haven't been to the store in a while. Some toast, maybe?"

"No, actually I don't think I could hold a bite." The heavy Scottish breakfast would easily anchor my butt to my chair. "Just the tea would be wonderful. It's a bit chilly out.

"Do you have a way to get to the store?" I asked, once she'd set the cups on the table and taken her own seat. "It just now hit me that Ian probably took your vehicle to...was it Aberdeen?"

"Yes, he did. I've been walking down to the wee market at the crossroads. It's got nearly everything."

I remembered the bitterness in Ian's voice the day I'd overheard him in that same market. Perhaps his hatred for Robert Dunbar and his position in Parliament went to the extreme.

"I get the feeling Ian doesn't like the Dunbars much," I ventured.

"What?" She gave me a puzzled look.

"Uh, well…" Oh great, Charlie, blow it right at the beginning. I realized the question must have come completely out of left field. I struggled for a segue but could only come up with the truth. "The first time I ever met Ian was just outside our cottage. I heard voices arguing and learned that they were he and Robert Dunbar."

Ramona chewed her lower lip.

"I would imagine there are a lot of people who don't care for him," I added, backpedaling to gain her confidence again. "Some of his votes haven't been the most popular choices, have they?"

She twisted the corner of a paper napkin into a point.

"Or so I've heard." I took a sip of tea. "Look, I guess local politics isn't really any of my business."

She put the napkin aside and picked up her mug. "I know you didn't mean anything by it, Charlie. I try to stay out of it myself. Plenty to do around here without getting into all that as well." She blew on the tea gently, then took a sip. "Ian usually stays out of politics himself. It's just the issue of the wool prices. Affects us so deeply, you know. We can't get away from it."

For the first time, her face folded into worry lines and she aged ten years. In twenty, she'd be a hard-edged middle-aged farm woman; the perky blond ponytail and functional-stylish denim overalls would give way to saggy tweeds and gray hair pulled into a tight bun. Knowing that her current existence would never change had to be disheartening. The temptation to grab for the brass ring, if one came available, would be nearly overwhelming.

I drained my mug and set it down.

"Look, I didn't mean to bring down the mood," she said.

Although her smile lit up, her blue eyes were just the tiniest bit too bright.

"Oh, you didn't. I shouldn't have brought up the subject. I apologize."

"Probably do Ian some good to be away for a few days," she said, "even if it's not under the best of circumstances."

I said goodbye a few minutes later and set out for the castle, feeling a mixture of pity for the shepherds' plight and horror at the idea that one of them might have taken revenge to this extent.

About halfway down the path to the gazebo, my cell phone rang. I jumped with the suddenness of it, my heart going into double-time. I groped in my jacket for it and the little tissue bundle fell to the ground.

"Hello?" I leaned over to retrieve my little evidence packet and placed it back into my pocket.

"Hi, hon, how are things?" Drake's voice came through a little too loudly. "Can you hear me okay?"

"Yes, fine. In fact, a bit loud."

"Sorry, is that better?" he said at normal volume. "I wasn't sure what kind of signal we'd get out here."

"You're at the rig?"

"Yeah. Mechanic's got the fuel line fixed. He's checking over the rest of the ship now."

"So you need me out there soon?"

"Not real soon. Couple hours maybe."

I shoved my sleeve up to look at my watch. That would also be about the time the Dunbars would be waiting at home for the noon call. I told him.

"Let's play it by ear," he said. "Somehow I need to get both ships off this rig before tonight."

Now what, I thought as we hung up. I saw myself being pulled in two directions. Sarah had already told me Robert expected me to go along when the ransom call came, help make the delivery and get Richie back safely. I thought about making one more plea with them to get the authorities to handle this, but knew it was probably futile. And Drake couldn't very well pilot two helicopters at once. My duty was to him and I'd have to tell the Dunbars so.

Unfortunately, it wasn't going to prove quite so simple.

TWENTY-THREE

ROBERT AND EDWARD were just pulling up in the Bentley when I rounded the corner of the castle. I walked over to the driver's door.

"Did everything go all right at the bank?"

Edward stepped out the passenger door and pulled a large valise from the back seat. He leaned vaguely sideways to counterbalance the weight of it as he carried it to the front door.

"Just as they asked. £50,000. Didn't say if they wanted small bills, but I got them anyway." Robert puffed a little as he slid out of the big old luxury car. "Banker raised a bit of an eyebrow. Man's known me forty years. Was thinking he'd never seen me do anything like this before, I know he was."

"Do you think he'll report it to the authorities?" I asked.

"No. Doubt it." A tiny crease divided his forehead. "Don't care anyway. Another couple of hours and we'll have Richie back. It'll all be over with."

I hoped so, but didn't quite feel his optimism. There were still a lot of things that could go wrong.

Robert and I walked together into the castle, where I noticed that Edward had casually dropped the valise in the entryway, the same way he'd done with his travel bag the other day. Robert hung his jacket on a peg, but I opted to keep mine on. Voices came from the kitchen and we followed them.

Edward and Elizabeth stood on opposite sides of the butcher-block island and the air between them was thick with electricity. I took in the scene and knew we'd interrupted some kind of heated exchange.

"Where's Sarah?" Robert asked, not noticing his daughter's flushed face.

Elizabeth turned away, facing the sink now. "Dressing. She should be down in a few minutes."

The three of us looked at a large clock that hung above the built-in china hutch.

Three minutes to eleven. I might as well broach the subject none of them wanted to hear.

"Robert," I said, "depending on when the phone call comes and what the instructions are, I may not be able to go with you."

"Nonsense, Charlie. We need you."

As if everything in the whole world revolved around them. I felt my blood pressure rising. I jammed my hands into my jacket pockets so my balled-up fists wouldn't be obvious.

"My hus—" I swallowed and forced my voice a few notes lower. "My husband also needs me. There are two helicopters and potentially several lives at stake out there, too." Stay calm, Charlie. "I've repeatedly suggested that you let the police handle this situation with Richie, but no one will listen. If Drake calls, I have to go."

My self-coaching wasn't working. Becoming hotter by the minute, I walked out. I brushed past Alasdair and Lewis in the corridor, their eyes wide and scared, and headed for the front door.

Outside on the stone steps, I paused and took a deep breath. Why was I letting this affect me so? I knew these people were completely self-centered. They would obviously expect everyone else to put their own lives on hold as long as there was a family crisis here.

But that's just it. It *is* a crisis. Richie's gone. We don't know where or who he's with or how desperate those people might be. I ran each point of logic through my head.

On the other hand, Drake's situation could easily become a crisis, too. If those men on the rig were intent on getting rid of the helicopter operators it wouldn't take much. The aircraft looked large and whirling and deadly in motion, but they were quite fragile when it came to their hundreds of moving parts. A simple act of sabotage could send a million-dollar aircraft and as many as six lives into the sea. I sank to one of the stone benches that flanked either side of the door, unmindful of the moisture soaking into my jeans, and propped my forehead in my hands.

The sun was beginning to show and I let it warm my back.

"Charlie?" Robert's voice sounded subdued as he sank down on the bench beside me. "I'll apologize if I sounded abrupt in there. Didn't realize you had so much on your mind right now."

"It's okay. I hadn't told you about the problems we've faced trying to keep Brian Swinney's helicopter business going out there." I recapped a couple of the incidents where the union boat operators had openly opposed us. "Your family has enough to think about at the moment."

"Wish there were something I could do," he said.

"Well, if you mean pulling some strings in some higher place than Parliament, I guess you could vote for Brian's mother to get well so he'd come back and run his own business. I'd sure rather be sightseeing and I know Drake wouldn't mind hitting a couple of those distillery tours." I worked up a smile. "Otherwise, I guess we just wait and see how everything plays out."

He patted my knee in a fatherly way. "It will, I'm afraid," he said, his mouth grim. "It will."

He stood and walked toward the Bentley, hands jammed in pockets, head bent. I kept my seat on the bench until he rounded the corner of the castle, then decided I better do something. Waiting isn't one of my stronger suits. Here I was, in the midst of two serious situations, unable to do anything about either one until a call came.

I paced the length of the castle twice, then spotted Sarah's rock garden on the other side of about two acres of lawn. I headed for that, thinking the extra walk would burn off some of my nervous energy. The tranquil spot should have calmed my nerves but I couldn't seem to make it happen. I climbed a narrow, winding path created to lead to the top of a small waterfall, which cascaded softly over a series of dark rocks to a serene pond below. Lily pads dotted the dark water and I half expected to see a tiny frog leap onto one and begin croaking out a little tune.

At the top of the rock outcropping I noticed an area where the tall grass lay flattened in a circular spot about a foot in diameter, the way a wild animal will leave an indent where it has slept. Odd. Other than squirrels, rabbits, and pheasant, I hadn't heard anyone mention many wild animals here on this part of the grounds. A larger animal, like a deer or elk, would leave a much bigger print anyway. A human butt had probably made this. I wondered for a moment if this was a spot Sarah would have come to sit.

Undoubtedly it was, except that this very place didn't offer any particular amenities. The ground was too rocky for comfort and the jutting rocks hid views of either the castle or the pond below. A flash of blue caught my eye. A candy wrapper. That pretty well confirmed that Sarah wasn't the person who'd sat here. So, who was?

I crouched on the matted grass for a moment. I could see the castle's turrets clearly, and a short stretch of the lane leading in and out. By rising to my knees and peering around the rocks, I could observe the parking area and the main door. Someone who wanted to spy on comings and goings at the castle could easily do it from here without being seen. My thoughts leapt to Ian Brodie.

But why would Ian need to watch the Dunbars? Unless he'd formulated the plan to take Richie and wanted to know when the boys left. It might have been a feat to dash to a concealed vehicle somewhere and follow them, but surely it wasn't impossible.

Movement below caught my eye. Sarah had stepped out the front door.

"Robert!" she called. Her voice carried clearly to me.

Robert, his head ducked into the trunk of the Bentley, hadn't heard. She called his name again and began walking toward the cars. She was halfway there before she got his attention. He snapped to attention and bumped his head on the lid of the trunk. I heard his expletive clearly. This, indeed, was the perfect spot for spying.

"Where's Charlie?" she asked him. "It's nearly time for the phone call."

"Well, she was out here somewhere," Robert said. "Just on the bench over there."

They both looked at the bench.

"Probably went back inside," he told her.

They turned and went into the castle. I felt like a real snoop watching the whole scenario, but it confirmed how easily sound traveled up the little hill, letting someone know what was going on. I pocketed the candy bar wrapper and followed the narrow trail down the other side of the rocks, making a complete circle around the pond. Beside it, there was a stone bench. This spot was clearly Sarah's haven when she came to visit the pond.

I made my way through the rest of the carefully arranged rocks and plantings and crossed the wide expanse of open lawn.

"Charlie! Oh, I was just wondering where you were," Sarah said as I entered the kitchen.

"Out walking," I said. "Trying to clear my mind for a few minutes."

I glanced at Robert and he sent an encouraging look my way.

"It's nearly noon," Sarah said.

Edward and Elizabeth sat at the counter, leaning forward on their stools, clutching mugs of coffee in their hands. Lewis had taken a seat on one of the other stools, one he'd pulled into a corner away from the others. Alasdair wasn't in the room. A portable phone sat in the middle of the large butcher-block island, with all eyes fixed to it.

"Is everything ready?" I asked.

Robert and Edward nodded. Elizabeth's knuckles whitened around her mug.

Lewis's face looked white and pinched, his soft freckles standing out like cinnamon on whipped cream. I blew out a breath, unable to take the tense silence.

"Could I get some water?" I asked Sarah. She nodded and pointed me toward the cupboard with the glasses. I drew a glassful from the sink and drank it in tiny sips.

Twelve o'clock inched by. One minute after. Two minutes after.

"I'm going to scream if that thing doesn't ring," Elizabeth said through clenched teeth.

At five after, the tension in the room had reached the breaking point. By ten after, an edgy weariness began to show on everyone's faces. By twelve-thirty, people were beginning to slump in their seats, weary of the wait.

"They're not calling, are they?" Elizabeth asked. "The bloody bas—"

The phone on the counter shrilled. A collective start bolted through the room. Six pairs of eyes stared at the innocent-looking white instrument. It rang again.

"Robert!" Sarah's voice was as close to hysterical as I'd ever heard it.

He snatched up the handset, pressed the button and listened.

"Yes?" His voice sounded over-loud in the dead silence of the room, where not a breath interrupted the quiet. "Yes. I understand. I will."

He held the phone in front of him with both hands for a few seconds before pressing the button that turned it off.

"What?" Edward's voice captured the word that nearly whooshed out of everyone else's mouth as we all began breathing again.

"They want Lewis to come."

"What?! That's ridiculous," Edward sputtered. "A teenager can't take this on."

We all stared at Lewis, who cringed into his corner. If his face had been white before, it was pure alabaster now.

"I—I—but, sir..." he said with a wobbly voice. "I can't drive. I don't have a license."

"That's right, stupid idea," Edward contributed.

"Drive what? Which car—"

"Depends on how far..."

The voices continued to pile upon one another until I couldn't make sense of any of them. Alasdair came in, looking like he wondered what the hell was going on. After about two minutes of the cacophony, I stepped forward and waved my hands, settling them into a time-out T.

"Folks, folks, time out a minute here," I said, working to keep calm in my voice. "Can we take a minute to analyze this?"

"Yes," Sarah said, "Charlie's the professional here. Let's let her handle this."

I groaned inwardly. Edward shot me a look that said he wasn't at all convinced of my professional abilities.

"I don't want to 'handle' it, but let's see if we can organize ourselves a bit," I said. "Now, Robert, what were the exact instructions?"

"We're to send the money with Lewis. He's to go to the Culloden Battlefield. He's to walk out on the field, follow the path to the area where the clan graves are, and put the bag behind the marker on the Clan MacDougal grave. He's to walk on to the Clan Fraser grave and meditate there a moment. Richie will join him there."

"I can—" Lewis piped up, but I shushed him with a hand signal.

"And how long do we have?" I asked Robert.

"They didn't say." His face looked stricken as he realized what he was telling us.

"Didn't give you a time for the rendezvous? That's crazy!" I said.

Voices in pandemonium broke out again. My mind whirled around a dozen possibilities. After a couple of minutes, things quieted and I found everyone staring at me again.

"Okay. Then we better get started now." I eyed the rest of them. "Lewis, what were you starting to say?"

"I can go to the battlefield. We went on a school trip once. I know the arrangement of the graves."

"Maybe the kidnappers didn't mean that Lewis must come absolutely alone.

"Maybe he's just to approach the graves alone," Alasdair suggested. "I could drive him to the battlefield."

"It's a big tourist attraction," Robert said. "Surely no one will be able to watch the car park and the graves too."

"I think we're forgetting the most important thing here," I said. "We can't just send two boys in by themselves. The kidnappers could be waiting for the perfect chance to snatch them as well. In fact, why else would they ask for Lewis to come alone, if not to grab him?"

Silence greeted that observation. Edward squirmed and I got the idea that he didn't really care that the other two boys might be in danger, if it meant a chance to get his son back. Alasdair and Lewis exchanged a glance, probably trying to build each other's confidence. Finally, Robert cleared his throat and spoke.

"What do you suggest, Charlie?" he asked.

"Aside from the fact that, if the police were handling this they would have some unknown faces to send in as guards," I said, "if it has to be us, I'm thinking we split up and cover as many bases as we can." I quickly outlined the rest of my plan.

TWENTY-FOUR

"COMMUNICATION IS going to be critical," I said, beginning to feel some of the authority they'd conveyed upon me. "Does each group have a cell phone?"

At their affirmative nods, I instructed them to pass all messages through Robert. Two-way radios would have worked better, where we could have kept everyone in touch on the same frequency, but we didn't have them. If all went smoothly, we shouldn't need them.

We exchanged numbers and five minutes later, Edward and Elizabeth left in Sarah's Land Rover. They would go to the battlefield and become two of the few hundred tourists who would be milling about the place. We gave them a ten-minute lead.

"Lewis, you and Alasdair will take the white Range Rover. Park where you can see the Land Rover, but not right next to it," I told them. "Lewis, take the bag of money. Alasdair, you wait in the car."

The two boys nodded. I watched Lewis lift the valise from the floor and my heart sank. He could barely pick it up. How was he ever going to walk inconspicuously through a crowd of people with it?

"I can manage," he huffed. "Just need to get me legs under me better." He hiked the case up to his waist and managed to get his arms under it. "See?"

At least he could walk, and without too much of a strained look on his face.

Robert and Sarah would follow in the Bentley, not exactly

an inconspicuous vehicle, but they would keep the boys in sight until they arrived in the parking area at Culloden.

I leaned in through the open window of the Bentley. "If Lewis looks too awkward carrying that bag, pretend to be a kindly stranger and offer to carry it for him," I suggested. "Nothing like having the museum people question him before he ever gets into the place." If they allowed bags in there at all.

"Right." Robert acknowledged the plan and drew himself up. "See you there."

I watched the two vehicles drive away. I would follow alone in my car, and I made it clear that I'd be peeling off and heading for the airport if Drake called. I glanced up at the rock garden once before getting into my rented Vector. If someone were regularly watching the place, they knew every move we'd just made.

Twenty minutes later I pulled into the parking area for the Culloden Battlefield and Museum. I spotted the white Range Rover, with Alasdair behind the wheel. His head swiveled back and forth, nervously watching the other cars. Don't be so conspicuous, kid, I thought as I drove past him and parked two rows away. The Bentley, empty, sat five cars away from the Range Rover. Sarah's Land Rover, also empty, had found a spot near the entrance.

I stuffed my few scraps of evidence—the two cigarette butts and the candy wrapper—into the glove compartment and locked it. Making sure that my cell phone was easily accessible in a jacket pocket, I locked the car and headed toward the visitor's center.

Overhead the clouds had fractured, leaving almost equal patches of blue and gray, and the wind had picked up considerably. A steady, damp-feeling breeze rushed off the surrounding low hills and swept across the open field. Set at wide distances, I could see the flags marking the positions of the two opposing armies back in 1746. The poor Highlanders had never stood a chance, losing 1200 men to the king's 300 on that bitter April day. It had all been over in forty minutes.

I hurried through the lobby of the museum and paid my entry fee. A docent tried to offer me the chance to view a film, see a reenactment of battlefield conditions in a field hospital, or tour the exhibits in two large rooms. I waved her off and went straight out the doors leading to the battlefield itself.

The wind whipped my hair across my face as I started up the path. A winding trail led the visitors around the perimeter of the entire field, but I headed right for the middle where a sign pointed the way to the clan graves. It was impossible to see any great distance. Tall shrubs and grasses forced the path to curve around small hillocks. I finally came to a gate, where I passed into the area where the majority of the clans had fallen.

Killed as they attacked, entire families had been slain in groups. Transporting the bodies back to their home ground, in spring's often blizzard conditions, over distances that could take weeks in good weather would have been impossible. Clans were gathered together and buried together, the frozen ground too impenetrable for adequate digging.

Now, more than two-hundred-fifty years later, earthen heaps marked each spot. A single rough-cut stone stood near each, naming the family of clansmen it contained. The stones were spread widely and randomly, and much of the area was surrounded by low trees and heavy shrubbery. I glanced at each, watching for MacDougal or Fraser.

MacDougal was the first one I spotted. It was one of the larger stones, before one of the larger mounds. I saw the black case behind it and only let my eyes stay on it a split-second. Acting as casually as I could, I paused and pulled a tissue from my pocket and blew my nose. In the damp, bitter wind, the act wasn't merely for show. I caught sight of Robert and Sarah looking down at a grave marker on the opposite side of the path, about thirty feet farther up. As planned, they were to make sure no tourist walked away with the bag. We didn't acknowledge each other.

I hurried along to the next marker, pausing again, wanting to blend in with the dozen or so other tourists in the area. At a bend in the path, I glanced back at Robert. He'd moved a little farther away from me, but was still within view of the MacDougal stone. As I followed the bend, I saw Edward and Elizabeth in the distance. Elizabeth's blond hair had given up its style and she finally looked like everyone else, windblown and mildly disheveled. I paused where I was and read some more markers. They slowly worked their way toward me.

"Nothing yet?" Edward said under his breath, as they passed on the opposite side of the path.

"It's still there," I said.

We passed without another word.

Another path cut away behind me, at a right angle to this one. It led to a large stone monument with a big brass plaque on its face. No one else was near it, so I headed that way. Circling it to be sure I was alone, I stood on the leeward side and pulled out my cell phone. I hit the button to speed dial the number of Robert's.

"Have you seen anyone you recognize?" I asked, keeping my voice low in the rush of the wind.

"No. You?"

Unfortunately, I hadn't. I wondered where Lewis was. I disconnected the call as another couple walked into view.

Farther down the main trail, I spotted Lewis standing in front of a marker. He stood with head bowed, hands clasped in front, looking meditative as per instructions. I kept up my slow pace, pausing at each grave, reading markers, until I stood at the same one with him.

I muttered the same question I'd posed to Robert, and he shook his head. His face looked miserable and I noticed that his hands shook. I wanted to pat him on the shoulder, but couldn't be sure who might be watching from the shrubbery.

"It'll be okay," I murmured. I had to move on as the other couple caught up with me once more.

Beyond the Fraser grave the path circled back over the main battlefield. Not wanting to get too far from the rest of the team or the money, I retraced my steps. Lewis remained at the Fraser grave and Robert was hanging pretty close to the MacDougal.

The others were milling about, looking uncertain. I kept my distance and stole a peek at my watch. It was nearing two o'clock. I thought we were all starting to get the same sickening feeling. Nothing was going to happen.

TWENTY-FIVE

AT THE MOMENT, there were no other people in sight but our small group. I motioned them together.

"I don't think it's going to happen," I mumbled. "Either we've been spotted, or this was a wild goose chase from the start."

"I agree." Robert's voice sounded like it was about to crack. "What do you want to do?"

"It's getting late and I need to get back to Drake," I said. "Let's make a show of rounding up everyone and leaving. It probably wasn't a good idea to bring this many people anyway."

Heads nodded, but only Edward's look was accusatory.

I turned back to Robert. "If you want to keep trying, I'd suggest that you have Lewis remain at the Fraser stone, as per instructions. Everyone else go home."

"I want to catch this criminal," Robert said. "I want Richie back, but it's not right that he simply get away with this. I want to catch him taking the money."

My cell phone rang. "Yes?" It was Drake.

"Time for me to go," I announced to the group. "Do whatever you want. My original suggestion still holds."

I met each of their eyes, but didn't get much of a feeling for what they would decide. I walked away.

Out in the parking area I glanced toward the white Range Rover. No sign of Alasdair. Now what was he up to? Dealing with these people was like trying to herd kittens. I threw up my hands in frustration and climbed into the Vector.

Drake had called from fifteen minutes out. He'd left the mechanic at the platform to keep watch on the JetRanger. He would pick me up at the airport and take me immediately back to the rig so we could shuttle both aircraft home safely.

Fortunately, Culloden wasn't far from the airport and I sped into the parking lot just as Drake circled on final. By the time he'd set down, I'd dashed into the office and grabbed my survival suit. I shuffled awkwardly into it while getting a quick briefing from Meggie. No phone messages, and yes, we would each be bringing back a full crew of workers from the rig.

Drake was jotting entries in his meticulous writing into his logbook when I climbed into the other front seat in the Astar. He pushed his mike aside to give me a quick kiss.

I buckled in and adjusted my headset while he radioed the tower and got clearance for takeoff.

"So, how was your day?" he asked, not knowing anything beyond the early morning phone call from Sarah.

By the time I'd filled him in on the ransom note, the clues I'd found, the visit to Ramona's, the ransom-drop phone call, and the abortive attempt to deliver it to Culloden, we had the rig in sight on the horizon.

"So, yes, it's been quite a day," I said. "I think I'm tired already."

"It's almost over," he said. "At least everything seems to be working fine on this baby now. And I put Joe on security detail with yours until we get back. I told him, no coffee breaks, no pit stops, nothing. Not to let that ship out of his sight for an instant. You'll be fine getting her back home."

"Any trouble from Brankin or his men?"

"Not a peep. I got a couple of dirty looks, but nobody said anything."

Drake guided the helicopter directly toward the south face of the platform, to the rig's helipad. He set the Astar gently onto its spot beside the waiting JetRanger. Joe, the mechanic, moved from his sentry post at the head of it and walked toward us. He came to my side of the ship and opened my door for me. Eight men waited in an orderly queue for their ride home at the end of their shifts, none from Brankin's inner circle.

"Crank up and we'll check our communications before I leave," Drake instructed me before I took off the headset and handed it over to Joe.

I ducked around the front of the Astar and unlocked the other ship. Drake waited, watching the area as Joe and I assisted our passengers. I went through the startup procedure, adjusted my headset, and radioed him.

"All clear, Delta-Delta-Alpha-Bravo. Go ahead, we'll be right behind you." His level voice came through clearly.

I pulled pitch and lifted slowly off the platform. Sweeping to my left, I made a wide berth for Drake. In another two minutes, he'd taken off again and he soon caught up with me, the two of us becoming a mini flight formation inbound, with our tails to the rig. I liked the symbolism of it.

I watched Drake at the controls of his aircraft and was reminded of the powerful attraction I'd felt the first time we'd met—he at the helm, and I a tourist out for a view of the beautiful island of Kauai. Now, here I was flying beside him. How far we'd come in these years. I caught him watching me and knew a very similar thought was going through his mind; we often do that. He raised his fingers to his lips and blew me a kiss.

I hung on to my little inner glow for the rest of the flight. It would have been nice to keep it for a few more hours and pretend we were honeymooners again. But I knew Drake needed to contact Brian Swinney and bring him up to date on his operations, and I really should check in at Dunworthy and find out where things stood with them.

We both landed outside the hangar and the crewmen dispersed quickly. Joe gathered his things and said goodbye. He had a train to catch and hoped to be home in time for dinner. Drake and I agreed that he would wind things up here—finishing paperwork and calling Brian—while I stopped at the Dunbar's.

All the vehicles were parked outside when I drove up to

Dunworthy. I crossed my fingers that this was a good sign, that they'd gotten Richie back and were now inside having a cheery family reunion. I knew the instant I rapped the heavy door knocker that it wasn't to be.

Molly pulled the heavy door open before I'd hardly lowered my hand.

"Oh, Ms. Parker, ma'am, they'll be so glad to see you!" Her full, young mouth settled back into the long lines it wore before she spoke.

"Is there any news?" I asked.

"Nothing good, I'm afraid."

I followed her to the drawing room where the men clenched whiskey glasses and the women cradled glasses of sherry. I accepted one without question.

"What's happened since the battlefield?" I asked Robert.

He ran a weathered hand over his brow, emitting a low groan.

"Actually, quite a lot has happened," Sarah said. She rose from her seat near the fireplace and came toward me. "We were just doing as you'd suggested, leaving Culloden, when another call came on the cell phone. The man directed us to another place."

"A park, actually, on the grounds of Inverness Castle," Robert said.

"This time he wanted Robert to bring the money."

"And come alone," Robert added.

"We did exactly as he asked," Sarah said. Moisture welled in her eyes.

"But you don't have Richie back, obviously," I said.

Edward slammed his glass down onto a table, jerking my attention to the other side of the room. "I've had it with these people and their wild chases. If I catch this man, I swear, I'll kill him."

Elizabeth didn't react. She'd sat in one position on an otto-man since I'd entered the room. Her elbows rested on her knees and her eyes bored at a spot on the carpet somewhere in the middle of the floor.

"This is ridiculous!" Edward ranted. "I can't believe the idiot, thinking he can put us through our paces this way."

"Clearly he is, Edward," Robert said, "so you may as well settle down."

Edward picked up his glass and drained it in one swig. "I'll be in the library. I've got paperwork." He set his glass down, none too gently, and stomped out of the room.

I wondered at the kind of man who would think to bring paperwork with him when his son had been kidnapped, but the others didn't look terribly surprised.

"So," I said, turning to Robert. "You gave up and brought the money back, I guess?"

"Well, I certainly wasn't going to leave it unguarded in a public place, not unless I had Richie safely in my care again. The bag is there." He pointed to a spot beside a small oval table.

"Not much we can do until we hear from them again," Sarah said as she picked up the sherry bottle and offered refills.

Robert poured himself another generous shot of Glen Livet and turned to me. "How's the progress on our other mystery, then?"

I went blank for a second. "Oh, the missing lambs? I can't report much there either, I'm afraid. I looked again at the two Ian and Ramona have, and there are no tags or distinguishing marks on either lamb."

"You went to Brodie's place?"

"Twice now. I've only noticed two lambs, but—"

"What did Brodie say about them?"

"He's not there right now. Gone for a few days to Aberdeen."

Robert's eyes narrowed suspiciously. "Quite the coincidence, isn't it? Him leaving right when Richie's missing."

I glanced at Sarah. Her face had gone about three shades paler. I was afraid to voice my own suspicions about Ian.

"His wife told me Ian's father had a heart attack and Ian had to go help with their farm." I suddenly felt torn about whether to mention the cigarette butts I'd found, or the candy wrapper. The cigarettes only indicated that Ian had come as close as the gazebo and that, in itself, was certainly no crime. Not to mention that they certainly weren't proof. No doubt millions of people smoked that same brand.

"Heart attack—that's a bit convenient, isn't it?" Robert said. His voice rose ominously. "Maybe two lambs weren't enough for the man. Had to really prove his point by coming for my own grandson!"

TWENTY-SIX

SARAH UTTERED a faint whimper and sank down to the ottoman beside Elizabeth. "You don't honestly think..."

"I don't know what to think," I said. After all, I'd had my own suspicions about Ian. "He really doesn't seem like the kind of man who would go this far." I thought of Ian working with his dogs, his brief tirade against the government policies on wool prices. He was angry, but I still saw him as a simple, hard-working man who just wanted to get a little bit ahead in this world.

"But...I sense there's a 'but' in there someplace," Robert said.

Literally. "I did find a couple of little indicators that someone may have been watching the house," I told them. "But without fingerprints or DNA evidence, they certainly aren't proof that the person was Ian."

"Come on, Charlie, who else would it be?"

"I don't know." I fought against letting my voice become too sharp. "You haven't given me much to go on here. You don't seem to feel you have any enemies, and I don't have the manpower to go out and canvass the neighborhood to find out otherwise. I only found out about the bad blood between you and Ian Brodie because I overheard an argument outside my window one morning." I took a deep breath and forced myself to speak more slowly. "I've repeatedly asked you to call in the authorities. They *would* have the manpower to investigate properly."

Sarah and Elizabeth stared at me, their eyes growing wider. Robert stomped across the room and picked up the telephone.

"Well, now that we know it's Brodie, maybe I will call them. Let them—"

The portable phone rang in his hand, startling all of us.

"Oh, bother," he said, hitting the button to answer the call. "Yes, what is it?"

He listened intently, the anger draining from his face.

"Yes. I've got it," he finally said and hung up.

"While it's fresh, repeat every word they said," I told him.

"He said, 'You failed the first test, idiot, but did much better on the second one. This will be your last chance and you'd better get this one right. Come alone. Go down Route B862 for exactly one-point-five miles beyond the sign that says Loch Ness Trail. At that point, there's a turnout on the left. Stop there and put the money into the waste bin.' Then he said, 'Have the money in a trash sack, not that stupid black valise you've been using.'"

So our moves had been watched.

"What about Richie?" I asked.

"Coming to that. He said, 'Drive exactly two more miles in the same direction and stop at the next turnout. Richie will be waiting there.' That's all he said."

"Nothing about leaving the police out of it?" I asked.

"I don't think we dare," he said. "They've obviously been watching everything we've done so far. And it's our last chance, he said."

"Unfortunately, I think you're right about that," I said. "Was it the same voice as before?"

"Pretty certain it was." He laid the phone on a table and rubbed his face with both hands. The stress of the day showed. "I better get moving. Sarah, find me a trash bag, will you?"

She rose automatically from her seat and went toward the kitchen.

"I'm glad they left Lewis out of it this time," I said. "I never was comfortable with the idea of sending him in there alone."

Robert knelt on the floor and scooped stacks of cash out of the valise. He transferred them to the black garbage bag when Sarah brought it a minute later.

"Dark soon," Robert said. "I'm sure they're counting on that."

"Perhaps Edward should follow in another car, just in case you need him," Sarah said.

I watched conflicting emotions cross Robert's face. He wanted to catch Ian Brodie in the act of taking the money, I knew. But he couldn't put his grandson's life at risk in the process. I wished we knew for certain that there was only one kidnapper involved in it, but we didn't and I didn't think we could take the chance that someone else wouldn't be watching the house to see how many of us left.

"Robert better walk out alone, get into a car, and leave. The rest of the cars, including mine, should stay here," I said. "I'll call Drake to let him know why I'm not home."

Robert pulled on a jacket and retrieved the keys to Sarah's Land Rover off the pegs near the door.

"Take your cell phone," I suggested. "At least you can keep us posted that way."

"Good idea. That road's pretty remote. One lane, and you take your chances with the oncoming traffic."

"Just be careful, love," Sarah said, stretching to peck a kiss onto his cheek.

Edward had emerged from the library, catching some of the commotion from the rest of us in the corridor. We watched somberly as Robert picked up the trash bag and headed out.

"I need to make that call," I told Sarah.

"Certainly, dear, just find yourself a quiet corner anywhere." She waved vaguely down the corridor.

Movement on the stairs at the far end of the hall caught my eye. Lewis and Alasdair came loping down in that gangly way only teenagers can negotiate stairs. The house was so large I'd forgotten about the two of them.

"May we take the Range Rover, ma'am?" Lewis politely addressed Sarah.

"No, sorry. Not tonight boys."

Alasdair's face tightened into an instant petulant scowl. Lewis fidgeted in his shoes.

"But ma'am," Alasdair argued, "we've got plans with some boys from school."

"I think you may want to stay here," she replied. "We've just received another call about Richie. Mr. Dunbar's gone off to fetch him home."

The two boys exchanged a pained look. A variety of arguments flickered across their faces.

"We can't take the chance of letting anyone else drive away," I said. "The kidnappers may be watching the house and we can't let anyone's movements foul up the plan."

"Right." Sarah pulled all the other vehicle keys from their pegs and jammed them firmly into the slash pockets in her twill slacks. "Everyone's in for the night."

"You'll want to be here when Richie gets home anyway, won't you?" Elizabeth asked. It was the first thing she'd said all evening.

Lewis glanced up at the taller boy. Alasdair smiled and spoke for both of them. "Sure. We'll be here."

They turned and went back upstairs.

"Not the most sociable young lads," Sarah muttered as she turned toward the kitchen. "Can't figure them out. Asked them this morning if they'd rather go home and they said 'no,' they wanted to be here for Richie. Now they don't seem to care."

"Kids—we just don't know what makes them tick, do we?" I said. I excused myself to make my call and went into the library, since everyone else seemed to have headed for the kitchen.

Drake wasn't thrilled that I was captive in the castle for a while, but said he'd make the best of it by raiding the fridge for some dinner. We talked a few more minutes, since we'd not exactly spent any time together all day. I wandered around the room, glancing at books on the shelves and bric-a-brac that probably pre-dated the founding of America. On one lower bookshelf I spotted a surprisingly modern collection of telephone directories. Idly fingering through them, I realized they covered most of northern Scotland, probably Robert's Parliamentary constituency. An idea flickered to life.

"Let's hope Robert and Richie come back within the hour and I'm safely home by bedtime," I said to Drake. "If not, I'll give another call to keep you posted."

As we were saying goodbye, I pulled the directory for Aberdeen from the stack. The yellow pages section looked pretty much like ours at home and I quickly found two hospitals listed in Aberdeen.

"I'd like to inquire about the condition of Mr. Brodie," I said to the elderly female voice that answered the first information number.

"Are you a family member, dear?"

"No, a close friend of his son's." I prayed that she wouldn't ask Mr. Brodie's first name because that would definitely give away the fact that I wasn't all that close.

"I'll put you through to the nurse's station," she said.

The extension rang four times before a harried-sounding voice picked it up. I repeated my question and was told that Mr. Brodie's recovery was coming along as expected and he would probably be released in a few more days. "Would you like to be connected to his room?" the nurse asked.

"Oh, that's all right, I'll let him rest."

So Ian's story was true. Although I didn't have absolute proof that Ian was at his father's bedside, it didn't seem likely that he could have counted on a heart attack to provide him with an alibi. So, if Ian wasn't the kidnapper, who was? And where was Richie right now?

TWENTY-SEVEN

I LOOKED AT my watch, imagining a very long evening ahead. I wanted to go home. I'd just jammed the directory for Aberdeen back onto the shelf when I spotted Molly standing in the doorway.

"Sorry, ma'am," she said. "Mrs. Dunbar said to tell you that we've put a cold buffet out in the dining room, in case anyone's hungry. You're to help yourself if you'd like something."

"Thanks, Molly."

She gave a quick nod and bustled off down the hallway. I couldn't remember if I'd eaten anything since the early breakfast and the mention of food made me realize I was starving. I stuffed my cell phone into my pocket and followed the long corridor to the family dining room. The sideboard contained platters of cold cuts and cheeses, plates of sliced fruit, and a mixed green salad in a large bowl. I made myself a quick sandwich and heaped my plate with salad and fruit.

No one else had touched anything and I found myself setting my plate down at an otherwise empty table. Again, I wished for the comforts of home—Drake and myself, with TV trays in front of the news channel and Rusty watching with liquid brown eyes for that one morsel that might fall to the floor. My throat tightened. It would be weeks yet before I'd realize that little scenario. Meanwhile, castle life would have to do. I took a deep breath and stabbed at my salad with a fork.

"Don't you dare say—" The loud whisper was immediately

cut off as the speaker pushed through the swinging door at the end of the room. Alasdair and Lewis gave me startled looks.

"Say what?" I asked, pinning them with my eyes.

Alasdair recovered first. "Say to Mrs. Dunbar that he's homesick," he said, jerking his thumb back toward Lewis. "Little crybaby wants to go home."

Lewis's face flushed. "Do not! I just said…" He stopped abruptly at a look from the taller boy. His eyes glistened.

"Hey, it's okay," I said. "I was just having the same thoughts myself. This is a pretty nice place, but it just isn't the same, is it?"

Alasdair headed for the buffet, making himself a sandwich that featured at least six layers of alternating ham and cheese and a generous slab of mustard. He wrapped it in a napkin and completely skipped the salads. Lewis put six strawberries on a plate and brought it to the table. He sat at the opposite end from me.

"I'm taking my sandwich back to the room," Alasdair announced. He gave Lewis a direct look and mouthed the word *crybaby*.

The younger boy turned away, eyes firmly affixed to the business of carving each strawberry into four pieces and forking them to his mouth.

"Lewis, it's okay," I said. "Don't let him get you down."

He shrugged but was saved from having to answer when Edward and Sarah walked in. Edward looked at his watch, apparently calculating whether Robert would have had time yet to reach the drop point. With a half-shrug, he headed for the food and proceeded to pile a plate full.

Sarah quietly crossed the cushy Oriental rug and laid her arm around Lewis's shoulders. With a grandmother's sense of what a kid needs, she gave him one strong squeeze but didn't say a word. She looked up at me.

"See you found something to eat. Everything all right?" she asked.

"It's great. Sorry I didn't wait for everyone else," I said.

"No, no," she said. "That was the point. Each of us can

eat when we're ready.'' She turned to Lewis. ''Did Alasdair get something?''

When he nodded she turned to the buffet herself. As she placed a few items on her plate, Edward sat down, his plate heaping. I noticed Lewis taking stock of the food and saw a little of his appetite come back. Without Alasdair's taunting influence, Lewis got up and made a second pass at the sideboard. This time, I was pleased to see, he made a decent sandwich for himself.

''I can't help wondering where Robert is right now,'' Sarah said, taking a seat next to me. ''Just can't get the whole subject out of my mind.''

''I doubt any of us can,'' I said. ''Not until we see Richie safely back home.''

Lewis stood, squirming, beside the table. ''Is it all right, ma'am, if I take this to my room?''

''Oh, certainly, Lewis.'' She waved him on his way.

''He's certainly more well-mannered than Alasdair,'' I told her.

''Oh, yes. Those three—what a team they've been over the years. Richie and Alasdair vying for ringleader, and little Lewis tagging along with the group. Remember, Edward, the time they took an entire batch of freshly baked biscuits out to give to the ducks?''

Edward, with his mouth bulging, shrugged vaguely. I sensed he wasn't exactly the kind of man who was home to witness all the kids' antics.

''And one summer Richie convinced the other two that his grandfather wouldn't mind if they drove the lawn tractor. Got the thing stuck in a ditch, and they had some answering to do when it turned out grandfather did mind.'' She chuckled at the memory.

''One year we had no renters in that cottage where the young couple is, the ones with the sheep. The boys decided they'd camp out in that barn. Woke up in the night to discover mice in their sleeping bags! They've not been much on camping out since then.''

Her mention of the Brodies reminded me of something that had crossed my mind earlier. I wanted to ask Ramona if she needed help with the animals tomorrow. By getting inside again, I hoped to verify a couple of things. I excused myself, placing my empty plate on a side table as Elizabeth came into the room. Her soft blond hair had a tangle in the back, as if she'd just gotten up from a nap.

I padded back to the library on the soft runner that went up the corridor and pulled my cell phone from my pocket. Somewhere…I knew I'd written down the phone number Ramona had given me, but I couldn't find it. Back to my purse, which I'd left hanging on one of the pegs by the front door. I took it back to the library with me and rummaged through the bits and scraps inside, finally coming up with it. Ramona answered on the first ring.

"Oh, Charlie, I'm glad you called."

"I heard Ian's father was doing better," I said. I hoped she wouldn't question exactly how I knew this.

"Yes, it's good news, isn't it? Ian was certainly glad to be home again."

"Home? At his parents' house?"

"Oh no." She laughed. "Home here, with me. Wherever we are, I guess that's how I think of it."

"Ian's back here? When did he get in?" I pictured his alibi suddenly being shot to pieces.

"Em', I'd say about mid-afternoon."

"Oh, well I won't disturb your evening together then," I said quickly. I envisioned Ian listening to the other end of this conversation and wondering who was grilling his wife.

"Well, he's not here at the moment," she said. "Ian's a true rancher, I guess. Had to get out right away and check on the flock. Out there in the dark now, he is, he and the dogs. Dinner's waiting, but it'll be cold before he gets any, I'm sure."

"I just called because I thought you might need help with the animals tomorrow," I said, watching my reason for getting back into their house float away.

''Oh, Charlie, that's so nice of you! But I guess we're fine now. You won't have to worry yourself with it.''

She gushed a little more about my being such a good friend, while I felt like a rat for sneaking around gathering evidence against her husband. We hung up with vague talk of shopping or a movie together sometime.

I sank into one of the library's cushy chairs. Was Ian really out tending the sheep in the dark? Or was he more likely driving down the Loch Ness Trail to meet Robert and collect £50,000? And what about Richie—where had he been all this time?

Voices nearby indicated that the family had finished their dinner and were beginning to gather in the drawing room, next to the library. It was a little after eight. How many more hours would we have to wait for news? I stretched and wished for Drake. Maybe, even if someone were watching the place, it would be okay for one car to leave—mine. Maybe I should feel like a selfish shit for thinking of myself instead of worrying myself sick over Richie's safety. Somehow, from the tone of the ransom notes, I had the feeling that this whole thing was more about the money than it was about harming the boy. I hoped I was right.

I strolled toward the drawing room, where at least the smell of coffee held some appeal. Sarah held a tray full of ornate silver service pieces, while Molly stood slightly behind her, bearing another with cups and saucers.

''Push those magazines aside, will you?'' Sarah asked the room at large.

I reached forward at the same moment Elizabeth did. We cleared a spot and Sarah proceeded to pour and distribute cups.

''So, nothing new?'' I asked, settling onto a large ottoman with my cream-laced coffee.

''Not a word.'' Sarah's face was losing some of its perpetual good cheer. She looked tired.

Edward and Elizabeth were barely speaking, and the two boys had disappeared again. I was just thinking what a dismal group we were when the phone rang. Cups rattled, then heads swiveled until Sarah discovered where the phone had been left. She picked it up cautiously.

"Robert!" She released breath she must have been holding for fifteen minutes. "Do you have Richie?"

TWENTY-EIGHT

WE ALL HELD OUR breaths, watching for a signal, a word.

"Oh." When it came, the word didn't sound positive. Sarah's normally cheery face drooped. "Here, love, tell Charlie." She handed the receiver to me.

"Robert? What's happening?" I asked.

"Nothing," he said. "I'm back in town. Couldn't get a cell signal out there. Too many hills around the loch, I guess. Thought I'd better call in case you've heard anything."

"No, not a thing. We're sitting here alternating between boredom and worry, wondering how it's been going with you."

"I put the money in the waste bin, as the instructions said. I went to the next turnout and Richie wasn't there. Waited a half hour. Searched a bit in the woods around but it's pretty dark. Moonlight doesn't make it through those trees very well. And I bloody well forgot to bring a torch with me." He took a noisy breath. "Only traffic out here all night's been two or three cars that whizzed right by."

"So, you've decided to come back?"

"Don't know what to do. Expect I better go back to the first turnout and collect the money. Someone'll be along by morning if I don't."

"Let me think about this," I said. If Robert's cell phone had been out of range, what if the kidnappers had tried to reach him and couldn't? That didn't make sense; we would have received another call here.

"Is the money sack still in the trash can?" I asked.

"Was ten minutes ago when I went by there. First thing I checked, by God."

"I don't know, Robert. It sounds like, for some reason, they just aren't going to make the rendezvous. What do you think?"

"Don't know. Just can't give up on Richie, though, poor lad. Cold, scared, I know he is."

"Maybe I can come out there and help you watch. Let's do this," I said, "you go back to the money drop and make sure it's there. Be visible, pace around, look perplexed."

"That won't be so difficult," he said.

"I'll leave here. If someone's watching the house, that won't look too odd. I'll pretend to go home, but I'll take a roundabout route and come down there. Once you see my car, you go down to the place where they said they'd leave Richie. Let's see if we can't get that boy home tonight."

My little pep talk, along with the hope that we were taking some action, seemed to perk up those in the room as well. I went back to the library and gathered my purse and cell phone. I placed a quick call to Drake and told him what we were doing. He insisted that I pick him up on the way.

Five minutes later, I was walking out the front door of the castle, making a show of thanking Sarah for dinner and telling her to call me at the cottage if she received any news. My eyes strayed to the rock garden as I approached my car, wondering whether a spy lurked there. I couldn't see anything in the shadows cast by the half moon.

I stopped at the cottage, where I went inside, again making a show of getting out of the car and seeming to be in for the night. Drake and I went around the place, turning on the bedroom lights and turning off the ones downstairs. We brought two flashlights and warm jackets. Careful not to make noise as we left the cottage, we tiptoed out to the car and kept the headlights off until we were ready to pull out of our lane onto the main blacktop. I could only hope that the kidnappers didn't have enough manpower to watch everyplace at once.

Traffic was light through Inverness. I drove and Drake brought out the map, finding us a way that would take us through a myriad of residential streets before catching B862 again. It was after nine-thirty by the time we hit the Loch Ness Trail. Thick forest lined both sides of the road. I watched the odometer and slowed slightly as we approached the first turn-out.

Robert's dark Land Rover sat there in the small space. He stood beside it, anxiously smoking a cigarette. He tossed it on the ground and stepped on it as I passed. That was the signal that he knew it was me.

"What's going on?" Drake asked in a muffled voice. We'd agreed that he would ride ducked out of sight as soon as we began to approach this point.

"We just passed Robert," I told him. "Our spot should be coming up soon."

Robert had told me that he'd noticed another turnout, larger than most, on the right side of the road. It would be just right for our needs. I found it, about a quarter mile beyond the money-drop site, but still well away from Robert's post where he should be picking up Richie. I pulled into the turnout and nosed the Vector into the brush as far as I dared. With the curve in the road, oncoming drivers shouldn't notice it. Even if someone got suspicious, they'd find out the car was a rental and would think some dumb tourists were out looking for "Nessie."

"Okay, we're ready," I told Drake.

We zipped into our warm jackets and each grabbed a flash-light. Between the thick trees we caught occasional glimpses of the lake with silver moonlight glinting off its surface. We crossed the one-lane blacktopped road and ducked into the woods on the other side. A vehicle approached and we squatted behind a rock. Robert's Range Rover sped past.

Once we were safely out of view of any potential traffic, we switched on our lights and headed into the forest. We stayed parallel to the road as well as possible through the thick growth and jutting boulders. It was impossible to be completely quiet—twigs snapped and branches brushed against us, damp-ening our jackets with dew. In about ten minutes I spotted the smooth ground of the turnout and caught the gleam of moon-light off the edges of the metal waste bin there.

I signaled Drake to slow up. We shone our lights around the area, looking for trampled grass, broken branches, or other signs of human occupancy. No one had been there.

"Now what?" I whispered. "I just thought someone would have been watching this spot, waiting for us to screw up with the money drop or something."

"Hard to figure why they'd go to all this trouble, the notes and calls and all, and then not show up for their money."

A car drove slowly by and we ducked. It didn't pause at our location, nor did the driver look our direction. I held my breath until its engine noise faded into the distance.

"Maybe it's got something to do with the witching hour of midnight," Drake suggested. "It's not quite eleven. Better get comfortable."

We found a spot where the ground wasn't as rocky and a cushion of leaves added some extra padding. Switching off the flashlights, we settled in. In a whispered voice, I told Drake about my calls to the hospital in Aberdeen and to Ramona.

"Don't you find it odd that Ian would come home after several days' absence and go out to his pastures after dark?" I asked.

"Well, I know when I'm away from you, outside is the last place I'd want to spend my first night back home." He reached out and squeezed my hand.

"Yeah, exactly. Ian and Ramona are young. They should still have the hots for each other. But she didn't even seem that upset by his being out." I sighed. "I don't know, just seems weird to me."

"So you think Ian could be the kidnapper?" he asked.

"He's certainly angry toward Robert Dunbar because of his position in Parliament. I heard him ranting on that subject several times. The Dunbars haven't shared anything else with me that leads me to any other enemies, and they've certainly been adamant about not bringing the police into this. Doesn't that seem strange? A man whose job involves the law, and he doesn't want to turn to them for help?''

"So what else have you turned up that might be leads?''

"Well, certainly nothing of use at the club where the kids went. The owners of the place don't remember Richie. The place was full of kids and he was just one of many. They said there wasn't any scuffle or violence that night. So if Richie left from the dance floor, he went without a struggle. For all we know, he might have walked down to his car for something and was accosted along the way. Here's where the police would have the manpower to canvass the entire neighborhood and track down a lot of the kids from the club. I just can't be everywhere.''

A sudden wave of helplessness washed over me. My throat tightened. What was I doing here anyway?

I took a deep breath and let it out. "Otherwise, the leads are few. Janie, the girlfriend, hasn't seen him. She's scared to death of what her father's going to do when he finds out she's pregnant, and she wants Richie back more than anyone at this point.''

The sound of a car engine broke the night but it rushed right past. No hesitation whatsoever.

"Ian seems to be our best bet on both motive and means. Someone's been keeping a close watch on that household and he's certainly able to do that.''

Something skittered through the leaves behind me and I jumped.

"Just a squirrel or something,'' Drake said. He put his arm around my shoulders and I leaned into him. "Hey, we could make out in the bushes,'' he teased.

"Yeah, and get caught with our pants down. Whoever's coming will surely do it at the least opportune moment.''

"Wish I had night vision binoculars,'' he said. "Bet you I'd spot Nessie out there.''

"You don't really believe in that monster stuff, do you?''

"No, but I'll bet you do. I'll bet you're keeping your eyes

right on that open space in the trees right there. I'll bet you're just waiting for something dark and slimy to…''

''Drake! Stop it! It's creepy enough out here without your helping matters.''

He slid his fingertips slowly from my shoulder to my neck, walking them underneath my hair and up my scalp. I reached for his ribs, the one ticklish spot on his body, and in seconds we were rolling on the ground.

''Shh! What was that?'' His whisper stopped me cold.

I sat up and stared into the night, all senses on alert.

''I don't know. I didn't hear anything.'' I barely breathed the words out, trying for absolute silence.

''Neither did I, but I got you to quit tickling me,'' he whispered, absolutely serious.

''Oh, you! For that—'' I reached again for his ribs.

Headlights rounded the curve suddenly and silenced us both. We dropped to the ground and watched as the car slowed, swerving erratically. Thumping boombox music surrounded the vehicle and shrieks of teenage-girl laughter reached us as the driver regained control and they zoomed past.

Drake and I lapsed into silence. Enough excitement for one evening, I thought. I just want to go home and climb into our nice warm bed. He pressed the button on his watch and the dial lit up.

''Just now midnight,'' he announced.

''I wonder how much longer we should stay.''

The early morning and very full day were beginning to tell. We huddled again and I felt myself becoming drowsy, despite the dampness creeping through the seat of my jeans. The moon reached its zenith. My eyelids drooped. No more than a few minutes passed, surely, but I snapped awake with Drake shaking me.

''Car!'' he whispered. ''It's pulling in.''

My eyes flew open just in time to flinch against bright headlights. Drake pulled me down flat against the ground. Gigantic tires scrunched through the gravel, not twenty feet from my face. The engine stopped and the lights went out.

"Wait, I think it's—" Drake began.

"Charlie! Drake!" Robert's stage-whisper came through clearly. "Are you out here?"

We stood creakily with stiff legs and numb rear ends. "Over here!" Drake answered.

Robert stepped out from the driver's door of the Land Rover and came toward us.

"Hate to admit it, but I think it's time to give up for the night. Take it there's been no action here?"

"Not a thing."

"Well, it's going on two," he said. His voice sounded scratchy and tired.

I couldn't believe I'd dozed off for nearly an hour and a half.

"Give you a lift back to your car?" he offered.

"Oh, no thanks," Drake said. "We could use the stretch."

Robert reached into the trash can and retrieved the sack he'd deposited there over four hours ago, and tossed it into his vehicle. Drake and I shook hands with him and turned toward the road. Without having to pick our way through the woods, the walk back to our car took only three or four minutes and we cranked up the heater the minute we got inside.

With Drake at the wheel, I dozed again until we made the turn onto the grounds of Dunworthy and the narrow lane to our cottage. I wasn't aware of much else as I shed my clothes and fell into bed, until the phone rang.

TWENTY-NINE

I ROLLED OVER with a groan. My legs and hips responded stiffly after our nighttime hours in the woods. Gray light filtered around the drapes and the room lay in shadows as deep as predawn. The bedside clock said nine-thirty and I came awake with a start. Had I really slept more than seven hours?

I reached for Drake before I realized he had leapt out of bed with the first ring of the telephone downstairs. His voice filtered up the stairway. I couldn't pick out the words. I slipped into a terry robe and ran my fingers through my hair in a small effort to detangle and get it off my face.

Nine-thirty?

I pulled the drape aside and peered out. Rain poured off the slate roof, puddling on the flagstone courtyard in back, dripping from the edges of the wrought iron furniture and cement railing that defined our small veranda. Heavy, dark clouds obscured the forest beyond. The turrets of Dunworthy Castle were shrouded in mist. I could have easily fallen back into bed for another three hours, but curiosity about the phone call pulled at me. I cinched the belt on my robe and headed downstairs.

Words here and there caught my attention, revealing that the call was about helicopter business. Although I wouldn't have to fly on a day like this, since I wasn't instrument rated yet, Drake might and I didn't look forward to sending him out in the soup if it wasn't necessary.

I gave him a peck on his bare shoulder as he stood at the kitchen counter wearing only his boxer shorts. Rounding the end of the counter, I rummaged for coffee and filled the machine with water.

From Drake's end of the conversation I gathered he was talking to Brian Swinney.

"Okay then, later," he said, ending the call just as the coffee began dripping fragrantly into the pot.

"Brian's back," he said. I couldn't read his expression but felt a wave of relief roll over me.

"To stay?" I asked.

"Probably not. His mother passed away and they had the funeral yesterday in London. He'll have to go back in a week or two to settle some legal matters."

"Sorry to hear that. About his mother, I mean."

"Meanwhile, he's planning to talk to the top guys with the oil company to find out how the union talks are going and to lodge a complaint about the harassment we're getting. I'll meet him at the office in an hour to go over everything together. Come along if you'd like."

"I better find out what's going on next door," I said. "I assume there aren't any new developments or they would have called. Unless the phone rang early and I slept right through it."

He shivered, noticing that the room was chilly and he wasn't exactly dressed for it. I opened my robe and pulled him into it.

"Now this is what I'd really rather be doing on a rainy morning," he said in a husky voice.

"Better than driving down to the airport in the rain." I rubbed against him.

"Maybe I could think of a way to warm you up real fast."

"Real fast," he said, scooping me into his arms and heading up the stairs.

"Think we'll manage more than a quickie anytime soon?" I asked him thirty minutes later under the shower.

He grinned and promised we would. The shower was a fast one and we moved into overdrive, toweling off and pulling on clothing. I dashed downstairs while he shaved and poured coffee into a travel mug, which I handed him as he reached for his rain jacket and keys.

"Drive careful," I murmured into his neck. "I'm counting on more of that soon."

He gave me a lingering kiss then reached for his favorite cap. "Soon," he said.

I watched him drive away, wishing I could slip back to sleep for another couple of hours but knowing I was too charged up to actually manage it. I closed the front door and returned to my coffee cup, from which I'd only managed two quick sips so far. Popping two slices of bread into the toaster, I decided a little breakfast was in order before checking in with the Dunbars.

Sarah answered the phone with a breathless hello on the second ring.

"Oh, Charlie, I'm so glad you called."

"Anything new on Richie?" I asked.

"No, I'm afraid not, dear. And now Robert's taken a chill. I'm just making him a hot lemonade for it."

"Uh-oh, I was afraid that damp air wasn't doing him any good last night."

"Can you come over?" she asked. "Surely we'll be getting some word today."

I felt myself hesitate. "Actually, Drake has some new developments going on out at the office." It wasn't exactly untrue. "And I have to be there for a while this morning." Okay, so that part was untrue, but I didn't relish another day of sitting around the castle watching Elizabeth worry, Edward complain, Robert cough, and Sarah fuss over the rest of them. "I'll have my cell phone with me," I told her. "Call me if there's any news."

"I will, dear."

The minute she hung up I began to feel guilty. I had the feeling Sarah was the glue holding the rest of them together—and keeping them from each other's throats. I knew she could use some moral support.

On the other hand, I had an uneasy feeling about things at

the oil rigs. Brian had been content to leave everything in Drake's hands until now. Despite pressing matters back in London he'd come home now. It made me wonder if the union situation was about to come to a boil.

I stewed over it while tidying up the cottage. If there were something I could do, I should be with Drake. I poured the rest of my coffee down the drain and grabbed my purse and umbrella.

The rain had let up slightly but the clouds still hung low, like fragmented wisps of cheesecloth over the tops of the trees. The lane was becoming muddy and I dodged a few puddles as I headed toward the blacktopped road. I was amazed at how quickly the storm had moved in and become heavy, considering that we'd watched the moon overhead past midnight last night. Typical weather over the North Atlantic, I figured.

For some reason, I'd had the image of Janie's fresh young face in my mind as I drove. A couple of days had passed and it nagged at me that she might have thought of something new, but couldn't work up the nerve to contact me. Since Drake wasn't expecting me at the airport I made a spot decision to detour.

As I reached the outskirts of Inverness, where the turnoff to the airport would take me to the northeast of the city, I passed it up and headed into town.

Downtown Inverness was just coming to life. Most shops opened at ten, and the clerks were just now setting merchandise in the windows and opening doors. The relentless drizzle wasn't keeping people indoors. Parking slots on the street were going fast, but I found one and managed to parallel park, despite the strange feeling of going at everything from the wrong side. I locked the car, popped open my umbrella, and walked toward the mall where Janie worked.

A supermarket provided the easiest entrance from the street. I resisted bakery goods and the candy aisle on my way to the back corner of the place, where an escalator rose to the mall's second level. The place felt deserted at this hour, with only a few shoppers wandering lackadaisically and glancing in store windows. I strolled into Up Beat and looked for Janie's silky blond hair along the rows of music CDs.

"Help you, ma'am?" a male voice asked.

I spun around to face a chubby young man of about twenty, whose spiky black hair looked freshly gelled and pimple-dotted face freshly scrubbed. His purple Up Beat knit shirt barely tucked into black slacks that were belted below the overhang of his gut.

"Is Janie working today?" I asked.

"Dunno." He turned toward the back of the store. "Hey, Bart! Janie on today?"

The manager, the same man I'd seen in here the other day, poked his head out of a back room.

"Supposed to be," he said. "Hasn't phoned in."

The clerk shrugged. "Guess she's not here yet."

"Mind if I look around and wait for her?" I asked. Like it would make any difference to him.

I glanced over the offerings on the first couple of aisles, finding a surprising number of American recording artists along with a large mix of British and other U.K. singers. I found myself meandering away from the rock and heading toward the more traditional music. Must be pushing middle age, I thought. I'd never warmed up to much of the sound-alike stuff popular with today's teens. In the section for traditional piano and guitar I did a double-take.

A familiar album cover leaped out at me. Dan Shelton, a really talented guitarist from New Mexico, had an entire section of his work here. I caught his music regularly on the radio at home, but had no idea he was an even bigger star over here. Amazing. I picked up the newest CD, one I didn't already own, and carried it to the counter, scanning the store for Janie as I walked through.

"Is this guy really hot here?" I asked the clerk, handing him the CD.

"Yeah, the older folks love him," he said.

Older than twenty. Excuse me, at thirty-three I don't think I'm exactly decrepit yet.

''So, Janie isn't here yet, I guess.'' I signed the credit card ticket he'd pushed at me.

The store manager turned from stacking some sets of tiny earphones. ''No, and that's not the first time recently. Girl better shape up or she'll not have a job.''

Outside, the rain had stopped although clouds still hung low over town. I stepped around puddles, walking up the pedestrian part of Church Street. I thought I'd parked the car two or three streets over, but couldn't remember the name of the one I was looking for, so I found myself pausing at each intersection, staring down the streets to find something familiar.

On the third try I spotted the Vector on the right-hand side of the road, just a few doors down. On the left, a flash of color caught my eye. Lewis's red hair. He and Alasdair were walking away from me. Without a thought as to what I'd say, I hurried after them.

THIRTY

THE BOYS WERE easily half a block ahead of me. Alasdair walked on the right, nearest the street. I noticed each boy was carrying two large paper sacks from McDonald's. Fast food breakfast, huh. Despite their teenage appetites, it looked like a lot for the two of them. I let a few other people get between the boys and me, deciding I might learn something by finding out where they went. With Alasdair's height it was pretty easy to keep him in sight.

Intent as I was on peering between people to see the boys, I missed the man who barreled into me, head-on. Dressed in full Scottish attire, including kilt, knee socks, dirk, and wool jacket, I wasn't sure how I'd overlooked him.

"Oh, sorry." He rushed past me, a leather bagpipe case in hand.

When I looked ahead again the boys were gone.

My heart rate picked up. I'd only glanced away for two seconds. How could I have lost them?

I hurried ahead, pushing past the few people who'd separated me from my quarry in the first place. My eyes darted around the area. They weren't across the street or ahead of me. They must have gone into one of the shops. A quick peek in the first one, a jewelry store, told me they weren't there. It was a tiny place with a U-shaped counter ringing all three interior walls. The second place was a kiltmaker, equally empty at a glance.

"Rats!"

The third doorway led into the Victorian Market. I rushed inside to find that it was a small shopping mall, T-shaped, with perhaps two-dozen stores and tiny booths lining the two central corridors. I walked the long side of the T but didn't find a trace of the two boys.

Exiting the market, I found myself facing the train station on Academy Street. Crowds surrounded it, and I just couldn't see myself fighting my way through to search there. And for what? I didn't have a clear idea why I wanted to catch up with Lewis and Alasdair anyway. No doubt they were merely meeting friends in town for breakfast. They'd been antsy the day before at not being able to get out of the castle. Today they were making up for lost time.

I crossed Union Street and found my car. It was high time I went ahead with the real business of the day, which was to help Drake at the airport.

Fresh drizzle began to hit my windshield as I drove away from the center of town and located the roundabout that would point me toward the airport. The familiar route always made me feel like miles of countryside would go by before I got there, and the effect was especially noticeable today with the low cloud cover and cocoon-like feeling inside the car.

The Air-Sea Helicopters van that Drake had been driving sat outside the small detached office building, alongside Meggie's tiny car and another I didn't recognize. Brian's personal car, probably. Next to the office, the hangar doors were closed, the building's gray exterior blending so well with the weather that it appeared almost ghostly in the mist.

I fumbled with my umbrella, trying to handle it and the car door and my purse and my keys all at once. This desert kid was still far from adept at handling wet-weather paraphernalia. By the time I'd crossed the graveled parking area and a stretch of grass that separated it from the sidewalk, my shoes were picking up dampness.

"Hi, Charlie," Meggie greeted as I walked in.

She'd turned the heater on and the office was cozy.

"Are the guys…" I started to ask if they'd taken flights, but saw Drake standing by a wall map just then.

"No," he said. "We're socked in. Rain's one thing, but the winds out there over the sea have picked up. It's pretty rough."

"Is Brian…"

"Went over to the hangar for a minute. He'll be right back and I'll introduce you."

I shed my damp jacket and purse and turned to Meggie. "Looks like you've got everything here back in shape," I said.

"Yeah, wasn't too bad," she said. Her dimpled smile belied the ordeal she'd been through just a few days ago. "I didn't want Brian to come back to a mess."

Here was Meggie, probably five years older than Janie, and about twenty years ahead of her in maturity. I thought of the possibility that Janie and Richie would decide to get married and raise their baby. The girl had a lot of growing up to do. Somehow, though, I couldn't see Edward sitting still for his son becoming trapped in a marriage at a young age. This was a man who'd have bigger plans for his boy. I didn't look forward to watching the fireworks when the Campbells faced that situation.

"…check it again." Drake's voice broke into my consciousness with something that seemed to require a response from me.

"Sorry, hon, I was drifting."

"I said that I was going to take you out and buy you a fabulous present," he said, trying hard to keep his face serious. "But, since you didn't act like you wanted it…"

"You did not." I turned to Meggie. "What did he really say?"

"He said that he'd take you out to lunch, and when you got back he'd check the weather forecast again."

"That sounds much more like it. And the answer is yes. Just for the record, the answer would have been yes if the question had involved a fabulous present, too." I mouthed a little kiss his direction.

"Mind if Brian's included in the lunch plans?" he asked.

"Maybe we could all four go?" I asked, looking at Meggie.

"Oh, not me, thanks. I just had something."

As if he'd been paged, Brian Swinney came through the door. I hadn't met Brian when we first arrived because he'd already been in London. Drake and I had taken our check flights with a government man from the Civil Aviation Authority. Brian could have been Drake's older brother, tall, slender, with salt-and-pepper hair, and a rugged face. The dark brown eyes framed in black lashes were the main difference. His grip was firm when Drake introduced us, his smile showing straight teeth and an inner warmth. I could easily see why the two men had become fast friends all those years ago.

Lunch plans decided, the three of us piled into the company van and headed back toward town. Brian had a favorite seafood place, one we hadn't discovered yet, and we ended up in a back corner of a large room packed with Formica tables and funky plastic chairs. Ours was one of the few spots with a half-wall divider, making it feel somewhat like a booth. With the possibility of flights this afternoon, we passed on the offer of ale and stayed with Cokes instead.

"Drake tells me you've found yourself in the middle of a mystery out at Dunworthy," Brian said, after we'd all ordered the lunch special, a grilled salmon.

I sketched out the barest outline of Richie's kidnapping, not wanting to bore him with too many details or admit how far I still was from retrieving the teenager.

"Funny bunch, those Dunbars," he said, taking a sip from his tepid Coke. "Always something going on with them, I think."

"You mean they've had other kidnappings in the family?" I asked, amazed.

"Oh, no, not that. Always something, though, it seems. Years ago—I was flying in the States back then—there was some scandal with Robert Dunbar's sister. Left her husband and ran off with an Italian count or something. Don't remember all the details. Then there was a big huff soon after that when Elizabeth married Edward Campbell. He came from some rogue branch of the clan that no one much respected."

The waitress appeared with our salmon and conversation

broke off for a few minutes as we lemoned the fish, buttered the bread, and took first bites.

"Have there been recent problems with the Dunbars or the Campbells?" I asked. "Something that would make an enemy mad enough to kidnap Richie?"

He leaned in over his plate. "Well, Robert Dunbar certainly isn't the most popular MSP in the country, I'll tell you. Regularly in the thick of things, he is."

"Like?" I knew about his unpopular vote on wool pricing, but wondered what else Brian might know.

"Oh, the thing we're into up to our necks right now," he said. "This business between the helicopter operators and the boat guys. Dunbar's vote on one bill took away the subsidies those boat operators have gotten for years. Now they have to compete like the rest of us, and they don't like it a bit. Owners wanted to cut wages to make up the difference but those union men pitched a fit over that."

"Any of them personally threaten Dunbar?" I asked.

He shrugged. "Wouldn't surprise me. It was a close issue. He and two other members cast the deciding votes."

"What about this guy, Brankin, who's been so vocal toward us? Is he pretty high up in the union?" Drake asked.

Brian took a bite of bread and worked it around in his mouth a moment. "Brankin's a thug. Pure muscle—below the neck, that is. Does what he's told."

"And he's been told to intimidate us?"

"Apparently so."

"I told Joe to save that fuel line he removed from the Astar," Drake said. "I want you to take a look and see if you think someone punctured it."

"Brankin might do something like that, but I tend to doubt it," Brian said. "For one thing, I'm not sure he's smart enough to open the service door, much less figure out which lines carry the fuel. I won't rule it out, though. Could have ordered someone else to do it. One of that little gang always hanging around him."

"He wouldn't have had time to study it much," Drake said.

"I'd landed out there and shut down just long enough to use the head and go over the schedule with Finnie. I wasn't inside more than ten minutes."

"Yeah. See, I think Brankin probably wouldn't have taken the risk of being caught in the act. He's more a dark-alley kind of guy. Catch you alone and whack you from behind. You want to watch yourself around him, that's for sure."

"Think he could have handled a kidnapping?" I asked.

"Wouldn't put it past any of 'em to grab some kid. Don't think Brankin could've planned the whole thing. And I really doubt he'd be the type to stick around and babysit the kid for days. Has there been a ransom demand?"

"Fifty thousand pounds."

He waited, silent, while the waitress picked up our plates.

"That's not much. Union guys would probably be wanting a lot more than that. But you never know. To a couple of the men, acting on their own, it might look pretty good to them." He picked up the check and raised his palm to wave off our money. His company credit card would cover lunch.

"Another thought," he continued after signing the slip, "is that they may have gotten word about you two living at Dunworthy. Hitting the Dunbars may actually be their way of hitting us too. Two birds with one stone kind of thing."

I hadn't considered that. I rode quietly in the back seat of the van on the way back to the office. I hated to think that Drake's and my work could have led these thugs to the Dunbar family.

THIRTY-ONE

VISIBILITY HAD IMPROVED considerably by the time we got back to the airport and I had a feeling it meant we had some flying to do.

Meggie greeted Brian with a handful of message slips. "Good to be home, eh?" she said with a grin.

While he flipped through the messages, wadding about every other one and tossing it into the trash, I decided to check in with the Dunbars. The phone rang ten or twelve times and I was about to hang up when a breathless-sounding Robert picked it up.

"What's going on?" I asked.

"Oh, Charlie, I'm so glad you've phoned. We…we've had a new development, a rather gruesome package."

"What do you mean?" I could hear raised voices and muffled confusion in the background. "Robert, what's going on?"

"I think you'd better come," he said. The line went dead.

I stared at the receiver in my hand for a minute. Gradually, the other three voices in the office worked their way back into my consciousness.

"Hon?" Drake was giving me a quizzical look.

"Do you need me here?" I asked.

"We were just discussing that," he said.

Brian piped up. "I think we can handle it. Problems?"

"Um, yeah, I think so." I looked back at Drake. "I think I better get out to Dunworthy. Stay in touch."

A nagging sense of unease fluttered through me as I started the car. What did Robert mean by *gruesome?* I couldn't begin to assess that comment, along with the commotion that seemed to be going on. I hit the highway, going well over the speed limit.

By the time I reached the turnoff to Dunworthy, my thoughts had run the gamut through the list of known Dunbar enemies, to the likelihood that they'd lost their sack of ransom money and still didn't have their grandson back. I raced up the lane, whipped into the parking area and killed the engine.

Robert met me at the door. "Brace yourself, Charlie," he said, placing a gentle hand on my forearm. "It's quite upsetting."

"What's upsetting? Tell me what's going on."

"We received another note this morning," he said. "And a package."

Was I going to have to drag it out of him one iota at a time? He saw my impatience. "The package contained a...a...finger."

"A finger? A human finger?" My head spun. "Let me see it."

"Are you sure? I mean, it's..."

"I think I better." Even as I spoke the words, the other half of me screamed out to go home and stay away from these people forever.

He took me inside and led me into the great hall. A small, white box, about three-inches square, sat on one of the inlaid tables. It looked like a jewelry box, the kind commonly found in any tourist shop, containing a brooch or pair of earrings. The semi-glossy finish might well contain fingerprints.

"Has everyone touched this?" I asked.

"Molly found it. And then I handled it as well. Once we found out what was inside, no one else wanted near it."

On the chance there might be a usable print or two, I didn't pick it up. I lifted the lid by two opposing diagonal corners, using the tips of my thumb and third finger, avoiding the box's flat surfaces. There inside, on a soft bed of cotton, lay a darkened, shriveled finger.

Lunch rolled over in my stomach but settled in place. I bent to get a closer look at the stiff digit. I guessed it to be the index finger of an adult. It lay on its cotton bedding, slightly crooked, bluish-gray with a longish, dirt encrusted nail. The severed edge had been cut cleanly with something very sharp. There was no blood to be seen.

"When did this arrive?" I asked.

"Don't know. Molly found it right here on this table this morning. Dusting the room, she was. Said she thought one of us had left it out. Glanced inside to find out whose it was. Nearly frightened her to death, poor girl." He shifted from one foot to the other, clearly agitated by the sight of the finger.

I replaced the lid.

"Oh, Charlie!" Sarah spotted me from the entry and wrapped me in a hug. "I'm so glad you've come."

"I just learned about this," I told her.

"Horrible! Elizabeth's had to be sedated. Edward's given her something and he's up there with her now. I told poor Molly to take the rest of the day off, but she says she'd do better by keeping busy. Afraid I feel the same way myself. Can't seem to sit down." Her hands fluttered as she spoke, and I noticed her eyes wouldn't look at the box.

"You said there was also a note?" I asked, glancing at both of them.

"Ah, yes," Robert said, fishing into the pocket of his cardigan for it. He handed me a slip of paper.

It looked like a half-sheet of typing paper, ragged where it had been torn in two, and folded to the size of the box.

"It was inside, lying on top of the…"

I unfolded it and read: *No more fooling around! We want our money NOW or you'll get your boy back in pieces. Your phone will ring at 1:00.*

"It's after one now," I pointed out. "Has there been a call?"

"No," Sarah wailed. "What are they doing to us?"

Robert put his arm around his wife's shoulder. "Trying to drive us mad with worry, I'd say. Can't believe we're dancing to their tune for three days now. Makes me want to have a go at them with my shotgun."

"No, Robert! You've seen what they'll do. Poor Richie, now he's missing a…" She gestured toward the box but still wouldn't look at it.

I took a deep breath. Somebody had to be the voice of reason here. "Okay, let's all calm down a minute. For one thing, I'm not at all sure that's Richie's finger. I'm certainly no expert, but that looks like it came from someone older and larger." I remembered Richie's almost delicate fingers as he'd talked to me outside the crofter's hut the other morning. The one in the box was definitely stockier and with a longer nail. "Secondly, we can't do anything until there's a phone call. We don't know what they'll have us do yet."

I turned to Sarah. "Do you have a small paper sack? I think we need to preserve the box with any fingerprints that might be on it."

She turned from Robert and hurried toward the kitchen.

"You realize that you'll have to call in the authorities now? They'll have to catch these people. Even if this isn't part of… well, what they want you to think it is, it came from someone. The police have to know about this."

He nodded a sullen acknowledgement.

Sarah came back with a small, flat shopping bag and I set it beside the box, again trying to only touch the corners as I worked it into the little sack. I folded the top down and picked up the repulsive bundle.

"We'll put this in a safe place until the police can look at it. I don't want anyone else to touch it."

She looked around for a suitable place, finally settling on an empty drawer in a Chinese chest across the room.

I looked at my watch again. One-fifteen. Before I could form the thought, a phone rang somewhere in another room. My stomach did a flip as Robert and Sarah both visibly started.

"Quick, is there an extension phone somewhere?" I asked.

"Take the kitchen phone, dear," she said to Robert. "I'll show Charlie the one in the drawing room."

We rushed down the corridor. "Get it right after the third ring," I told Robert.

Sarah pointed to an old fifties-style phone on a table in the corner of the celery-green room. I let it complete its third ring, then gently lifted the receiver. Robert's "hello" came through. I shifted the mouthpiece away from my face so my breathing wouldn't come through the line.

"Last chance now, old man," said the voice at the other end. "You got our little ft, didn't you?" I listened intently, trying to analyze the sound of it.

"Yes." Robert's voice was small, strained.

"Go back to that trash can on the Loch Ness Trail. You'll find a note. Do what it says. Come alone, no police." The line went dead.

I replaced the receiver gently, closing my eyes to capture the sound I'd just heard.

The gruffness of the voice, the pitch, the words.

"Char—"

I put up a hand in a "stop" motion toward Sarah.

That voice. There was something very familiar about it. I let my mind absorb the sound and form a picture. I thought I knew who we were dealing with.

THIRTY-TWO

ROBERT HURRIED INTO the room. "You heard what he said? I better get going."

"I want to figure out a way to go with you, without letting them know I'm there," I said. "Can you gather the rest of the family?"

Sarah hurried toward the stairs to get Elizabeth and Edward, while Robert and I headed to the front door.

"I think it's someone close by," I told him, "someone who knows our moves."

"Brodie. We figured that out," he said.

"No, we didn't. I know you'd like to suspect him, but I have my doubts." I watched him raise the seat of a bench in the entry and pull out the plastic sack of money. "There's a spot up by the rock garden that gives a perfect view of the castle, including the door and the parking area. I think some-one's been watching the family."

The others joined us in the entryway, including Molly. I briefly outlined what I wanted them to do. Staying close to-gether in a group, we walked outside.

As planned, Robert made a show of opening the back door of the Bentley and tossing the sack of money into the back seat. I ducked under his arm and crawled onto the floor of the back. Robert climbed into the driver's seat and we were off. I could only hope that the others would play out their portions of the little scene. The plan was, if they walked back inside together, anyone watching wouldn't realize that I wasn't with them.

I settled into a more comfortable position on the floor of the luxury car. It handled the dirt lane smoothly and truly glided once we came to paved roads.

"Everything all right back there?" Robert asked over his shoulder.

"Just fine. As we get closer, don't look back at me. Let me know if you see anything unusual."

I settled in for the ride. It would probably take at least thirty minutes, and I found myself becoming drowsy by the time Robert alerted me that he was making the turn to the Loch Ness Trail. In a few minutes I felt the car slow and stop.

"The voice said there would be a note," I said. "Can you see it?"

"Not yet," he said. "I'll get out and look."

His door opened and closed. I fidgeted on the floor of the back seat, not daring to raise my head.

"Got it," Robert said as he slid into his seat again.

"Any sign of anyone watching the area?" I asked.

"Nothing. Here's the note."

"Don't pass it back here," I cautioned. "Read it aloud."

Paper crinkled and he cleared his throat. "That was step one. Keep driving south to Fort Augustus. Put the money in the trash can at the petrol station on the left. Walk across to the restaurant directly across the street. Go through it and out the back door to find Richie. You have twenty minutes."

"How do they know what time we're picking this up?" I asked, throwing logic into the problem. "Pass the note to me, down low."

Robert started the car and thrust the paper through the space between his seat and the door. He began driving as I flattened the sheet. Again, it was written on plain typing paper, the letters in block printing that looked like someone's attempt to write with their off hand so it wouldn't be recognizable. I stuffed the note into my jeans pocket.

The car picked up speed and I braced myself, dreading the possibility of a head-on crash on the narrow, twisting road. An eternity passed before Robert announced, "Fort Augustus, three miles."

"Any other cars in sight?" I asked.

"Not a one."

"I have to straighten my legs for a minute or two," I groaned. I raised myself to a position where my butt could rest on the edge of the seat while my legs stretched fully extended to the floor on the opposite side of the roomy old car. Tingles shot through my ankles and feet. I wiggled them to get feeling back. The view outside was pretty much like the rest of the Loch Ness drive, thick forest with occasional glimpses of the lake on our right.

"Any thoughts on what I should be doing while you're walking across the street to that restaurant?" I asked.

"Can't very well let anyone see you lying on the floor back there, can we?"

"When you get to this petrol station, see what the layout is like. Maybe there'll be a place you can park off to the side, away from the pumps."

"Guess that would be logical," he agreed.

A sign indicated that we were one mile from Fort Augustus, so I ducked back out of sight. I felt the car slow down considerably.

"There's the station," Robert said. "On the left." The car glided over the driveway bump. "There's a spot near the toilets. I'll park there and walk the money over to those bins by the pumps."

"Anything in here to cover me up with?" I asked. I felt suddenly vulnerable to view by anyone strolling by who would surely wonder why a woman was crouching behind the driver's seat in a parked car.

"Jacket?" he suggested. "Could toss mine over you."

The vehicle lurched as the front tires hit a bumper of some kind. He cut the engine and opened his door, while I made myself as tiny as possible and wrapped around my purse into a Charlie-ball.

"Ow, what was that?" I muttered as something hard in Robert's jacket hit me on the head.

"Oops, cell phone. Guess I better take it with me." He retrieved it and spread the jacket softly over me. It blanketed me in a cloud of darkness and a residue of men's club smells—cigar smoke and aftershave, underlaid with a wisp of male sweat. I hoped he wouldn't be gone long.

The plastic garbage bag crinkled, electric locks clicked down, and the car door thunked soundly shut. I tried to mentally map out Robert's progress, imagining how long each step would take and how soon I could again uncurl. By the time I'd imagined him dropping the money bag, crossing the street, and walking toward the back of a restaurant I'd never seen, my knees felt like they'd been crimped in a vise. I sneaked a look at my watch and saw that he'd only been gone two minutes. I watched the second hand creep around until that became three minutes. This was a dumb idea.

I should have had him drop me off a couple of blocks away and I could have found a surveillance spot within view of the money bag. By now, they'd probably snatched the cash and taken off. Here I was, not seeing anything, and there was Robert, waiting for Richie, who probably wouldn't turn up at all.

From somewhere in the depths of my purse, my cell phone rang. I whacked my elbow on some hard surface as I struggled to unzip the bag while remaining wrapped around it like a piece of bacon in a rumaki appetizer. My mind raced to the possibility that Sarah had received word of Richie at home, or that Robert had gotten lost in crossing the street. I finally managed to fumble for the phone by feel, and get the correct button pressed in the half light under my jacket cloak.

"Hello?"

"Charlie? It's Meggie."

My brain took a very long moment to process. "Meggie?"

"At the office?"

"What's wrong?" Nothing could be right if Meggie called me now.

"I can't raise Brian or Drake on the radio," she said in a shaky voice.

"Are they in flight?" I asked.

"I think so. Last word was that they were lifting off in five minutes. That was thirty minutes ago, and I've been trying to call them since."

"What're your procedur—" I heard a key in the Bentley's lock. "Hold on a second, Meggie."

"Blast it!" Robert said. "More instructions."

The sack of money flew over my head and landed with a thump on the back seat.

"Just a second," I told him. Turning back to my phone, I said, "Meggie, do you have safety procedures to follow?"

"Em'…"

"Some policy on what to do when an aircraft is considered late?"

"Yes, somewhere around here."

"Find them. Usually you're supposed to wait about an hour. Keep trying the radio and call me back if you can't raise a response in that amount of time."

"Can you come…"

"Not at this moment. I'm…I'm not sure what's happening. I'll check back when I can catch my breath." I clicked off before she could say anything more.

I realized the car was in motion again. Unburying my head from the cigar-reeking jacket, I took a deep breath. "What's happening?" I asked.

"Damn it all," he spouted. "They called again. I'd done everything just right. Dropped the money, walked through that little restaurant across the road. There was a back door, straight through the place, and I went out there. Phone rang."

"What did they say?"

"Same voice as before. Said 'Good work, old man. You *can* follow instructions. Now go get the money and drive up to Drumnadrochit.' Course by now I'm frightened that someone else may have picked up the money."

"Where's Drumnadrochit?" I asked.

"Other side of the loch. About halfway back to Inverness. Tell you, they're driving us in circles."

I curbed a flash of irritation. "Did he give you a deadline?"

"Twenty minutes again. It's okay. Better road this time."

I felt the luxury car pick up speed as we left Fort Augustus behind. I unrolled myself and sat up partially. "Keep your eyes on the other cars. Watch for anyone who's watching us. I want to stay out of sight, but I can't stay in a ball forever."

"I'll keep my distance from the others," he said.

"So, what's at this next place and what're we supposed to do?"

"Drumnadrochit. It's what you Americans would call a tourist trap. Place where the Loch Ness boat cruises board. Museum there, lots of shops. I'm to park by the museum and take the money to the high grass by the Nessie lagoon. Then I go into this one shop and buy something. When I come out, Richie's supposed to be standing by Nessie."

"Standing by Nessie? You mean he holds still?"

"Ach, big plaster dinosaur is what it is. Tourists love to take their pictures standing there." His glance shifted from the road ahead to his rearview mirror, to his side mirrors. "Don't know if it's anything, but there's a white vehicle back there. Been staying even with us, back a half-mile or so. Keep your head low."

I told him my idea of getting out at some point before the drop off place so I could watch the money sack, but we agreed that it wouldn't be smart to do that if another vehicle was keeping ours in sight.

"Watch him," I said. "If he's still back there as we get to the outskirts of town, I'll furl myself back up on the floor."

"Better start furling," he said. "We're nearly there and that car is still behind us."

I didn't relish having the smoky jacket over my head again, but supposed it was inevitable. The tires crunched over gravel and we went up a slight incline.

"Car park's here," Robert said. "And the white car just zipped past. Didn't turn off."

"I wonder... No, I better not take the chance. I'll stay in here again."

He angled the car into a slot and reached over the back of his seat. "I'll be back soon," he said, tucking the jacket over me and reaching for the money sack.

Again, the heavy car door slammed with a solid thunk, sealing me in tightly. I pulled my cell phone from my purse once more and dialed the Air-Sea number.

"Meggie? Any word from Drake yet?"

THIRTY-THREE

I HELD MY BREATH, not really wanting to hear the answer.

"No, ma'am, and it's been nearly an hour now."

"What do your instructions say?"

"Overdue aircraft are to be reported when they're an hour late," she said. Panic edged very near the surface.

"Do you have phone numbers to call?"

"Yes, right here on my list." I heard papers crackling in the background. "Do ye think I should start calling them?"

"What was your last communication from Drake?"

She repeated what she'd told me earlier.

"You've been trying all this time to raise him on the radio? What about his cell phone? Have you tried that recently?"

"No, I'd forgotten about that."

"Okay, try that. I'd come in, but I'm stuck right now. Call me back if you're able to get him." I hung up.

Strident footsteps approached the car and I felt the driver's door being yanked open. "Damn their bloody hides," Robert shouted. The vehicle sagged as he flung himself into his seat. "Another call!"

I felt my temper rise along with his. "What now, for pete's sake?"

"Back to Inverness."

"Robert, I've got another potential emergency unfolding. I may have to abandon you at some point." I filled him in with just a few sketchy details.

"I'll get us into town as soon as I can," he promised. "If those bastards don't keep running us around, this should be over soon." He backed out of the parking slot and took off with a spurt of gravel.

And if they do, it's over for me anyway, I thought. My husband's aircraft that's missing out over the water is more urgent than whatever little game's going on here. I flung off Robert's jacket and dialed Meggie again.

"Oh, Charlie! I'm so glad you called." The relief in her voice was palpable.

"Did you reach him?" I held my breath.

"Barely. Well, what I mean is, yes."

"What did he say? Where are they?"

"The connection was very bad. I mostly heard a lot of noise on the line. But he's on the way."

Tentative relief washed over me. "That's it? No indication of how soon he'd land?"

"I'm sorry, Charlie. There was just so much noise on the line."

"It's okay, Meggie. I'll be there as soon as I can." I looked at my watch. It was nearly five. "Please stay at the office, okay?"

"Oh, yes, ma'am. I wouldna' leave until I know they're safe."

"Thank you. I'll get there somehow." I clicked off the call and raised my head to speak to Robert. "How far to Inverness?"

"We're making good time. Another ten minutes."

"What do we do when we get there?" I tugged my attention back to the current problem.

"Take the money to the churchyard and leave it in the doorway to the rectory. Richie will be near the Dunbar family plot."

"This time we're going to end this thing," I said through gritted teeth. "One way or another."

Robert didn't respond. His knuckles were white on the steering wheel.

THIRTY-FOUR

LATE AFTERNOON SHADOWS stretched across the town. It wouldn't be fully dark for a while yet, but the streets had that end-of-day feel to them. Shops were closing, people scattering to their homes and after-work pursuits. The number of cars on the street had dwindled considerably.

"Park a few blocks away," I suggested to Robert. "This time we'll lead."

He found a place near the train station, a small lot where he could get the Bentley off the street. I reconfirmed which churchyard we were talking about. I'd passed it on my walk a couple of days ago. He again picked up the sack and left. I checked my watch, gave him five minutes, then quietly crawled out of the car.

Standing on my own two legs again sent a half-dozen pops and creaks through my joints, from spine to toes. I shook my legs and stretched my arms, the human version of a dog shaking the kinks out. I scanned the surrounding area for anyone paying special attention to the car, but everyone appeared to be busy with their own missions. I set out on mine.

The church stood on a slight hill, alongside the river, bordered by streets on three sides, a narrow alley on the fourth. I crept down the alley, which was nearly dark in the late shadows. It cut through the hill, sloping downward toward the river, with a stone retaining wall that allowed the church and its tiny cemetery to stand on nearly level ground. By the time I came to the fenced graveyard, the retaining wall was over four feet tall, placing the gravestones in easy view. I peered through the black wrought iron fence that topped the retaining wall.

Rows of headstones staggered in drunken imprecision across the plot, which was probably less than an acre in total size. I squinted at the deep shadows, working to discern shapes among the stones. Some were relatively short, while others stood high and majestic and expensive. I expected the Dunbar markers to be the latter. Movement to my right caught my attention.

Robert Dunbar emerged through a doorway in the church. His white hair gleamed in the dying light. His dark silhouette stood still for a moment, both arms down at his sides. I watched him take one sideways step and drop the plastic sack beside the stone doorpost. He walked on, heading purposefully toward his goal.

In the shadow of an obelisk marker about five feet tall, I spotted a huddled figure, waiting. It was male, dressed all in black. Richie Campbell watched his grandfather walk through the center of the cemetery.

THIRTY-FIVE

MY EYES DARTED to the doorway where Robert had dropped the money. I knew what was about to happen and I had to stop it.

I turned and raced back up the alleyway to the street. There was no way through the iron fence except to go into the building. Shit! How would I find my way around in there?

The front doors faced the street. I ran up the few steps and yanked open one of the double doors. I found myself in a vestibule with four doors, two in the wall directly in front of me, one in each of the narrower end walls. I took the one on the left, figuring it was at least on the same side of the building where I wanted to end up. A startled priest stepped back when I jerked the door open.

"Does this lead to the graveyard out back?" I asked, somewhat breathlessly.

He nodded. "Straight down this corridor, turn left at the end."

"Call the police," I said.

He stared, uncomprehending.

"Now! There's a kidnapping underway." I turned and ran the length of the stone hallway.

The left-hand turn he'd indicated only led me to more choices. Two more closed doors faced me. I chose the one on the right, again hoping it led in the general direction I wanted. It pulled inward and I found myself on a small stone porch, under a slight protective stone overhang. The plastic sack lay on the ground about ten feet ahead of me. I ducked into the shadows as I watched two black-clad figures approach it.

The taller one picked up the sack, hefting its weight, chuckling. He handed it to the shorter guy and said, "See there? We did it."

"No you didn't," I said, stepping from my concealed spot. They both stared at me, mouths slack.

"This was really a stupid stunt," I told them.

Lewis slumped, dropping the bag on the ground. Alasdair made a grab for it, but I reached it first. He spun and bolted for the fence.

THIRTY-SIX

A SECOND FIGURE dashed from the middle of the churchyard somewhere and ran for the fence.

"Robert, stop him!" I screamed.

Alasdair grabbed the top of the five-foot iron fence and pulled himself to the top. The spear-pointed finials at the top grabbed at his clothing and I heard a rip as he rolled himself over the top and fell to the ground on the other side. It must have been a ten-foot drop at that point, and the breath tugged out of him.

With a deadly glare at Lewis, I warned him, "Don't move." I took off running after the second boy, who also looked determined to make the break.

"No, Richie," I yelled, tripping over a headstone and windmilling my arms to catch myself. "It's too far!"

He paused for a fraction of a second. Seeing me, he leaped for the fence. His timing wasn't as good as Alasdair's and he missed, his right hand slipping off the top rung, his chin grazing one of the spear points. Blood spurted across his face and neck and he fell to the ground.

I hopped two more headstones and rushed to his side. His face was a white moon in the twilight, the blood flowing blackly as it poured down his neck.

"Here, Richie, lie down," I said, willing my voice to remain calm. "Let me look at this." I turned his head to the side and pressed my fingers against the side of his neck. It was slick with blood and his breathing had become shallow.

"Robert, get an ambulance," I shouted over my shoulder.

Blood continued to run past my fingers. I yanked at Richie's t-shirt and ripped the tail of it. The small scrap that came away wouldn't do any good. If he'd cut his carotid artery he'd probably bleed out in a few more seconds. I pressed hard with my bare fingers.

"Now!" I screamed. Left handed, I ripped away more t-shirt material. I pressed it to the wound and felt it saturate way too quickly. In the distance sirens undulated.

THIRTY-SEVEN

ROBERT DROPPED to his knees beside me. "Help is on the way," he said.

I lifted the sodden scrap of cloth and tried to see the wound in the failing light. The source of the flow was at the edge of the boy's jawbone. A brief gash of white showed through before blood covered it. I turned the cloth over and reapplied pressure. Richie groaned.

"I think it missed the carotid," I said, "but just barely." Where were the paramedics?

I looked up to see the priest I'd passed earlier coming toward us, his arm around Lewis's shoulders. The boy's freckles stood out against his marshmallow-white face, even in the twilight.

"Did you call for help?" I asked the priest.

"As you asked."

"Go back inside and direct the paramedics out here. This is a critical situation." I looked again at Richie. "And send the police after that other kid, the one that jumped the fence."

He turned, leaving Lewis staring at Richie's supine form, his dark eyes looking empty as black holes in his skull.

"Will he be okay?" he asked.

"I don't know, Lewis." Richie's eyelids fluttered and he lost consciousness. "I don't know."

THIRTY-EIGHT

BLUE AND WHITE LIGHTS flashed along the lower street and rounded the corner. I looked at the wound again. The blood flow had slowed, thank goodness. I ripped off another patch of shirt and applied it. Richie's face was whiter than I'd ever seen on any human.

A commotion behind me told me that help had finally come. Bright lights shone across the grass, and I looked up to see four uniforms making their way between the headstones.

"Over here!" Robert shouted.

"We'll get him now, ma'am," a deep male voice said. "What's happened here?"

I scooted aside, letting them get to Richie. With a tight throat, I told them briefly what had happened.

"Okay, good job," the paramedic told me.

Robert reached for my elbow and I let him lift me and walk me to the side of the action. On the other side of Richie, pushed aside by the medical people, Lewis stood with tears running down his face. My throat tightened at the sight of him, scared and alone. For some reason, I started shaking.

THIRTY-NINE

ROBERT'S ARM tightened around my shoulders as I worked to pull myself together. Congealing blood stuck my fingers together and I absentmindedly rubbed them on my jeans. Little incidents fell into place, telling me what had happened—the two boys coming back from the club a day late, the large bags of fast food, the constant misdirection done by cell phones. I just couldn't figure out why. Why three boys from well-to-do families would go this far for money their parents probably would have given them.

My cell phone rang. I couldn't believe I'd forgotten Drake.

My purse had landed near the fence. I pounced on it. Stepping away from the crowded hubbub, picking my way between headstones, I fumbled for the right button.

"Drake?" I answered.

"It's Meggie." A high edge of panic tinged her voice.

"Meggie, what's wrong?" A wad rose in my throat, making my voice come out strangely.

"They're back," she said. "But...there's...there's a problem. Charlie, you better get here." Her voice broke.

FORTY

"MEGGIE, WHAT PROBLEM? What's the matter?"

Hiccupping sobs punctuated indecipherable words.

"Meggie, hang on. I'm coming. I'll be there right away."

Something that sounded like assent came through the line, then she hung up.

I stumbled over a grave marker, caught myself, and hurried into the church. There was not a soul in sight. I rushed through, to the street—thinking, driving, pushing. No car. How would I get there? The train station was only two blocks away. Surely there would be cabs...

Every negative thought went through my mind as I ran. One of the aircraft had gone down, Drake was hurt, Drake was gone.... Tears blurred my vision and the squeal of brakes jerked me back to reality. The driver gave me an impatient look—crazy American, looking the wrong direction and stepping off the curb. I crossed in front of him, swiping at my eyes with my sleeve.

Four cabs waited at the stand in front of the train station. I ran to the first one. The driver looked up, took one look at me and recoiled. He rolled up his window and drove away. I forgot how I must look. My clothes and hands were covered in blood. The next cabbie rolled forward, glanced, and kept rolling. I ran to the end of the line, into the shadows, to the last cab. Whipping the back door open, I jumped open.

"Please, there's been an accident," I said in a whoosh of pent-up breath. "I have to get to the airport."

"No problem, mum," the man said, not even looking at me. He gently steered the car around the others lined up at the curb.

"Hurry!" I softened my voice. "Please."

"Sure, mum. I'll get you there." He punched the accelerator and I fell back against the seat.

I looked down. My phone was still in my hand. Bringing up the speed dial for Drake's cell phone number, I pressed it and listened to the quick set of chirpy beeps. It rang four excruciatingly slow times before the automatic voice came on. "We are sorry, the cellular phone customer you are—" I clicked off in disgust. I dialed Air-Sea's number. Maybe I could get something coherent out of Meggie now. The phone rang repeatedly. No one picked up and the answering machine didn't kick on. My gut clenched a little tighter.

The ride to the airport felt endless, although according to the cab's little clock the driver managed it in record time. I directed him to the left, around the main terminal toward the general aviation facilities.

"Oh my god," I whispered.

The entire area in front of the hangar and office buildings was jammed with the flashing, pulsing lights of emergency vehicles.

FORTY-ONE

I THREW SOME MONEY at the cab driver and ripped open the door. Stumbling over a parking barrier I ran into the melee.

The two helicopters sat on the tarmac, in roughly their normal places. The Astar had landed at a cockeyed angle to the building, not the usual precision ninety-degree positioning Drake usually achieved. Meggie stood to one side of the JetRanger, her skirt fluttering in the breeze, hugging herself with arms clad only in a thin sweater. I started toward her. Then I spotted the gurney beside the Astar.

Oh, god, Drake.

I ran toward it.

Paramedics crowded around the wheeled stretcher; a flight helmet lay on the ground beside the aircraft's skid. The flashing lights flared off the windshield, giving the helicopter a frightening, evil-eyed look. Onlookers ringed the scene, shifting with curiosity. I threaded my way in, pushing people aside until I reached the nose of the Astar.

The body on the gurney wasn't moving. Salt-and-pepper hair. Blood on the flight suit. A scream rose in my throat.

"Charlie!"

My head whipped around to find him. Drake rushed to me and took me in his arms. Relief weakened my knees.

"Oh, thank god," I mumbled into his flight suit. He hugged me until my ribs creaked.

"What happened?" I asked, pushing back to look into his face.

"Brian's been shot—" His eyes widened as he looked closely at me. "Charlie! Blood—what's happened to *you?*"

"Richie. We got him back. I'll tell you later." I pointed at the gurney, my hand shaky. "Brian's shot? What—who?"

"Don't know for sure," he said. "I...can't think too straight. It was all I could do to bring him in."

"Let's see if we can find out something," I said. Belatedly I turned to him again. "You're not hurt, too, are you?" I backed away and looked him over. No wounds that I could see.

Meggie spotted us and rushed over. "Oh, Charlie, it...it's so awf—" She burst into tears. Drake and I both put our arms around her.

"It's okay," Drake soothed. "You did everything just right."

"When you called..." Wracking sobs interrupted every few words. "I didn't know...I mean, I dialed.... Just glad they came..."

"Me too," he said, "me too." He rubbed her back and found a handkerchief somewhere in a deep pocket.

"They're taking him," I said.

The paramedics had covered Brian with a blanket and strapped an oxygen mask to his face. Drake trotted over to them as they pushed the gurney into the ambulance. I saw him exchange a few words with one of them. He stood back while they cranked up their sirens and roared away.

"Come on," I said to Meggie. "Let's find out what we can do."

A police officer had approached Drake by the time we got to him and I caught the end of an exchange that had something to do with examining the Astar.

"It'd probably be easier for you to do that indoors," Drake said. "I'll have the maintenance man put both aircraft into the hangar."

The officer nodded then turned and gave my clothing a long, hard look.

"Separate incident," I said. "A kid with a bad cut."

I could tell he was torn between questioning me further and making sure evidence on the helicopter wasn't destroyed. Since Fergus was in the process of hooking up the tug to tow away the aircraft, the evidence won out.

"We better get to the hospital," Drake said. "Brian's condition isn't good. Meggie, you don't have to come if you don't want to."

"I do," she said. "I wouldn't relax at home, not knowing."

"Lock the office. We'll all take the van," he said.

I hugged him again as she walked away. "I know this is selfish," I said. "But I'm so thankful it wasn't you."

"Probably just sheer luck," he said, holding me tightly. "I don't think that sniper cared which he got. He tried for both of us."

FORTY-TWO

THE EMERGENCY ROOM bustled with activity. Drake inquired at the desk about Brian, and was told that we couldn't see him yet.

I'd just asked about Richie Campbell, when a pretty, red-headed woman approached the desk.

"I'm Karen Swinney," she said breathlessly. "My husband was brought here."

Drake turned to her. "Karen, I'm Drake. This is my wife, Charlie."

Karen's creamy complexion was marred by red blotches. Her workout attire suggested that she'd been at exercise class when she got the call. Her flame-red hair was pulled back into a ponytail and a headband circled her forehead. When the woman at the desk told her she couldn't see Brian yet, her face crumpled.

"Sit over here with us," Drake said, guiding her elbow.

She allowed herself to be led to a chair beside Meggie, where she stared in disbelief at a point in the middle of the room. Drake started in gently, telling her what had happened so far. Since it was the stuff I already knew, I quietly excused myself to go check on the situation with the Dunbars.

Richie was in another cubicle, where I found him lying on an exam table, an IV in his arm, and a neat row of stitches under his jawbone. His color looked a hundred percent better although dark circles made his eyes appear that they were sunken into deep pools.

"Cut missed that main artery by mere centimeters," Robert said, coming to my side. I hadn't seen him in the corner.

"What were you boys thinking?" I asked Richie.

His eyes closed and a tear slid from each, running sideways to his short sideburns.

"Dunno. Stupid, wasn't it?"

"Yes, it was."

"Boring summer…just thought it'd be fun to watch 'em squirm." He wiped at his eyes and pushed himself up a little higher on the bed.

"Why didn't you just run off and join the circus? Why put your family through this torture?"

"Wasn't meant to be torture," he responded, more fire showing in his eyes. "More like a scavenger hunt."

"But you didn't need the money—what was that all about?"

He shrugged. "Lewis wants to get into a good college. Alasdair—he's itching to get out, travel, do some adventures. Me? Dunno."

"And Janie? Was she in on this? What was she getting out of the deal?"

"She wasn't part of this," he said, raising his voice. "Don't blame her." His gaze skittered away, fixing on the floor. "Guess she'll get nothing but a quick abortion from it."

I heard Robert's gasp. I turned to see that his face had gone somewhat gray. Poor man, he was learning a few new things about his grandson tonight.

"Where are the rest of the family members?" I asked Robert. "Have they been here?"

"Talked to Sarah awhile ago," he said, dragging his eyes away from Richie's supine figure. "Told her only what you see here—doctor says the boy can go home in a little while, after they get a bit more fluid into him. Didn't go into the rest of it. Guess that's for later."

"Well, I'll leave you to it. I've got another emergency here in the hospital," I told him. "One that, unfortunately, is more serious than this."

I turned to walk away and nearly collided with a man who'd just come around the edge of the curtain. Ian Brodie was standing in my path.

FORTY-THREE

HE GAVE MY bloodied clothing a startled look, then turned his face to Robert.

"Sorry to intrude, sir. I just heard about the boy."

I stepped aside and saw Ramona behind him, around just the other side of the curtain divider.

"Brodie? Why—" Robert sputtered slightly. I knew he'd held firm to the idea that Ian had something to do with Richie's kidnapping and was having a hard time assimilating his appearance now.

"I've returned the lambs, sir," Ian said. He shifted from one foot to the other, twisting his knit cap in his hands.

Robert's face registered absolute confusion.

"My wife, sir, she made me...uh, she made me see the error of me ways. I might disagree with your politics, sir, but it don't give me the right to take your property."

I glanced at Ramona's face. A tiny smile of pride flickered there, until she noticed I had seen it. She blushed, pink with embarrassment.

"The lambs," Robert finally said. "Well, thank you for returning them." He stretched out a hand to the other man.

I stepped outside the curtain and faced Ramona. "You made him come all the way down here to say this?"

"Well, we went to the castle first. Had the lambs in tow. I told Ian he had to face up to this. Mrs. Dunbar, she told us what had happened with the boy and that it might be late before Mr. Dunbar got home." She shrugged. "This wasn't easy for Ian, but I knew it would be even harder in the morning."

"Look, I've gotta' go," I said. "But I'll stop by soon."

She smiled and squeezed my hand.

Down the hall, I walked into the waiting area to find a doctor in messy scrubs facing Drake and Meggie and Karen.

"I'm so very sorry," he said.

For an instant it felt as if the air had gone out of the room. Then Karen's wail pierced the air.

"No—"

We all felt it. That Brian was gone had to be impossible. We'd just eaten lunch together. He and Drake had just flown back from the rig. Drake's lower lip trembled and he pulled on it with his teeth. Meggie covered her eyes with her hands and sobbed.

FORTY-FOUR

In the way grieving people tend to do, we clung together. From what had looked to be a long night in a hospital waiting room, we'd suddenly gone to having nothing at all to do. The bustle went on around us but we stood like a tiny island, waves of noise crashing over us. The doctor offered to show us to a quiet room for a few minutes peace, but Karen shook her head. "Home," she said.

Drake slipped an arm around her shoulders and guided her toward the door. I pulled some tissues from a box on a small side table and handed them to Meggie, then led her to follow Drake. My mind couldn't seem to go beyond one tiny, mundane thing after another. The reality of the big picture was still too much to accept.

Thank goodness for Drake's calm presence. He led us out to the van, safely buckled the ladies into their seats, and drove through the quiet dinnertime streets of Inverness to Brian and Karen's cute stone house with its tiny garden out front. It was the only residence on the street that stood in darkness.

Karen moved automatically, finding her keys, switching on lights, plucking Brian's discarded jacket from the back of a chair and hanging it in the closet. Meggie and I couldn't seem to think what to do. We perched at the edge of the sofa like birds ready to take flight at any minute. I felt as though I could neither sit still nor do anything useful. Drake offered to make dinner or go out for something but no one wanted anything. Finally, we settled around the dining table with coffee.

"I have to know what happened," Karen said. She sat with

her hands wrapped around her mug, drawing warmth from it more than actually consuming it.

"I don't exactly know," Drake told her. "I'm sure the police will investigate fully. Brian and I had taken off together from the rig, just before sunset. We were in radio contact, just shooting the bull, commenting on the beautiful evening."

I wanted to ask whether there'd been trouble out at the rig but I held off.

"I was in the JetRanger, slightly ahead of Brian. We'd been in the air about thirty minutes or so, and he radioed a weird call. Sounded like a curse word or something. I didn't get it and asked him to repeat. That's when he said, 'Oh my god, I'm hit.' " His voice caught and he took a long sip of his coffee. "I said, 'Say again? Hit?' and he told me something had hit him in the shoulder or the chest."

Karen's face had gone white.

"You don't need to—" Drake said, squeezing her forearm.

"No, please tell me."

"Well, we were over water, no place to set down for at least fifteen more minutes, so I just kept talking to him. He insisted he could make it to the airport. He was getting pretty fuzzy by the time we saw the runway lights, and I talked him through the landing." He faced Karen and took both her hands in his. "I've never seen a guy do anything like it. He kept that aircraft under control and made a near-perfect landing. I don't think he gave in to the pain until he saw the ambulances."

"Who would do this?" It was the question on everyone's mind, but Karen voiced it.

"I don't know," Drake said. He gave her a very condensed version of the bad feelings we'd encountered from the boat operators. "I'm sure those are the first people the police will want to look at."

A look of steel hardened Karen's face. "I never thought they'd go this far," she said. "Brian didn't either. He knew those men were trouble, but this…"

"I know," Drake said. "I know."

I felt eager to get him alone, to ask questions about things

Karen probably shouldn't hear. While the others talked about calls to family members, making funeral arrangements, I pondered the possibilities. There didn't seem to be anyone other than Brankin and his bunch who would have either the motive or the opportunity to take shots at a helicopter over the sea. Helicopters, I corrected myself.

Surely they'd fired shots at both ships. If they'd hit both, odds were good that neither would have made it back. They'd have vanished into the water and no one would have ever known what happened. A wave of goosebumps rippled over my skin.

FORTY-FIVE

"PLEASE, DRAKE," Karen was saying. She stood up and went into the kitchen. "No...what am I saying? I can't ask you to do it."

"What's the problem?" I asked, scrambling for the vital bit of conversation I must have missed.

She brought the coffeepot and began refilling cups automatically. "It's the wording in that bloody contract. I didn't like it, from the time Brian signed it."

I glanced over at Drake as Karen set the coffeepot down. He sent me a tiny shrug.

"He didn't tell you?" she asked Drake.

He shook his head.

"We don't get paid unless we complete the contract. September first. We owe them two more days of flying."

"That's outrageous," I said. "It's completely unfair."

"It's the way the contract was written." She sat down again and patiently laid it out. "It's a ninety-day contract. We received one half payment upon completion of the first forty-five days. Upon completion of the other forty-five days, we get the balance. If we don't complete it, nothing."

Skepticism must have registered on my face because Meggie chimed in. "It's true, Charlie. The contract's filed at the office. I remember depositing the first check when it came."

I couldn't believe Brian had agreed to such a ridiculous clause, and I had to believe an attorney could make a good case against it. But then, we were in a different country and I couldn't be sure.

"So, if we just fly two more days," Drake said, "the contract is complete and you get the money."

"Right. But, Drake, I can't ask you to do that. I'd manage somehow," Karen said.

Meggie looked alarmed. She didn't want to say it, but I'd seen a good-sized stack of invoices on her desk, accounts for fuel, maintenance, and office expenses that were waiting for payment. Without that big check there was no money to cover them.

I nodded subtly at Drake. He had my support.

"Karen, don't you worry," he said. "We're going to do it. Come on, two more days won't kill us."

The words slipped out before he could stop them. He hastily tried to cover, but the truth was that we all knew even one more flight very well could do exactly that.

FORTY-SIX

HOURS LATER Drake and I finally found ourselves alone, back in our own cottage. We'd arranged for a neighbor to stay with Karen overnight, and we'd dropped Meggie back at her car parked at Air-Sea's office. Drake and a mechanic had checked over both aircraft but found no damage other than the one bullet hole in the Astar's window. One shot, so perfectly placed that it had ended Brian's life. If the trigger had been pulled a fraction of a second sooner…if the helicopter had been a quarter of a mile off course…those millions of tiny details that make things come together in that precision confluence of time and place that we often call fate.

We'd no sooner closed and locked our door than Drake and I reached for each other. Suddenly, we both felt the need for contact. A crushing kiss, clothing ripped away, and a desperate conjoining on the sofa—the need overwhelmed everything else. With the dissipation of the initial passion, we climbed the stairs, trailing our discarded clothing with us, where we took the time for a second union, stroking, murmuring, loving.

Somehow it was midnight when I pulled myself toward consciousness enough to notice the bedside clock. I realized we'd not eaten anything for more than twelve hours and the easy camaraderie with Brian over our lunch swept over me with a melancholy blow.

"Let's find something in the kitchen," Drake mumbled, as if reading my mind.

I dabbed away the moisture in my eyes and slipped on my robe. Downstairs, we poured glasses of wine and fixed a plate of cheese and crackers, which we shared snuggled close together on the couch.

"Have we just done a totally stupid thing?" I said after the initial hunger pangs died.

"I thought it was a totally pleasurable thing."

"You know what I mean. Those guys won't stop. Agreeing to help Karen might have been really dumb."

"We're going to take every precaution," he said. "It won't hurt anything to spend a few extra hours double-checking both aircraft. And the police already know who they need to question."

"How do you know that?"

"Because I called them and I named names."

"When?" I didn't remember a minute we'd been out of each other's sight all evening.

"Right after I landed, as soon as I knew there'd been shots fired. That's a federal offense here, or however they refer to it, just like at home. I called Fergus from the hospital and he told me the police and aviation authorities were all over the aircraft."

"And? Did they find anything?"

"Nothing they shared with him, of course. But we'll see. I intend to find out all I can before we put our lives at risk."

It was sometime around two before we settled into bed, but the gray light of dawn lightened the edge of the drapes before I finally dozed.

I awoke with a fuzzy feeling that something was terribly wrong, the feeling that comes from a mixture of grief and alcohol. Last night's events came back at me and I groaned, not wanting to start the new day. That's when I realized Drake's side of the bed was empty.

I patted the cool sheets, not finding him, and forced myself to sit up, pounding headache and all. In the bathroom I splashed cold water on my face and slipped into my robe. The cottage was too quiet and the fuzziness left me as I called out and got no answer.

Downstairs, the coffee was still warm and a note stood

propped against the canister. *You didn't get much sleep,* it said, *so I tried to be quiet. Sarah Dunbar called and I told them to leave you alone. I'm at the hangar. See you later. Love, Drake.*

I poured a mug of coffee and sipped it black, willing my head to clear. Everything was still too fresh—the harrowing experience of holding back Richie's flowing blood, the sight of all the flashing lights at the hangar, Brian's death. A dull ache pervaded my body.

I needed to call Sarah and find out how things were going. I hoped they'd caught Alasdair and that all three boys were in for some punishment. But first I needed a shower. My stomach did a queasy roll. No, first I needed food. I scrambled two eggs and toasted a couple of slices of bread. Somewhat fortified, I spent twenty minutes in the shower where I shampooed and conditioned my hair and took the time to shave my legs. Dried, brushed, and with a touch of lipstick I felt like a new person.

I dialed Dunworthy and was surprised when Elizabeth picked up.

"Oh, hello, Charlie," she said, sounding distracted. "We're just leaving for London." She instructed someone in the background to carry something to the car. "Here, I'll have you speak to mother."

"Charlie! I'm glad you called," Sarah said. "Did Drake tell you I'd called? He said you were up very late, dear."

I confirmed it, but didn't tell her exactly why.

"We've had an eventful night and morning," she said. "Do you have a moment to pop by? I can fill you in."

"Well, maybe just a moment," I said. "I think we have a pretty full schedule for the next couple of days."

I hung up, wondering why she couldn't just fill me in over the phone, but I dutifully got in my car anyway.

"Robert's driven Edward, Elizabeth, and Richie to the airport," she told me, once we'd settled at the kitchen counter with cups of tea. "I'd like to say things will be different from now on, but I doubt it."

"What's happened?"

"All three boys were arrested last night," she said. "Charged with extortion, fraud, and mutilation of a corpse."

"Ah, I'd wondered where the severed finger came from."

"From what I gather, Alasdair has a friend who works in a mortuary. The police didn't tell us everything, but they were already aware of the crime."

"But you said Richie's going home with his parents?"

"And the other boys as well. All the parents posted bond. We had quite the fireworks last night when Robert and I found out. Tried to make the case for letting the boys suffer their punishment, but parents today don't see it that way, I'm afraid."

"Don't want them scarred for life, right?" I said, knowing that's how it would be at home.

"Personally, I'd scar his little bottom," Sarah said. "Don't take me wrong. But I happen to think those boys are getting a clear message from this, and it's the wrong one."

I couldn't disagree. We nursed our cups of tea and I filled her in on a bit of the rest of the evening, making light of the possible dangers Drake and I could still face. We made one of those tentative dinner plans for one evening after our work was done, before we left for home.

AT THE AIRPORT, I found Meggie at her desk. Every time I tried to ask her a question the phone rang. After I'd listened to her third explanation that, "Yes, the company was still in business," I managed to get in a word. She indicated that Drake was over at the hangar, so I left her to the phones and I trotted over to the other building.

The tall double doors stood open and a group of men crowded around the Astar. I recognized Joe, the mechanic from Edinburgh, and Fergus, but the others were strangers, men from the police or aviation authority, I guessed. Drake spotted me standing in the wide doorway and motioned me to where he stood, beside the other helicopter.

"JetRanger checks out okay," he said. "So far the only thing we've found on the Astar is what we knew about last night, the one bullet hole in the window. Once they've finished, Joe and I can clean things up a bit and she'll be ready to fly.''

"Are you ready?" I asked.

He became somber, but nodded. "You?"

"Sure." One of the things occupying my thoughts at four this morning had been the possibility of my own demise in the same way Brian had met his end. I'd decided that the thugs really weren't after me. They wanted Brian out of business and they'd effectively achieved that. Drake and I could stay long enough to finish the current contract, but Karen had already stated that she would sell the aircraft once we were done. One more small helicopter operator driven out of business. It wouldn't make a big difference—not until we were all gone anyway.

FORTY-SEVEN

I HUNG OUT IN the office, watching Meggie answer the phone and generally wondering how everything would turn out, until Drake poked his head in a couple hours later.

"Ready?" he asked.

"As I'll ever be." I pulled on my gear and followed him out to the tarmac.

Drake introduced me to the four men who were standing around the two aircraft.

They were Michael, Rob, Alex, and Duncan, but I had no idea which name belonged to which generic face by the time the introductions were finished. Three were police investigators, I gathered, and one from the CAA.

They intended to ask a lot of questions out at the rig and we were to be their transportation. I got Rob and Alex as my passengers, both police, whom I gathered hadn't done much helicopter travel and none of it with a female pilot. I pretended not to see their nervous glances as I escorted them to the JetRanger and strapped them into their seats.

I listened to Drake's radio transmission to the tower, then followed with my own, obtaining clearance for takeoff.

The sky was clear blue today, a steady wind tracing the last of yesterday's clouds and rain. I fought the headwind out to sea and focused my attention on keeping to my GPS course as I aimed for what would look like a microdot in the vast blank blue of the North Atlantic. Drake's faster machine provided a good lead, but he was soon far enough ahead that I couldn't count on visual contact to accurately get me there.

By the time I arrived at Rig 6, Drake had landed and his passengers were emerging. Colin Finnie stepped out of his office as I brought the JetRanger to her spot softly. My two inspectors let themselves out, each with a relieved nod of thanks in my direction, and I began my shut-down procedure. The group of men disappeared into Colin's office.

"What's the plan?" I radioed Drake, who was also waiting for his rotors to wind down.

"Guess we're out here until either Colin or the police are ready to send us back."

Two HOURS LATER we were still standing by and I found myself keeping an eye on the sky. Light cirrus, probable precursors to another storm, now covered the afternoon sky. As quickly as they'd moved in, we were likely to see more rain by midnight.

"Well, this is certainly fun," I told Drake, "but I need to find the girls' room." We'd shed our survival gear and moved over to his ship to stretch out in the roomy back seat.

"Good luck. I doubt there're too many women visiting this place. You'll probably have to take your chances with something generic."

And don't count on it being any too clean, I figured as I stepped down and headed toward the building. As I'd discovered from previous visits, a hallway ran beside Colin's office and led deep into the structure of the rig where a variety of other rooms helped facilitate the operation: map rooms, meeting places, kitchen facilities, and dorm-style bunkrooms where the men lived on their seven-day shifts. I spotted the generic blue sign with its stick-figure people denoting the toilets. As Drake predicted, there was just one and I tapped gingerly on the door before opening it.

The underlying roar of drilling equipment, generators, and heating fans masked any response that might have come, so I pushed gently at the door and called out. Empty, thank goodness. I ignored the row of dingy urinals against the right wall, not wanting to know their true condition. Nudging each stall door open, I finally found one I thought I could bring myself to enter.

I was midway through the process of unzipping my jeans, when a voice froze me in place.

"Don't think that's the end of it, lady."

FORTY-EIGHT

I FOUGHT BACK the electric charge that shot through me as my heart started again with a thud. I clutched at my clothing and tried to peek through the crack where the door met the stall. There wasn't one, it was a tight fit.

"End of what?" I said, trying to gather my thoughts and see if I could recognize the voice.

"Trouble. You keep comin' out here, you got trouble." The man kept his voice low, almost a growl.

I re-buttoned my jeans and tugged my t-shirt down. "Two more days," I told him. "We won't be here after that."

His menacing laugh chilled me. I heard a sound I couldn't immediately identify, a splashing. At the foot of the stall door a splatter of liquid dotted the floor and ran toward my feet. I jumped back, crowding myself into a corner by the toilet. The man was urinating on the door!

"What—you're crazy," I shouted.

The laugh continued and the splashing stopped. The door to the hallway whooshed shut on its closer. I flung open the stall door and made little zig-zag steps to avoid the wetness. The hall was empty.

What was that all about, I wondered. Some kind of primitive marking message, or the more direct way of saying "piss on you." I ran toward Colin Finnie's office and pushed my way in. Finnie and two of the inspectors looked up at me.

"I just received a threat," I said. I filled them in, including all the details.

One of the inspectors headed for the hall, while the other—

Alex, I think it was—began asking questions and jotting notes on a small notepad. I told him of the previous threats—subtle, not so subtle, and those staged to look like accidents. "These guys are serious about getting us out of here," I concluded. "They have to be the ones who fired on Brian yesterday."

"Yes, ma'am," he said, "according to your husband's statement, we've pinpointed the place from which the shots came. Now we're searching marine records to learn which boats could have been there at the time."

"Do you think you'll be able to do it?"

Colin spoke up. "Well, we're able to eliminate certain of the union boats because they were at the various rigs, and there are witnesses."

"But every single boat that might…?" My skepticism rose.

"We've got good leads," Alex said.

"Brankin's been the most vocal toward Drake and me," I said, "but it wasn't his voice I heard just now."

"Be assured that we're keeping a close eye on Mr. Brankin," Alex said. "But we also want to get whoever's behind him, giving the orders."

Satisfied that I'd told them everything I could, I went back outside to tell Drake about this latest threat. Both helicopters sat on their pads, but Drake was nowhere to be found.

FORTY-NINE

I CALLED OUT and got no answer. A cleaning rag lay beside the JetRanger, one that I kept in the cargo compartment for little spills. The compartment door was closed but unlatched, and the window cleaner and roll of paper towels stood inside, out of the box we always strap down during flight. Drake must have started to clean the windows on the aircraft and needed to go inside for something. I felt a tiny jab of annoyance because we'd agreed that one of us would always stay by the ships.

It was already after three o'clock and the clouds continued to build. I was impatient that we weren't getting underway more quickly. I wanted to be safely back on land before dark. I sat on the skid step and planted my elbows on my knees, making myself take a few deep breaths to relax.

By the time thirty more minutes had passed, my relaxation techniques had all run out and I was feeling decidedly put out with my husband. Had he simply decided to have coffee and shoot the breeze all day with someone? I looked up to see Alex and Duncan approaching.

"Nearly ready, then?" Alex asked. "We've done our interviews."

"Where's Drake?" I asked. "Was he with you?"

"Haven't seen him," Duncan said. "I think Bill's in the map room, checking something. Maybe he's in there."

"Look, someone should stay by the aircraft, just to be sure there's no one prowling around. Can you go inside and tell him we're ready to leave?"

Alex volunteered, so I took a few minutes to finish the job Drake had begun, wiping down the front windows on each helicopter and stowing the cleaning supplies securely. Ten minutes went by. Twenty. My pique quickly turned to worry.

Our two other passengers, the third inspector and the aviation man, emerged and stood there with Duncan comparing notes. I was about to ask one of them to go looking for Alex and Drake when Alex came out of the building.

"I can't find him," he said. "At least he's not in the main common rooms here."

"We better get Colin's help. He knows this rig inside out."

Colin quickly rounded up a crew of ten men to help with the search, while he got on the phone and called to various parts of the huge rig to see if anyone else had seen Drake. "Why don't you wait by your helicopters, Charlie," he said. "That's most likely where he'll go."

I trotted back to the aircraft where my four passengers now shuffled, clearly as eager as I was to get going. I circled the JetRanger, performing my preflight inspection, not wanting to stay any longer than we had to. I didn't like the increasingly violent waves on the roiling gray water. I walked to the edge of the helicopter pads. This one corner of the rig consisted of the flat concrete surface we landed on each time. No railing or barrier protected anyone who might come too close to the edge. I looked down and realized with sickening clarity that anyone who went over the edge right here would hit the sea a hundred feet below and surely be dashed to death against the massive pilings. My stomach heaved.

I stumbled backward, needing to put distance between the edge and myself. What if Drake had...

FIFTY

"CHARLIE!" A shout brought me back to reality. "Charlie, didn't you hear me?" Colin Finnie walked toward me, waving me to come. "We found him."

I looked up to see Drake emerging from the building, hair disheveled but otherwise looking as neat and trim as ever in the khaki flight suit he always wore under the bulky survival gear. I wanted to run to him and just hold on but the three inspectors crowded around him first.

"...some little closet," he was saying as I came close. He stretched an arm toward me and circled my waist with it. The hug conveyed a degree of relief that he wasn't sharing with the officers. He continued, "I don't know if I could identify the man. It was just one of the oil workers. He came out here and told me my wife needed help and he'd show me where she was. He led me down a couple of hallways and I was beginning to wonder what on earth Charlie would be doing this far down. I think I was about to question him when this right hook came out of nowhere. I saw stars and figured out he was shoving me into a small space and closing the door on me.

"It was pitch dark in there and by the time I felt around for the door I heard him locking it from the outside. I'd been pounding on it ever since."

"It was a storage closet back near the generator room," Colin explained. "You can barely hear anyone shouting right in your ear there. No wonder we didn't hear you."

"I was threatened in the bathroom, too," I told him, not expanding on exactly what had happened.

"Well, I don't care if it causes problems for Karen in getting paid or not. We're not flying out here again," he told Colin. "It's not worth risking our lives."

The three police inspectors looked visibly relieved. "Naturally, we can't order it, sir," Alex said, "but we were about to make a strong recommendation to that effect."

Only Colin seemed unhappy. He'd come to rely on the convenience of the two aircraft, but I was beyond caring. The man who'd lured Drake to his temporary prison might have just as easily knocked him unconscious and thrown him over the platform's edge. In fact, he might have planned to detain us until dark and do exactly that. I edged in closer to Drake.

"Let's get out of here," I whispered to him.

We bade Colin goodbye, assuring him that we didn't bear him any ill will. Drake suggested that he take the four passengers with him in the Astar, lightening the load for the slower JetRanger. The CAA man had a plane to catch back to Edinburgh so we suddenly had a deadline. It took less than five minutes for everyone to be in their seats and for the welcome whine of turbines to wind up. I let out a big pent-up breath as we both cleared the rig and headed for open sea.

Despite the darkening sky and slight turbulence as the wind picked up, I felt unexplainably light. Richie Campbell's kidnapping ordeal was over. The helicopter contract, while an exciting experience, had caused more worry than joy and I was glad to be free of it. Within the hour we would drop off our passengers. Drake would still have to explain to Karen why we wouldn't finish the last two days of work for her, but the more I thought about it the more sure I felt that she'd have a strong case for being paid for the work done up to this point. Even a big, powerful oil company surely couldn't withhold payment for time that had legitimately been flown. For right now, I wanted a hot shower and nice dinner out with my husband. Someplace with dark, quiet booths and good wine.

A subtle change in sound grabbed my attention, then the piercing, constant tone of the low rotor horn. My eyes darted to the instruments. My N1 compressor speed was dropping rapidly as the pulsating engine-out horn joined in. Oh shit. Engine failure.

I looked for Drake. The Astar was ahead of me, out of sight now in the deepening gloom.

I keyed my mike. "Mayday, mayday, mayday. Delta-Delta-Alpha-Bravo. I'm going down in the sea." I glanced at my GPS and read off the coordinates. I repeated the message twice. No response.

I looked down at the rolling sea, knowing that I had no choice. I might survive this if I could pull off a perfect auto-rotation, and if the floats could keep the fragile aircraft upright.

The procedure came back to me, those dozens of times we'd practiced them in training. I went through the steps in my mind, my hands automatically guiding the cyclic in minute moves. The steel gray water came closer and closer, rolling with sickening undulations that threatened my sense of direction. I fought to keep the horizon in sight as the airspeed slowed to less than eighty. I squeezed the trigger to inflate the floats. There was a loud bang on both sides of the helicopter as nitrogen exploded into each of the floats, expanding them along the length of each skid. I brought the helicopter's nose up and felt the skids touch water. This is it, either this thing will float or I'm about to go under. I'd never felt so alone in my life.

FIFTY-ONE

THE SWELLS WERE a good three feet high and it was all I could do to keep my eyes above them. I threw the fuel shutoff valve, shutting down the engine and pulled on the rotor brake to stop the blades. I hoped the tiny craft would stay afloat until Drake could circle around and get me. Had he heard my mayday? Did he have any way of plucking me out of the sea without endangering himself and his passengers? I didn't think so.

As I repeated my radio call, a wave higher than the rest crashed against the side of the aircraft. The whole thing leaned precariously.

Okay, Charlie, think. This thing probably won't hold until someone gets here. I jettisoned my door. If the aircraft went down I sure as hell wouldn't be able to push against the throbbing sea to get out. I unbuckled my harness and made sure my survival suit was zipped to my throat. I remembered to reach back to the center post between the front two seats and activate the emergency locator transmitter.

Another wave rocked the ship.

"I'm in the sea, I'm in the sea," I called out over the radio. As a third wave tipped me dangerously toward the passenger door a small shriek slipped out. I prayed that Drake, the Coast Guard, or someone out there was getting this.

I climbed across and pushed open the passenger door stepping gingerly onto the skid. There was a life raft in the cargo compartment, just behind the rear passenger door, a brilliant place to store something a pilot would need to reach quickly under emergency conditions. I'd be sending a letter to some egghead at some factory when I got out of this—if I could get to the raft first.

I gripped the doorframe with my left hand and edged my way aft. Another wave sent the ship rolling and the door slammed down on the back of my hand. Tears sprang to my eyes automatically and I almost lost my only grip on the slick surface.

Take a breath, Charlie. Don't let go. A momentary picture of the depth of the cold gray water popped into my head. Specks danced before my eyes. "No!" I shouted to the sea. My fingers grasped for the cargo-door latches. They were just beyond my reach.

I opened the back door and was able to use the doorjamb as a hand hold. I edged aft again until I finally reached the cargo door, pulled it open, and grabbed the raft in its red carry bag. The effort threw me off balance and I toppled backward into the icy water.

The impact and the surprise took my breath away. By sheer luck a strap on the raft became snagged on my wrist. I reached out and hugged the package to my chest with my right arm, wrapping the left around the aircraft's skid.

Now what? Survival instinct told me that I'd be better off inside the aircraft, as long as it stayed afloat. I clambered back up onto the float and in through the passenger door, panting with the effort.

I gripped the life raft packet with one hand and the edge of the seat with the other.

Once the ship rocked back level I yanked at the oversized zipper on the raft's carry bag. A bright red plastic handle popped free. It would inflate the raft with one good yank. Outside, Charlie. Don't do it now. I threaded my arm through a carry-loop on the end of the bag. If I had to bail out of here I better have this thing with me.

For the moment the aircraft bobbed placidly on the water, like a kid's bathtub toy left behind.

I picked up my discarded headset. "Does anybody copy?"

I shouted into my microphone. "Mayday, mayday, mayday, does anyone hear me?"

Fuzzy static came back. I had no way of knowing whether a voice went with it or if the thickening weather was responsible. I tried again with the same result. Just as I was about to change frequencies to try for a clearer channel, I looked up...

A huge wave, higher than the cabin.

It crashed over the helicopter, rolling it over. My world became milky gray as the wave engulfed my little cocoon. As the helicopter hung by the floats, upside down on the surface of the water, I was thanking myself for jettisoning that door. I pulled my upper torso through the opening, dragging the life raft with me. I rested my elbows on the now-inverted floats for a second, gasping for air and spitting out water.

Almost in slow motion the sea began swallowing the aircraft as the pop-out floats broke away from the helicopter. I felt the flotation of the survival suit take over as the helicopter sank out of sight into the murky depths. I swallowed panic, refusing to think about the depth of the cold water, the vastness of the open sea.

FIFTY-TWO

I GRIPPED THE life raft bundle in my arms, working to get my bearings. A wave swept over my head, plastering my hair to my face. The bundle threatened to pull me under. Get some air in that thing, Charlie. I raked the wet hair out of my eyes with my free hand, blinked away salt water, and groped for the red handle on the raft. My first pull fumbled weakly as my muscles turned to liquid.

"Harder! Damn it!"

I summoned my strength and gave it a real yank. The reaction knocked me backward. The raft whipped into full buoyancy in about a half-second. My arm slipped from its hold on the bag, though, and I found myself ten feet away from the bobbing yellow pillow. In the gloomy light, it looked like it was floating away from me.

"No!" I shouted. I swam for it and managed to grip one of the nylon web handles on the side. Another swell lifted the raft and me and plopped us back. I scrabbled to get a grip over the fat, rounded edge of the little boat, working with both arms and both legs until I finally managed to throw myself over the edge to safety.

Relative safety, I reminded myself as another wave doused me. Twilight was coming on fast. I better figure out what to do next if I was to survive this night.

Strapped to the inside of the raft were a few emergency supplies—a bailing scoop, two flares, a signal mirror, a water-proof poncho the size of a deck of cards, small first aid kit, and a packet of desalinization tablets. I put the scoop right to work while I tried to figure out what to do with the rest. It would be senseless to use the flares until I had good reason to think someone might be out there to see them. The roll of gauze and two aspirin could wait until later, and the waterproof poncho would be pretty useless if the survival suit failed.

Scared and miserable, I hunkered down. It was going to be a long night.

FIFTY-THREE

THE MIND DOES funny things when the situation looks hopeless. Mine flitted through events of the past few days, dabbled in fantasies of being home on our deck in Albuquerque sipping margaritas in the sunshine, and truly wanted nothing more than to be warm and dry and in bed with Drake.

The sky deepened to pitch black and the sea became an oily-looking black pit, dipping me up and down in my yellow craft which now looked more like faded gray. I concentrated on not thinking about it, or about the beautiful JetRanger now lying at the bottom. It was all I could do to concentrate on this minute in this little raft; I couldn't deal with the contemplation of my environment. I didn't want to think about how long I'd been out here. The longer the better, I reasoned. It would mean help could be coming along any time now.

My watch was waterproof but I couldn't see it in the absolute blackness. By now Drake knew I hadn't followed him to the airport, but unless he'd received my radio call, he wouldn't know where to find me. The aircraft's ELT might be signaling away merrily, if it worked under water. I had no idea.

A gust of wind caught my attention and I hurriedly stuffed the emergency supplies back into their waterproof pouch attached to the wall of the raft. More gusts whipped at my head and a light rain began to fall. In the distance a bolt of lightning tore through the air and the rain finally got serious. I pulled the survival suit's hood over my head and ducked under the poncho like a turtle going into its shell. My eyes tingled but I wasn't going to give in to tears. Not yet.

The squall roared overhead and the rain drilled a steady staccato on my plastic fashion wear. I felt wavelets around my boots and realized it was filling the raft with water.

Shit.

I groped for the bailing scoop and worked to stay up with the downpour. The rain continued to come in waves, heavier then lighter, stronger, weaker. Bailing gave me something to do, even as I struggled and slid on the slippery rubber. I caught myself once, reaching over the edge to dump water, nearly being upended over the edge.

My hands had gone numb, my boots were squishy with water, and my eyelids wanted to close. Just burrow under the poncho and go to sleep. I struggled against it. Drowsiness was a sign of hypothermia. I couldn't let myself give in.

I moved around, bailed water, set little tasks for myself like counting the seconds between lightning flash and resulting thunder. The storm was moving away and I read that as a positive sign. The rain gradually dwindled to a sprinkle but the roar of the wind grew louder. I pushed my hood back and blinked away moisture. Did I see lights?

My arm continued to bail water automatically as I scanned the sky. Glints off the raindrops made visibility tricky. I wiped at both eyes. Yes, something out there flashed.

The regular strobe of an aircraft light. It crossed from just off the left side of my raft to my right. "No, don't go on," I yelled. "Wait!"

The flares.

I crawled to the pouch of emergency goodies. My numb fingers fumbled into the pouch, finally coming up with one of the sticks. My eyes didn't leave the flashing strobe. Circle back, circle back. The little prayer repeated through my head as I tried to remember the instructions for the flare. A heavy red arrow pointed toward one end. I aimed it away from my body and pulled. The slender tube spat out five fireballs.

Please see them. Something warm ran down my face as I whispered the words.

FIFTY-FOUR

FOR A MINUTE I didn't dare look. I imagined the lights flying on, some light plane unaware of me. I squinted my own tears back and looked again. Now there were three lights, the white strobe, a red, and a green. The red was on my right. He was headed toward me. I grabbed the other flare, ready to use it if the aircraft veered off course. But it didn't.

It came steadily toward me and I realized part of the roar I'd been hearing was the sound of twin turbine engines. An intense light shone down on the water, moving too slowly. The whop-whop of rotor blades beat the air.

"Aim over here!" I yelled. I stood up and waved my arms madly.

Gradually the light came closer, sweeping back and forth across the rolling water. I popped the other flare, sending the signal flames in the direction the helicopter should take to reach me.

The beacon light landed on me.

I nearly landed face-down when I attempted to jump up and down in the raft, so I crouched on my knees and kept waving my arms. The rotor downwash nearly flattened me as the yellow RAF Sea King hovered directly overhead. I couldn't look directly up into the blinding light, but voices carried clearly down to me. Orders were shouted and a sling winched down.

"To your left, to your left," a voice shouted up to the crew.

It was Drake's voice.

I looked up and saw him just above me, riding the rescue

sling and waving arm signals to the men above. It felt like forever, but he finally touched me.

"Oh my god, Charlie, are you okay? We were frantic."

"Pretty good, actually," I answered, sounding like we'd just bumped into each other at a cocktail party.

"Oh, baby, I should have never flown ahead. I should have kept you in sight," he said.

"You couldn't have known," I said, burying my face in his neck. "It turned out okay."

"Here, we gotta' get you up. Step right here. Okay, let's get this behind your waist." He directed me on how to get into the sling then made a cranking motion for the men overhead to reel us in. Being treated like a salmon had never felt so good.

I held my breath on the ride up, dreading the very idea of another plunge into the water. After a quick scramble to get ourselves out of the sling, Drake directed me to a seat against the bulkhead. The rescue team slid the door shut and the pilot transitioned smoothly forward, heading for dry land. That's when the shakes set in.

FIFTY-FIVE

BY THE TIME we reached the airport three blankets had begun to warm me, but mostly it was knowing that Drake and I were together again, both alive and well, that kept me going. I was ready for a huge dinner, I realized—right after a bath and dry clothes. I wasn't ready for what awaited me.

A dozen or more reporters rushed toward the RAF helicopter the minute we opened the side door. Microphones probed at us like unrelenting feelers and questions flew.

"How do you feel, Ms. Parker?"

"Wet." How do you think I feel?

"What happened out there?"

You want me to admit to losing a million-dollar aircraft at sea? Or shall I tell you what I really think, that a bunch of thugs aren't above murder to get their way? "It was a harrowing experience."

"Whose fault was it that your helicopter went down?" This from a BBC blondie.

Drake squeezed my shoulder. "We better get inside. No further questions," he said, steering me gently and pushing a path through.

In the office, Meggie greeted me with a mug of hot coffee. I downed about half of it before peeling off my heavy survival suit. Underneath, my jeans and shirt were damp and I had no dry things with me.

"Let's get you out of here before the authorities descend on the place," Drake said. "Meggie, you ought to go on home, too. Do not say a word to anyone who asks you about this. I mean it. We've got to find out what really happened before a bunch of rumors start flying.''

"Oh, absolutely," she said.

Drake peered out through a slat in the mini-blinds. "Reporters haven't gone away. Look, I'll walk you both out to the cars. Don't say a word and just keep going. Drive away. If anyone follows you, Meggie, I want you to call me.''

We switched off the lights, ignored the ringing telephone, and walked out as a group. The reporters were less friendly this time. Microphones jabbed at us and questions flew in loud self-important tones. Drake kept an arm around each of us females and steered us to the cars. We shielded Meggie as she climbed into hers.

"Drive fast, go straight home, and lock your doors," he told her.

She nodded and raced her engine. We did the same and were somehow able to get away from the airport without one news van on our tail. I didn't relax until we'd closed ourselves into our cottage. Drake picked up the phone as I hastened upstairs, shivering again from the bone-deep cold.

An hour later, after a long soak in the hottest water I could get from the old plumbing, I joined him downstairs. He'd put together a quick supper of soup and crackers, and I'd washed the seaweedy smell from my hair. I wolfed down two bowls of soup and a glass of wine and suddenly couldn't keep my eyes open another minute.

Drake tucked the covers around me and kissed me goodnight, saying he was too keyed up to sleep yet. I hardly heard the words as he gently closed the bedroom door.

I rolled over to find bright sunlight edging the drapes. I reached for Drake, not wanting to give up the warmth of the bed just yet. His side was empty. My eyes shot open. His side was still neatly made; he hadn't come to bed at all. A jolt of alarm shot through me. No coherent answer came. I yanked on my robe and doubled-timed down the stairs.

"Coffee?" he asked. He stood in the kitchen in the same

clothes he'd worn yesterday. Sun streamed through the windows, accenting the deep bluish shadows under his eyes.

I let out a large breath. "Scared me," I said, "waking up like that." I slipped into his offered embrace. "You okay?"

"Yeah, better now. Couldn't stop thinking all night." He reached for the carafe and poured me a mug of coffee.

I took it and watched him rub both hands over the dark stubble on his face.

"Aside from yesterday's horrible experience, which is over with, by the way," I said, "what were you thinking about that took ten hours to sort out."

He turned away from me and opened the refrigerator door. "What I'm going to do," he said. "Want some toast?"

"No, I don't want toast." I set my mug on the counter, harder than I intended.

"What do you mean, what you're going to do?"

He closed the door deliberately. "About the men who tried to kill you." His gaze held steady, his mouth formed a grim line.

"Hon, this wasn't personal. They weren't after *me*. They want Air-Sea Helicopters to quit flying. They achieved that. They ought to be real happy right now."

"So why didn't they sabotage my aircraft? Why yours? Why did the guy corner you and threaten you? Why did they lock me away, if not to get to you?" His eyes flashed, the green flecks sparking.

"I don't know," I admitted. "Pick on the weaker thread, maybe?"

A little of the tension went out of his shoulders as he reached again for his mug.

"So just what do you think you'll *do?* Isn't it really a matter for the authorities?"

"Apparently not. I called Alex, the cop that was with us, last night after you went to bed. He seemed surprised that I thought Brian's shooting and your helicopter going down might be related."

"What?"

"Yeah. They seem to see this…your accident…as an aviation matter, some malfunction of equipment. Brian's is a murder and they're working on that."

"And they don't at all make the connection between all the threats from the union guys and their very real hatred of the helicopter operators?"

"Two different things, he told me. Not to worry, the aviation authorities will make a thorough investigation, he said, and he's sure Air-Sea's insurance company will also get involved." He topped off each of our cups. "They'll all probably question you to death. It's not going to be fun."

"I'll tell them exactly what happened," I said. "Starting with the threats we got from the beginning."

"You can expect to be picked apart, hon. Don't take this too lightly. Especially when the insurance company comes into it. They're not going to pay out nearly a million dollars without trying to wangle out of it first."

"Will they bring the aircraft up from the bottom?" I asked.

"Don't know. Might depend on how deep it is out there, how expensive an operation that might be."

I caught sight of my reflection in the shiny window of the microwave. A deep furrow pulled my eyebrows together and my mouth was now set as grimly as Drake's.

"Hey, let's get on to something else," he said. "Maybe we should go tour a distillery or something today."

I nodded without answering.

"I gotta' shower and shave," he said. "I feel like dirt warmed over." He gave me a quick hug and headed for the stairs.

I toasted a slice of bread and chewed on it while my mind chewed on everything else. There had to be some proof, something we could find that would bring Brankin and his thugs down once and for all. Only problem was I couldn't figure out how we'd do that without going back out to the rig again.

Then the phone rang.

FIFTY-SIX

IT WAS KAREN SWINNEY, calling to let us know that Brian's funeral would be tomorrow. I jotted down the name of the church and time of the service. I'd no sooner hung up than it rang again. I got it halfway through the first ring, assuming Karen had forgotten to tell me something.

"Ms. Parker?" The male voice sounded official. I knew I should have let the machine start screening the calls. I reluctantly acknowledged him.

"Charlotte L. Parker?"

"Yes. Who is this please?"

"I'm Hugo Fitzwater with the Civil Aviation Authority. I'll need to meet with you and get a statement about yesterday's incident. At your convenience, of course."

Of course. Unfailing British politeness.

"Would this afternoon be all right?" Polite but firm.

I agreed and, given the choice between his downtown office and the Air-Sea offices at the airport, chose my own turf.

"One o'clock, then?"

It was nearly ten already and I decided it was about time I got dressed for the day. Back upstairs, Drake was just emerging from the shower.

"Guess the distillery tour's off," I called out. "CAA wants to see me at one. You'll come with me, won't you?"

He stood in the bathroom doorway, towel poised halfway to his face. "Think you're ready?"

"No. But then I can only tell him the truth, relate the experience. They'll investigate, won't they? Find out whether the ship was sabotaged or this was just incredibly coincidental timing?''

''Hard to say just what they'll do. You know how I feel about bureaucratic jerks with power. I tell 'em only what they need to know.'' He pointed his index finger skyward. ''Remember, a bureaucrat is not your friend.''

I chuckled while I rummaged through the closet for some clean khakis.

''You know, I think I'll wander over to the castle for a few minutes. I should check in and see how everything's turning out with them.''

''Let me know what time you want to head for the airport,'' he said. ''Remember, we're down to one vehicle this morning.''

''Why don't you catch a little nap, hon? We can leave about twelve.''

I ran a brush through my hair and gave my lips a smear of color.

Sarah grabbed my hand, leading me into the entry. ''Oh, Charlie, I'm so glad you've come. What on earth happened out there, dear? I tell you, I about went into shock when the story came on.''

''On? It's on the news?'' I should have figured. Whether I talked or not, those reporters were determined to say something.

''Oh, my, yes. There's a film of Drake leading you through a crowd of people. Well, I wouldn't have known it was you because you didn't look so great, but they said an American woman pilot so I knew it must have been.''

I quickly recapped the basics, making light of the terror I'd felt as the aircraft sunk under my feet and skipping over the part where I'd been convinced I would freeze to death in the black ocean.

''Well, let me give you some tea,'' she said, bustling me toward the kitchen. ''I've just put the kettle on.''

''How are things going with Richie?'' I asked, as we settled at the counter with tea in delicate china cups and slices of angel food cake.

Sarah raised her eyes, as if some god on the ceiling might give answers. "They'll get no punishment, I'm sure, those boys. Robert doesn't think we should press charges for the fire at the crofter's hut. Said they were just smoking and it was an accident." She took a tentative sip of her tea. "Already Alasdair's parents have paid some kind of money to the family of the dead person whose finger was cut off, and kept the thing very hushed publicly. That young man is going to be trouble, you watch. They've been covering for him and getting him out of his little jams all his life. One day…"

"And Richie?"

"His cut's healing, so well you'd hardly know it's there Elizabeth tells me. I worry for the boy, Charlie. It's another case of discipline too little and too late. Edward simply won't allow 'the child' to end up with a criminal record. 'Child'— hah! I tell them he'd better start learning some lessons the hard way. But they don't listen to me. Think I'm just an old idiot."

I laughed and patted her hand. "You're no old idiot," I said. "I think you've got the most sense of the entire bunch."

"Oh! I nearly forgot, dear. I found a little something for you." She hurried out of the kitchen and returned with one hand behind her back. "Since you refused payment for your services in locating Richie—"

"I really didn't—"

"Since you won't take money, I wanted you to have a permanent memento of Scotland. Something positive, that is." She held out a flat box about twelve inches square, wrapped in an attractive blue and green plaid paper and tied with a fluffy red bow. "Go on, open it."

I preserved the bow and the paper and lifted the lid. Inside was a wooden plaque with an intricate crest in pewter.

"It's the family crest of the Clan Davidson," she explained. "And on the back…"

I turned it over.

"...that's a short history of the origins of your family name."

I swallowed a lump. "It's just beautiful, Sarah. Thank you very much."

We finished our tea and I realized it was time for me to face the music. With a vague plan for dinner one night soon, several more "thank you's" on both sides, and a firm hug, I left Dunworthy.

FIFTY-SEVEN

I SNEAKED A PEEK at my watch, under the edge of the desk. Two hours of questioning by the CAA man, Hugo Fitzwater, and my energy was flagging. We'd not covered any new ground after the first thirty minutes.

"And so, you don't know whether it's possible that someone might have tampered with your aircraft during the time you were at Rig 6?" he asked for the fourth time. His small blue eyes stared at the notepad on his lap.

"No, I don't know it for a fact. It might have simply been a mechanical failure," I said for the fourth time. Everything about the man, from his jowly round face to his white shirt that stretched to the bursting point over his round gut, was beginning to irk me.

"Had there been any unusual occurrences in the past few days?"

Unusual occurrences. Well, that might include a man dashing in front of Drake as he came in for a landing. It might include someone following me into the bathroom, whispering threats through the door, and marking their territory. It could also include somebody luring Drake down a corridor, punching him in the face, and locking him in a closet. But we'd been over all that.

"Other than the things I've already told you about, I can't think—" My breath caught and Fitzwater looked up at me. Oh my god, there certainly was something.

"Ms. Parker?"

"The flight manual." I took a deep breath. "The JetRanger's

flight manual was missing one day. I had to wait while Meggie brought up the current weight and balance on the computer and printed me a new one. We never did find the original.''

Fitzwater sat up straighter and scratched notes furiously on his pad.

''The flight manual contains instructions specific to each aircraft,'' I said, more to myself than to him. ''The warning notices, the procedures…''

I felt a rush of adrenaline, the kind of excitement I get when a case-breaking idea hits. ''We have to get out to the rig,'' I told him. ''Now. Drake will fly us out there. We have to search the crew's quarters.''

Even as I said it I realized how hopeless an idea it was. Brankin surely wouldn't keep anything so incriminating in his room. Where was Drake? He'd dismissed Meggie for the day then discreetly vacated the office so Fitzwater could talk to me. I grabbed the phone and punched in his cell phone number.

''Now, wait a min—'' Fitzwater sputtered.

''Get the Astar ready,'' I said. ''We have to get out to the rig. No, first, call the police. Tell them it's urgent to get a warrant to search Brankin's home. He must live in town somewhere. It's the flight manual, Drake, that's the evidence we need.''

Bless him, he didn't question me.

''Don't you see?'' I pleaded with Fitzwater. ''With the flight manual, somebody like Brankin or his buddies would have the information they needed to disable the aircraft. If we can find it, that's proof.''

''I just don't know that we need—''

It hit me that the man was looking for a way out of going on the flight. He was afraid, of something.

''If you don't want to go, that's fine. Drake's already calling the police. He'll fly them out there, they'll search the place, and wrap it up. The CAA isn't going to care who gets credit, as long as they establish guilt, right?'' I knew good and well that any bureaucrat worth his salt cares more about getting credit than just about anything else on earth. I'm sure he couldn't give a damn who was guilty, as long as his name was on the final paperwork. I stood up. "We're finished with questions here, aren't we?"

"For my report..." he began. "Well, I suppose I should take a look at that manual."

I crossed the ramp to the waiting Astar, knowing that the odds of those union thugs keeping any incriminating evidence was extremely slim. They'd probably looked through the book, found the information they wanted, and ditched the thing into the sea. But I had to know. There was no way I could simply accept an accident on my record, chalk it up to a mechanical failure, and let them get away with it. A man was dead, his widow probably bankrupt, and I'd nearly gone to meet the Great Kahuna. Someone was responsible.

Alex and Duncan stood by the nose of the Astar, while Drake circled, performing his preflight inspection.

"How'd you get them here so fast?" I asked, catching up with him near the tail rotor.

"Fancy footwork," he said with a smile. "Actually, they were already here. Next in line for questions. You just barked out your orders and hung up so fast I didn't have time to tell you."

"Oh."

He squeezed my hand. "It's okay. If we can pin down these crooks nothing would make me happier. Unless we could do it without another ride out to that platform."

"I know. Think I have any desire to fly across that open water again?"

"You gotta' get back on the horse sometime. You're taking this one."

Dread welled inside me but I made myself do it. We packed Fitzwater into the two center seats in back, with Alex and Duncan flanking him. I climbed into the pilot's seat and Drake took the front jump seat.

"Take a deep breath. You can do this," Drake said after switching the intercom so only we two could communicate. "If you're unsure of anything, I'm right here."

"Don't let that CAA guy hear you."

My insides fluttered as the turbine engine spun up and I guided the craft into the air. By the time I set her gently onto the pad at Rig 6 my confidence level had soared. A new set of nerves took over once we landed. Colin Finnie greeted us, a puzzled look on his face.

Alex pulled out a folded sheet of paper. "Warrant to search the crew quarters," he said, shoving it back into his jacket.

I thanked him silently for being willing to bluff his way in because I knew there was no way he could have gotten a legal warrant that quickly. Somehow I knew he'd have one by this afternoon though. Leaving Duncan to keep an eye on the aircraft, the rest of us turned toward the building.

Finnie showed us through the door and down a hallway lined with bunkrooms.

"Brankin's?" Alex asked. Finnie pointed to one corner.

The room was set up in quarters, bunks two-high in each corner with lockers beside them. Each locker had some form of identification on it, most just a piece of masking tape with a last name penned on it. Eight beds to a room, eight lockers. Presumably, toilets and showers were communal and somewhere else along the hallway.

"We need to cut that lock," Alex ordered, pointing at Brankin's locker. Colin left to find a bolt cutter.

"The other names in here," I said, "I recognize most of them. Robson, Barrie, and Ewing are all buddies of his. And I think Tolliver was another."

Drake quickly circled the room, giving each bed a cursory search—running his hands over the blankets and under the pillows, flipping the mattress up. He unearthed a decent collection of girly magazines but no flight manual. By the time Colin returned we were standing near Brankin's locker again.

The brawny Alex nipped the lock in one motion and cast it aside. He quickly patted down the clothing and upended the boots and shoes. A shelf above the row of hangers held books and papers, and Alex put them out en masse and threw them onto the bed. He went through each item, but I knew at a glance there was no flight manual among them.

FIFTY-EIGHT

"WAIT, WHAT'S THIS?" I asked, noticing that each lower bunk had things stuffed under it.

"Trunks," Colin answered. "Each man has a trunk for his larger gear—survival suits, diving gear, stuff he doesn't want to pack and take home between shifts."

Alex pulled Brankin's trunk out and quickly did away with the lock. It contained just what Colin had said it would. No flight manual.

Fitzwater was beginning to look impatient, thinking no doubt that he'd had to endure two flights for nothing. Alex, though, wasn't ready to give up yet.

"Which of these other men are part of Brankin's boat union?" Alex asked Colin.

"Everyone in this room," Colin answered.

Three lockers later we hit paydirt. The manual with my aircraft's tail number sat right there in Tolliver's locker.

Tolliver, the quiet one who'd always hung at the fringes of Brankin's group. The one who wouldn't be nearly as suspect if he quietly moseyed toward the ship. Probably the one with enough brains to read the manual and figure out what to do.

"Look at this," Drake said, flipping through the manual.

He'd opened it to the page of preflight cautions, those little warnings that come with everything from hair dryers to ladders to aircraft. The warnings that show up after fatalities. He pointed to a passage underlined in blue ink.

"This warns that the B-nut on the fuel control line has to

be tightened to exact specs. If it's only finger-tight it can vibrate loose during flight.''

"What does that mean?" Alex asked, saving me from the embarrassment of admitting that I didn't know either.

"The engine starts okay, can even fly perfectly well. But if that nut works its way loose, fuel pressure drops, engine speed falls off. The pilot suddenly has no power. The low-rotor horn is usually your first warning.''

As I'd discovered. Fitzwater was nodding.

Drake continued, "Tolliver could have loosened the B-nut with a wrench, then tightened it just finger-tight. If he didn't give it much of a twist, he could have been pretty sure it would come loose before the aircraft completed its flight.''

Alex took charge. "Are these men on duty today—Brankin, Tolliver, Ewing, Barrie, and Robson?" he asked Colin. With a positive response, he turned to me. "Charlie, Drake, you might as well go out and guard your helicopter. I need Duncan in here with me.''

Fitzwater followed us, saying something about the police being able to handle the apprehension quite well. He made directly for his seat in the back of the Astar, ready to take the load off and get going. Drake and I stood by the ship's rounded nose, wondering aloud just how the two police inspectors intended to get themselves and five suspects back to shore. Our seven-place aircraft certainly wasn't going to handle all ten of us, especially since Fitzwater counted as two.

"Either have to take 'em by boat," Drake said, "which, under the circumstances, I doubt they'll want to do, or call in the RAF again. The Sea King will hold nineteen.''

"So, maybe we can leave soon?" I suddenly felt tired, ready to stay home awhile. Drake's eyes showed his lack of sleep too. The vision of pulling the drapes closed and sleeping the afternoon away in each other's arms held a lot of appeal.

"Let's at least preflight this thing," he said.

We began making the rounds of the aircraft, looking it over, checking the tightness of hatch covers. I was at the tail when a door slammed. I glanced around the side of the aircraft and spotted Brankin, his eyes wild and aggressive. He stared at me.

FIFTY-NINE

BEFORE MY BRAIN registered what was happening, he launched himself across the landing pad and grabbed my arm. He wrenched it upward behind my back.

"Filthy bitch!" he growled into my ear. "Ain't gettin' me arrested."

I flailed at him with my other fist, but each time he merely yanked harder on the captive one. It felt like my shoulder was coming out of its socket.

"Drake!" I screamed. I didn't see him.

Brankin shoved me ahead of him, muttering curses and grabbing at me until he held both my arms firmly.

"Drake!"

"Shut up!" He moved as if to hit me in the face but thought better of it as he'd have to let one of my arms go.

I kicked at his shins and tried to twist out of his grip but the man was unbelievably strong. He kept shoving me across the concrete pad and I realized what he was doing.

We were headed right toward the edge of the platform. A sickening feeling rose in my throat as I remembered the straight plunge, a hundred fifty feet into the sea.

"Brankin! Stop!" Drake's shout rang across the open expanse.

It was a nice try, but Brankin only shoved harder. We were no more than six feet from the drop-off. I planted my heels against the concrete, trying to push against Brankin as hard as he was pushing me, but he was clearly stronger. My boot heels formed twin black skid marks as the distance narrowed.

I couldn't see Drake but his voice sounded closer this time. "Brankin, wait, let's talk about this," he said. "Charlie didn't do anything to you."

A nasty growl, right in my ear, was the only response.

"Drake! We're almost at the edge!" I shouted.

"Max, don't do it." The voice got Brankin's attention and he turned slightly. Tolliver, with Alex and Duncan beside him, stood ten feet or so from the door to Colin's office. "Hurting the lady won't do you any good."

Brankin's grip loosened a tiny bit but it was all I needed. I swung my right arm free and spun, catching him on the left ear. Drake rushed at me from the side, grabbing me around the waist and diving for the center of the helipad. We both went down, just in time to see Tolliver head toward his friend. Brankin, however, wasn't going to be talked into surrendering. He regained his footing quickly and ran for the edge of the platform.

We heard his scream as he plunged.

SIXTY

RAIN DRIPPED OFF a dozen umbrellas as we stood around Brian's coffin. The day was perfect, as funerals go. Such occasions fit gray, drizzly days when people gather for unhappy purposes. Our black clothing against the bright green grass in the churchyard made us look like a bunch of ravens waiting around the newest delicacy in a field. A spray of white roses draped the mahogany coffin and the only touch of color in the somber place came from the minister's purple vestments worn over his black coat.

Karen looked older, tired, emotionally void. A daughter stood beside her, a young woman of about twenty. I tried to remember if I'd been told her name, but couldn't come up with it. At any rate, it probably wouldn't matter after today.

We'd booked a flight home at the end of the week, giving us a few more days to cram in any sightseeing we wanted to do, say goodbye to the friends we'd made here, and pack. Truthfully, I was looking forward to a long dose of New Mexico sunshine and the warm, doggy smell of a hug from Rusty.

The minister finished with whatever he was saying and people began to file away, stopping to offer Karen their hugs, handshakes, or warm wishes. Drake and I hung back until the end.

"I don't know if this helps," I said, "but they've caught the killers."

Her mouth opened slightly as she looked at us through dark glasses.

"Five men were arrested yesterday at the rig. Well, I should say four were arrested and one thoughtfully rid the world of his own presence.''

"Of the men who were arrested," Drake said, "one admitted to being the man who fired the shots from a boat."

"One of the guys pretty much told the whole story, about how the union leaders set up a campaign to get rid of the helicopter operators. They figured if they put strong intimidation on one, everyone else would back away and just let them have all the business. We were just unlucky enough to be the one they targeted."

"Did they say anything about..." Karen paused, looking for a good way to ask.

"The money's coming," Drake said. "Colin Finnie gave his word that he'd see to it that you get paid for all the flight time actually done. Said the oil company likes to sound tough in their contracts, but they can't really withhold payment."

"And most likely the insurance company will cover the downed aircraft. The CAA man told us it's up to them to decide whether they want to try to bring it up and inspect it. His report will conclude that the craft went down due to an act of sabotage and that the perpetrators have been apprehended."

Her face crumpled. "Thank you so much," she said. "You've both been so much help."

Her daughter put an arm around Karen's shoulders. "Let's go home, mother," she whispered.

I looked up at Drake as we followed them toward their waiting limousine. "Yes, let's."